THE
HEART
THAT KNOWS

BY
CHARLES G.D. ROBERTS

INTRODUCTION BY
CARRIE MACMILLAN

Formac Publishing Company Limited
Halifax

Copyright © 2002
by Formac Publishing Company Limited

All rights reserved. No part of this book may be reproduced or transmitted in any form or by any means, electronic or mechanical, including photocopying, or by any information storage or retrieval system, without permission in writing from the publisher.

Formac Publishing Company Limited acknowledges the support of the cultural affairs section, Nova Scotia Department of Tourism and Culture. We acknowledge the financial support of the Government of Canada through the Book Publishing Industry Development Program (BPIDP) for our publishing activities. We acknowledge the support of the Canada Council for the Arts for our publishing program.

Cover illustration: *Westcock Parsonage*, G. Roberts (watercolour on cardboard) Fort Beauséjour Collection, Parks Canada.

National Library of Canada Cataloguing in Publication Data

Roberts, Charles G. D., 1860-1943
    The heart that knows / Charles G.D. Roberts.

(Formac fiction treasures)
ISBN 0-88780-570-1

    I. Title. II. Series.

PS8485.O24H48 2002   C813'.4   C2002-903374-8
PR9199.3.R5269H43 2002

First published in 1906, L.C. Page & Company, Boston.
Series editor: Gwendolyn Davies

Formac Publishing Company Limited
5502 Atlantic Street
Halifax, Nova Scotia B3H 1G4
www.formac.ca

Printed and bound in Canada

Presenting Formac Fiction Treasures
Series Editor: Gwendolyn Davies

A taste for reading popular fiction expanded in the nineteenth century with the mass marketing of books and magazines. People read rousing adventure stories aloud at night around the fireside; they bought entertaining romances to read while travelling on trains and curled up with the latest serial novel in their leisure moments. Novelists were important cultural figures, with devotees who eagerly awaited their next work.

Among the many successful popular English language novelists of the late 19th and early 20th centuries were a group of Maritimers who found in their own education, travel and sense of history events and characters capable of entertaining readers on both sides of the Atlantic. They emerged from well-established communities which valued education and culture, for women as well as for men. Faced with limited publishing opportunities in the Maritimes, successful writers sought magazine and book publishers in the major cultural centres: New York, Boston, Philadelphia, London, and sometimes Montreal and Toronto. They often enjoyed much success with readers 'at home' but the best of these writers found large audiences across Canada and in the United States and Great Britain.

The Formac Fiction Treasures series is aimed at offering contemporary readers access to books that were successful, often huge bestsellers in their time, but which are now little known and often hard to find. The authors and titles selected are chosen first of all as enjoyable to read, and secondly for the light they shine on historical events and on attitudes and views of the culture from which they emerged. These complete original texts reflect values which are sometimes in conflict with those of today: for example, racism is often evident, and bluntly expressed. This collection of novels is offered as a step towards rediscovering a surprisingly diverse and not nearly well enough known popular cultural heritage of the Maritime provinces and of Canada.

INTRODUCTION

Charles G. D. Roberts' *The Heart That Knows* (1906) is a powerful novel of affirmation expressed through a magnificent language of place. That place is the Tantramar region, Roberts' childhood home until he was fourteen, and his imaginative and emotional centre throughout his lifetime. Again and again in his poetry, from the early "Tantramar Revisited" (1883) to the late "Westcock Hill" (1929), as well as in his fiction, Roberts returned to Tantramar to express his deepest and most powerful feelings.

Born in 1860, Roberts was raised in Westcock in the southeastern corner of New Brunswick at the head of Cumberland Basin, one of the major branches of the Bay of Fundy. Roberts was the son of the Rev. George Goodridge Roberts, Anglican rector of Westcock, Dorchester and Sackville, who instilled in Roberts a love and appreciation of literature, art and music, and a strong pride in his country. His father read to him from an early age the classics of English poetry and allowed him access to the library at the parsonage. Roberts learned to play the piano and organ at St. Ann's, the little wooden church set in the spruce woods on the Dorchester road, and had instruction in painting at the Ladies' College, Mount Allison University, two miles away in Sackville. When

Canada achieved nationhood in 1867, the seven-year old boy shared the spirit of excitement and promise that characterized the early Confederation period.

An immensely important legacy of the Westcock years is the freedom Roberts had to explore the outdoor world of Tantramar. The parsonage included a glebe farm where Charles helped to plough, sow and harvest, kept his own special breed of chickens and raised a ewe and a calf. Beehives sat on the terrace at the front of the rectory, beyond which was the family's vegetable garden. Behind the house was the spruce grove where Roberts explored paths and observed plants, birds and animals. Below the house, across the Wood Point Road, visible from Roberts' bedroom window, was the incomparable broad vista, the "miles on miles" of Tantramar, of sky, marsh, sea and dyke. Here twice a day surged the forty-foot tides of Cumberland Basin. Bordering the Basin were miles of ancient dykes first built by the Acadians in the mid-seventeenth century, to reclaim and protect from the sea the marshlands and their blowing grasses. Across the bay lay "green-rampired" Cumberland Point and the ruins of Fort Beausejour, down the road from Mount Whatley, where Roberts' uncle, the Rev. Donald Bliss, served his parish and where Roberts searched the fields and overgrown fortifications for artifacts from the days of native habitation and French occupation. This landscape would provide the observant child with the foundation for a literary career that included the writing of nature poetry, historical novels and animal stories, which embodied a deep abiding love for this place.

Introduction

The Tantramar childhood was succeeded by a sound classical liberal arts education at the Fredericton Collegiate School (1874-76) and the University of New Brunswick (1876-79), where Roberts earned BA and MA degrees. At Collegiate Roberts was particularly fortunate in his literature professor, George Parkin, who had recently undertaken postgraduate studies at Oxford University and brought back with him an enthusiasm for the latest in English poetry, particularly that of the Pre-Raphaelites. Poetry, as shared by Parkin with his young protégés, was a living form, one in which they were encouraged to participate. Roberts spent free hours with Parkin and fellow aspiring poet Bliss Carman, his Fredericton cousin, walking the riverbanks and woods of the city, reading and discussing poetry and dreaming of a life in literature.

In 1880, at twenty, Roberts' literary career was launched with the publication of *Orion and Other Poems*. Although he had not yet found his characteristic voice, which was one of emotion powerfully fused with vivid description of landscape, *Orion* demonstrates Roberts' mastery of poetic verse forms. The precocious young author sent his volume to several prominent English and American authors, two of whom, Matthew Arnold and Oliver Wendell Holmes, returned letters of encouragement. After Roberts completed his MA he married Mary (May) Fenety of Fredericton, whose father had published *Orion*.

Roberts was now ready to pursue a literary career, but what opportunities were there for the young Canadian literary aspirant of his day? Certainly, it was not possible to live solely from writing, and Roberts searched for a career that would complement his literary interests. He served briefly as editor of the Toronto periodical *The Week* (December 1883-February 1884). Then for ten years he was a professor at King's College, Windsor, Nova Scotia. Both careers, however, proved stressful and the pressures on his time left little opportunity for writing. At *The Week*, where he met other Canadian writers, including Archibald Lampman and S. Frances Harrison, there were the inevitable constant deadlines. At King's Roberts not only had a demanding teaching schedule but he was also responsible for activities including sports and the literary Haliburton Club in which he served as president. Future writers H.A. Cody, Robert Norwood and H.H. Pittman, all of whom were Roberts' students at King's, would pay tribute to the significance of Roberts' inspiration and tireless support of their early literary careers. As well, Roberts' study at King's was open to visiting literary friends including the poets Bliss Carman and Richard Hovey from New England, the novelist Sophie Almon Hensley from Halifax and Roberts' sister, the poet Elizabeth Roberts MacDonald from Fredericton.

Adding to the pressures of his work, financial insecurity hung like a dark cloud over King's during Roberts' years there. This led to heavy teaching loads and poor salaries. In 1892 Roberts described his state of mind to Bliss Carman: "Get away we must. Have change we must. Readjust the focus of life we must. We must soar out of our present fetters." Given all these circumstances, it is remarkable that Roberts produced three major poetry collections between 1885 and 1896.

Introduction ix

In addition to his career frustrations, other concerns beset Roberts at this time. His wife May had little interest in poetry and was not very supportive of his writing. To be fair to May, much of the raising of the Roberts' four children, the management of the household and catering to frequent literary guests fell on her as her husband pursued his academic and literary careers behind the study door. It is not surprising that she might at times have been resentful. May's ambivalence about her husband's literary life, combined with Roberts' tendency to pursue other women, led to tensions within the marriage. As well, Roberts' cousin and closest friend, Bliss Carman, was living a comparatively free bachelor life in Boston, where he edited a succession of magazines and enjoyed the supportive Boston-Cambridge literary milieu. A self-declared vagabond (Carman and fellow poet Richard Hovey had written books entitled *Songs from Vagabondia* and *More Songs from Vagabondia*), Carman wrote frequently to Roberts, keeping him abreast of the exciting cultural and social life south of the border. Carman regularly summered in the Maritimes bringing with him his American literary friends, pitching tents in the Roberts' backyard. Carman's literary vagabond life was attractive to the overburdened Roberts.

By the 1890s a large and literate reading population, combined with the advent of less costly printing technologies, resulted in huge book sales for publishers in the United States, particularly in Boston and New York. Canada did not as yet have the population and the financial or cultural confidence to support such a strong publishing industry. If

Roberts wanted to live as a writer with an assured, regular income, and enjoy the exciting literary currents of the day, he would have to go to the United States.

In 1897 he left May and the children in a small house in Fredericton, where they were not far from their Roberts and Fenety relatives, and moved to New York. Initially he assumed responsibilities as assistant editor of *The Illustrated American*, but eventually he lived fully off his writing, though always precariously. Although he promised to send for his family when he could support them in New York, he never did so. Instead, over the years he took bachelor digs in various upper-floor furnished studios with addresses such as West 9th Street, East 58th Street and Fifth Avenue. He went home for Christmas and occasional holiday visits, sent funds and had his children visit or travel with him as he was able. He seized the opportunity when time and finances allowed to travel to Cuba, England and Europe. More than a decade after World War I, in which Roberts served as a major in England and France, he returned to Canada to establish his home in Toronto.

Notwithstanding the opinion of the modernist poets, including F.R. Scott and A.J.M. Smith, that Roberts' generation of writers were stuffy and outmoded, Roberts himself was celebrated by the Canadian literary establishment as the grand man of Canadian letters. He was fêted by the Canadian Authors' Association and the Royal Society as the father of Canadian poetry, and was in demand from coast to coast for recital-lecture tours and at summer Chautauquas. As well as being elected president of the Canadian Authors' Association (1926), he was the first recipient of the Royal Society's Lorne

Pierce Medal for Literature (1926) and a pension from the Canadian Authors' Foundation Fund (1931). He was conferred with a knighthood in 1935 and given an honorary degree by Mount Allison University in 1942. May died in 1930 and in 1943, a month before his death, Roberts married his young literary assistant and protégé, Joan Montgomery.

Except for brief visits, Roberts never returned to live near the Tantramar. However, in his memory and imagination he never left the marshlands. They sustained him in difficult times, when the pressures of family, finances and work were strong. They offered subject matter for his writing. And it was through the Tantramar landscape that Roberts explored some of his most profound themes and feelings.

In its poetic strength and passion *The Heart That Knows* stands out from the competent and somewhat formulaic bread-and-butter historical romances of the author's New York period. Roberts wrote the bulk of the novel in 1906 in a quiet hotel near Matanzas, Cuba, where he had gone at the suggestion of his old Fredericton friend, the poet and banker Francis Sherman, who was with the Royal Bank of Canada in Havana. The novel was published by L.C. Page in Boston and Copp Clark in Toronto. A stimulus for the work was the death in 1905 of his beloved father, teacher and mentor, "the wisest, kindest, most wholly admirable man I shall ever know." This death set in motion a process of profound personal reconstruction:

> *The Heart That Knows* is the most intimate and personal of all my prose works. Westcock and Westcock

parsonage and all the surrounding country are faithfully described; 'the Rector' is a true picture of my beloved father; the Rector's wife, a loving portrait of my mother; many of the other characters are from life; many of the incidents — actions of my father — are fact; and much of my own boyhood is in the boyhood of Luella's little, irregular son.

Another factor that likely contributed to the power of the novel is that Roberts was struggling with a profound disappointment in love when he wrote it. Late in 1904 Roberts learned that the woman with whom he was "badly in love," the New York journalist Mary Fanton, cared for his brother, William Carman Roberts. It is almost certain that the love poems in Roberts' *The Book of the Rose* were written for Fanton. In December 1906 she married William.

His father's death, combined with the proximity and inaccessibility of the woman he loved, made the years 1905 and 1906 particularly difficult. The strong themes of loss and separation experienced by the principal characters in *The Heart that Knows* — Luella, Jim and Seth — are feelings with which Roberts contended at this time. Evidence of Roberts' reminiscent and nostalgic frame of mind is found in such resonant details of place as the "faint sound of a church-bell, elusive and sweet as a fading memory" (11) and "this shining world of green earth and yellow sea" (4,5). The entire first chapter, in which ebbing tide and deepening night reflect Luella's gradual realization of the pain of loss and loneliness, is weighted with Roberts' own feelings of sadness and loss.

Introduction

At the emotional and spiritual centre of the novel is the beloved rector who is struck in the heroic mould, that of the muscular Christian, popular in the fiction of the day. A physical paragon, he defends the honour of Westcock when a man from Truro threatens to win the 'putting-the-stone' at the annual Foresters' picnic. He discovers the fire that threatens to consume the barquentine *G.G. Goodridge* and mobilizes the work force to save the ship which will as a consequence bear his name. His physical prowess, however, is an emblem of more important qualities of character and of heart. The rector sustains his flock by defending it from injustice and prejudice, by nourishing it intellectually and emotionally. It is to the parsonage that Luella turns when she is abandoned by Jim. At the parsonage she finds support, even when it is revealed that she will bear a child out of wedlock. The rector is "as intuitive as a woman" (67) and "a shrewd as well as a tender watcher of the human heart" (16). The rector and his wife have faith in Luella's love of the man to whom she was betrothed, and openmindedly consider that she is married in God's eyes. They also have faith that the child she bears is Jim's, and refuse to doubt Luella's character, as others in the community do.

The scholarly rector takes Jim Calder and later, his son Seth under his wing to instruct them in navigation, thereby equipping them to advance in their careers as seamen and to sail the world. Moreover, the rector's influence transcends place and time: it accompanies Jim and Seth in their travels. The two are brought together emotionally shortly after they meet, as their hearts are engaged with similar feelings of love of home and memories of the rector by the sight of *G.G. Goodridge* in the waters off Singapore. Memories of the rector's instruction and character guide their undertakings in their travels. Mrs. Goodridge, whose character is based on that of Roberts' mother, Emma Bliss Roberts, also supports the heart. More outspoken than her husband, intuitive and less innocent in her judgment of others, she is filled with anger when she learns that Jim Calder has sailed without marrying Luella, and bursts out: "It's all that Melissa Britton . . . The hussy!"(72) She stands up fearlessly to the sewing circle, insisting that Luella is a good and honest girl, the victim of a hideous wrong(124), and she takes her business away from Abner Beasley when he casts Luella out of his house. Her home is always open to Luella and her son.

The characters in the novel are aligned in terms of those who have faith in human nature and those who obstruct the ways of the heart. The word "heart" occurs over thirty times in the novel. Those who sustain the heart, in addition to the Rev. and Mrs. Goodridge, are Luella, who remains faithful to Jim and raises his son with love, and Sis Bembridge, a powerful, almost mythic woman, a witch figure and "law unto herself." (34) Among those who attempt to thwart the heart is the rigid Mrs. Calder, Jim's mother, whose "prim, uncompromising," "aggressively clean" (30), orderly and sterile home offers an image of her inability to share her possessive and jealous love of her son with Luella. The church ladies' sewing circle is a further impediment to Luella's happiness in her hour of need. Regardless of the fact that some of these women or their daughters have found themselves in situa-

Introduction   xv

tions similar to Luella's, they harden their hearts to her predicament and ostracize her. Like her Uncle Abner, whose concern is for his business and reputation, the women of this small-town society are presented as the social and moral arbiters of their world. And well they should be. After all, if the institution of marriage is not upheld, what will become of women's position and security in patriarchal society where marriage and family are women's one destiny?

The alignment of the characters with the theme of the heart is reflected in a language of gardens in the novel. Mrs. Calder's garden is geometrically contained and unimaginative. Luella's garden is the richest and fullest in Westcock, tended with love and care, "bearing the earliest blossoms of the year, and the latest" (44) and shared with others in the community, particularly the parsonage and the church. Sis Bembridge's garden thrives with practical vegetables, and powerful "yarbs" with which she ministers to the health of the community. In Roberts' novel the characters who are close to the fecund land and nature of Tantramar are those who know the heart.

For Roberts the Tantramar of the parsonage and the good rector is a world set in the place and time of his childhood, a world of happiness and innocence, far from the cares that beset him in maturity. Roberts could never go back to the Tantramar. Indeed, the Tantramar he describes in the novel may never have existed except in the innocence of childhood and in the imagination of the poet. The Tantramar is an image for Roberts of qualities of character and heart that are elusive in the world of social reality, in the world of maturity, cities and daily grind. Only in the Tantramar of his imagination can Roberts find the elusive qualities that he values. We are reminded of his poem "Tantramar Revisited" in which he insists that he "will not go down to the marshland, — / Muse and recall far off, rather remember than see,— / Lest on too close sight I miss the darling illusion, /Spy at their task even here the hands of chance and change." This is the function of the Tantramar for Roberts, a world of the imagination where he can preserve all that he most values, that bulwarks the forces of doubt and negation, just as the sturdy dykes of Fundy bulwark the powerful tides. This is the power of Roberts' poetry of Tantramar, and of the poetic novel *The Heart That Knows*.

It is informative to compare Roberts' novel with an almost exact contemporary, Lucy Maud Montgomery's *Anne of Green Gables* (1908). Both novels employ the Maritimes as a setting, both use mythic patterns of quest combined with realistic detail, both present a child who overcomes restrictive social forces, leading to redemption, and both assert the value of and longing for human connection, for love and home. As writers, Roberts and Montgomery, in the face of the social ruptures of the modern age, affirm and situate the values of the heart and of place in the Maritimes of their childhoods.

Roberts is one of a very few Canadian writers in his day who wrote novels that presented sympathetically "the woman who is a mother but not a wife." Joanna E. Wood's *The Untempered Wind* (1894) presents a rural Ontario woman whose situation is very much like that of Luella; Myron Holder raises her son on the margins of society, ostracized by the severe matrons of the town. Canadian-born Grant Allen's *The Woman Who Did* (1895) presents a central character who resists what she considers to be the hypocrisies of conventional marriage. Thomas Stinson Jarvis's *Geoffrey Hampstead* (1890) presents a woman who falls victim to a villainous seducer. Roberts himself had already written a novel in which there is obscure paternity, *The Heart of the Ancient Wood* (1900). In his story "On the Tantramar Dyke" (1903), a kind of embryonic version of *The Heart That Knows*, he experimented with the deserted woman figure. Roberts, in presenting sympathetically women who err against society's law, expressed, not surprisingly given his interest in the wild, a concern about the rigid line that is drawn in his day between the primitive and the social. In *The Heart That Knows* Roberts offers a critique of the narrow, hypocritical and sometimes cruel vision of conventional morality, of the double standard by which men and women are judged. He demonstrates in his novel a compassionate and liberal attitude toward women and their moral burden. It is possible even to describe *The Heart That Knows* as a subversive novel. Critics in Canada at the turn of the century for the most part did not receive favourably fiction that presented vice, depravity or any departure from prescribed social values. Literature, it was believed, should uplift and instruct. Roberts' subject matter demonstrates a more modern and socially engaged writer than was evident in his earlier nature poetry.

When *The Heart That Knows* was published it tended to be lumped together with Roberts' other novels as another popular, if tender, romance. Perhaps that is why it did not raise moral hackles, as might have been expected. Also, the suffering meted out to Luella is intense, and in the end she gains some respectability through the implied marriage to the father of her child (there was a limit to how far Roberts would or could go to challenge propriety). The advent of modernist tenets in the 1920s and 1930s did nothing to advance the novel's reputation, although the Saint Botolph Society of Boston reprinted it in 1923 as a story of "the fisher and sailor folk of the Bay of Fundy." Only with the reprinting of the novel in Mount Allison University's Ralph Pickard Bell reprint series in 1984, with an introduction by Michael J. MacDonald, did the novel begin to receive serious critical attention, but only from a limited audience. The publication of the novel by Formac Publishing offers an opportunity to launch it back into the world, where it can be judged beyond the narrow standards of modernism, and where its power, beauty and affirmation can be appreciated by a new and wider audience.

Carrie MacMillan
Mount Allison University
2002

CONTENTS

CHAPTER		PAGE
I.	WHEN THE SHIP WENT OUT	1
II.	THE BARQUENTINE G. G. GOODRIDGE	13
III.	THE WEDDING THAT WAS NOT	20
IV.	HER LOVER AND HIS MOTHER	30
V.	WHAT MELISSA WANTED	41
VI.	MELISSA'S MASTER-STROKE	51
VII.	LUELLA'S FRIENDS, AND OTHERS	64
VIII.	"OLD SIS"	78
IX.	LUELLA AND THE BLUE HEN	88
X.	THE INTERVIEWING OF JIM'S MOTHER	103
XI.	THE SEWING-CIRCLE	111
XII.	ABNER BAISLEY'S BILL	128
XIII.	TURNED OUT	135
XIV.	JIM AND MELISSA	147
XV.	TO SOUTHERN SEAS	153
XVI.	MELISSA'S TRIUMPH	159
XVII.	THE SPELL OF THE EAST	174
XVIII.	AT MRS. BEMBRIDGE'S	180
XIX.	DOWN TO THE "BITO"	197
XX.	THE RECTOR SPEAKS OUT	207
XXI.	SETH AND HIS SCHOOLMATES	218
XXII.	SETH BEGINS TO UNDERSTAND	230
XXIII.	THE MEANING OF THE WORD	239
XXIV.	HIS FATHER'S NAME	249
XXV.	THE SEED OF VENGEANCE	258
XXVI.	THE FORESTERS' PICNIC	268

Contents

CHAPTER		PAGE
XXVII.	INSULT	285
XXVIII.	SETH GOES TO SEA	298
XXIX.	THE MATE OF THE MARY OF TECK	309
XXX.	THE FIGHT IN THE DANCE-HALL	319
XXXI.	THE BO'SUN'S BELAYING-PIN	329
XXXII.	THE RECTOR AND TIM LARSEN	337
XXXIII.	SETH'S FATHER	349
XXXIV.	WHAT THE HEART KNOWS	363
XXXV.	THE BREATH OF THE TIDE AND LILAC BLOOMS	374

THE
HEART THAT KNOWS

CHAPTER I.

WHEN THE SHIP WENT OUT

An unremitting wind, blowing down the vast and solitary green levels of Tantramar, bowed all one way the deep June grasses over the miles on miles of marsh. A tall girl, standing alone on the crest of the dyke, — the one human figure visible in the wide, bright-coloured emptiness of the morning, — caught its full force and braced herself sturdily against it. It flapped the starched wings of her deep white sunbonnet across her face, twitched out a heavy streamer of her flax-blond hair, and pressed her thin, blue and white calico gown close upon the tenderly rounded lines of her slim young figure. The soft, insistent noise of it, mingled with the sound of the shallow, dancing waves that swept along past the dyke-front, confused her ears and partly numbed her thought. But her eyes, which were large, and of a peculiarly positive porcelain blue, were fixed with anxious strain upon a ship riding at anchor far out across the yellow waves. That ship, a black-hulled barquentine on the yards of whose foremast the white sails were being broken out, was evidently the one thing her eyes took note of in all the spacious scene.

The scene was all space, — all high, light colour, wind-washed brightness, and loneliness. Toward the southeast, where the girl was looking, and in a vast sweep around the southward horizon, spread the tawny, tumbled waters of Fundy, eternally vexed by their terrific tides. Beyond the ship — leagues beyond, and across the yellow water — rose the low blue hills of Minudie. To eastward outspread the interminable light green levels of the Tantramar marshes, with the dark green spur of Fort Beauséjour thrust out to fence them off from the marshes of the Missaguash. Further around to the left the grassy solitudes were cleft and threaded by the many-winding channel of that most mutable of rivers, the Tantramar, just now at full tide, and pouring its pale, copper-coloured flood into the bay almost before the girl's feet. The windings of the river — which twisted hither and thither as if it had forgotten its way — made bright, reddish yellow slashes and patches over the wide green of the marsh.

Still further to the left, along the foot of the uplands which ran diminishing northward, a far-off group of roofs, with a couple of church spires and a cluster of masts, showed the little town of Sackville on its gently billowing hills. Much nearer, a promontory of wooded upland bore, half-hidden in its front, an old colonial mansion, "Westcock House," with horse-chestnuts and Lombardy poplars ranged majestically before it. Outspread behind the watcher on the dyke lay a mile-breadth of the same light green marshes, traversed by a meandering creek which came to the sea reluctantly, close at the girl's right. It pierced the massive barrier of the dyke by an *aboi d'eaux* (or "Bito," as the country-folk called it), and formed a tiny port for the boats of the shad-fishers, whose high, brown net-reels sentinelled its borders. The broad belt of marsh, secure behind its rampart of dyke, ran off in long curves toward the southwest, and terminated at the rocky, oak-crowned heights of Wood Point. Behind it, trailing out sparsely along the tilled slope of the upland, and dotted here and there with dark fir-groves, lay the southerly portion of Westcock village, the rest of it hidden from sight behind a shoulder of dark fir-groves.

The marshes, at this season of early summer,

were covered with a three-foot growth of timothy and other fine hay-grasses. Here and there, for acres at a time, the grass could not bow and turn blue evenly before the wind, because it was stiff with the blooms and tangled leafage of the great red clover. Here and there, too, instead of the rosy stain of the clover, vast patches of blossoming vetch, entwined with the grass stems, spread a wash of undulating purple over the pale green. For the most part, however, the levels bore no colour but green, vivid and pure when the grass stood up in a rare lull of the wind, but bluish and beryl-pallid as the bending tops revealed the lower surfaces of blade and bloom. Along the twisting banks of the creek, along the inner bases of the dyke, along every deep but narrow drainage ditch, and along both sides of the rutted road of dry mud which led, a rusty streak across the green, from the little haven of the shad-boats to the far-off, sunny uplands, ran wild roses, their leafage of yellowish bronze now thick strewn with golden-hearted blossoms of pale pink. Everywhere, in a riot of summer exuberance, hummed and foraged the great black and gold bumblebees. Brown marsh-hawks winnowed low over the grass-tops, quartering every grass-packed acre for the field-mice which scurried among the grass-roots. And over all this shining world of green earth and yellow sea hung a low-vaulted sky of light, pure blue, the blue of thinned cobalt.

For nearly two hours the girl had waited on the wind-swept dyke, watching the ship. She had been expecting to see a boat put off from the ship's side, and head for the mouth of the creek. The tide had crept in yellow over the red flats, till it brimmed the creek mouth with its broken, white-topped waves and washed foaming along the bases of the dyke below her feet. After half an hour she wondered and grew impatient. Then, at slack of tide, she began to grow angry, — for Jim had asked her to meet him out here on the dyke at high tide that they might talk over certain matters of intimate concern at safe distance from eye and ear of the village gossips. That night, in Westcock church, a great event was to take place, before the sailing of the ship on the morrow's ebb; and Luella felt that on such a day, when she had so much to do, it ill became her lover to be late.

But when, after this long waiting, the girl saw that the ship was beginning to make sail, anger gave way to an anxiety which soon grew to a terrible fear. A child of the fisher and sailor folk of Fundy, she read the signs only too well. The tide was just on the turn. Presently the tremendous ebb would begin and for six hours the vast Chignecto Basin, which forms the head of Fundy, would disgorge its tawny waters toward the ocean, till its level would be lowered by some thirty or forty feet, the tortuous channels of Tantramar and all its tributary creeks would be changed to glistening, red, steep-sided chasms of mud, and league upon league of oozy, red-gold flats would lie uncovered between the water and the dykes. Luella saw that, with wind and tide agreeing, it was a most favourable time for the *G. G. Goodridge* to set sail, and work her way out from the shoals and mad currents of the upper bay. The *G. G. Goodridge* was what is known as a " barquentine," a ship of three masts, the foremast carrying yards and square sails, — square-rigged, that is, — and the main and mizzen masts schooner-rigged, with booms and gaffs. When Luella saw the canvas spreading white on the yards of the foremast, she could not long delude herself. She could not see the men at the windlass, heaving the anchor, but her overtense ears hypnotized by the implacable drumming of the wind, seemed to hear the far-off chantey and the rhythmic creaking of the windlass. Soon the ship began to forge slowly ahead, and she knew that the anchor was up. Then a jib was broken out, bellying full; and then up went the great white mainsail, gleaming marvellously in the sun. The *G. G. Goodridge* was now a half-mile from her anchorage, and gathering headway. In a few minutes she was fairly hidden in her cloud of canvas, careening majestically, and passing down the bay with the full favour of wind and tide. Only too well Luella knew how long would be the voyage thus begun before her anguished eyes. She had talked it all over, and over, and over with Jim. The *G. G. Goodridge* was bound for Montevideo with a cargo of fish and deals, there to discharge, and perhaps take freight for around the Horn and up the Pacific Coast to Valparaiso. From some Peruvian port — Luella could not remember whether it was Arequipo or Callao that Jim said — she would load with nitrates for Liverpool, and then, possibly, return to New Brunswick, after an absence of perhaps two years. Luella knew that Jim Calder was aboard the vessel now passing so swiftly from before her eyes. Three weeks ago that day he had signed his papers as second mate of the *G. G. Goodridge*. For two years he had been Luella's acknowledged lover; and it had been a pledge between them that they should be married when Jim got his papers as mate. The wedding was to have been that night. And Luella was to have sailed with him on the morrow as far as St. John, there to bid him farewell, and return to Westcock to await his home-coming.

When, at last, the whole overwhelming significance of what had happened penetrated her numb brain, Luella sank down into a huddling heap upon the dyke, staring dry-eyed, and clutching unconsciously at the long strings which tied her sunbonnet beneath her chin. In her unheeding grasp the bow came untied. Instantly the wind twitched the sunbonnet from her head, carried it flapping and turning out to sea, and dropped it into the huddle of yellow waves. The great coils of her hair came unpinned, and streamed out, pale flaxen yellow and softly rich, like silk. But Luella did not know that her sunbonnet was gone. She was unconscious even that she had sunk down upon her knees. She only knew that Jim was on that vanishing ship, — that he had gone without a word to her, — that not for two years, at the very best, could she hope to see him again, — that there would be no wedding that night in the little Westcock church, — and that a formless horror of fear and shame and anguish was drawing near to engulf her. Her set lips, slowly turning gray, uttered not a sound, as she stared steadily after the fleeting cloud of canvas. At last, it disappeared around the lofty shoulder of Wood Point. When it had vanished, she sprang to her feet with a cry, caught at her heart, and made a motion as if to throw herself into the water. Death, at the moment, seemed so simple a solution, and the only effective one. But while she had been watching the ship the tide had been ebbing in fierce haste, after the fashion of these tides of Tantramar; and where, the last time she took note of things, the waves had been tumbling at her feet, spread now a dozen rods of mud flat, oozily glistening in the sun. She could reach the water only by wading knee-deep in slime. The picture of what she would have looked like if she had flung herself from the dyke forced itself upon her, and she sat down suddenly, with a hysterical cry. In this the first perilous moment of her despair, she was saved. Then her strong will, and the sanity of those who have lived simply and naturally, came to her aid. She turned her back upon the water, took one desperate look at the far-off uplands and the houses of the village to which she must return, then descended the inner face of the dyke, and ran and threw herself face down in the deep of the grass.

For hours she lay there, hidden from all eyes but those of the marsh-hawk, which now and then winged over her to fly off to one side with a sudden heavy flapping and a shrill piping cry of astonishment. The girl's brain was too numb to think, but it was scorching dry with grief, and amazed injury, and terror of a future of humiliation which she realized only as a monstrous, uncomprehended nightmare. She lay with her eyes shut, and covered by her hands, and tearless, but with her parched lips half-open. Over and over, but with the futility of utter inconsequence, her brain clutched at every conceivable or inconceivable explanation of the blow which had fallen upon her. Over and over, with deadly repetition and never any possible advance, she recalled and dwelt upon and squeezed to dryness every word of her last talk with Jim, only the afternoon before, — when he had been all tenderness and loyal passion, she all trust and forward-looking gladness, in spite of the weary two years of separation which she had braced herself to face for his sake. While her heart and brain were surging with the tumult of her pain, outwardly she was as still as a dead thing. A bright-striped garter-snake, hunting among the grass-stems for mice and crickets, came suddenly upon her, and darted away in frightened writhings. And later, a foraging yellow weasel, hardly less sinuous and soundless than the snake, stole around her with unfriendly eyes for nearly half an hour.

Meanwhile the yellow tide retreated down the glassy flats till the noise of the waves quite died away, and there was no sound on the air but the hum of the bumblebees and the swish of the wind in the bowing grass. The sun rolled slowly across the light blue arc of sky, and sank below the fir-crested ridge of uplands behind Westcock village. The sky grew one transparent orange blaze over the ridge, barred with three long, narrow, horizontal clouds of purest crimson. The crimson died slowly to cold purple, the orange blaze to tenderest lilac and lavender; and the zenith took on the green of a clear sea that washes over white sands. The wind died suddenly. The uplands grew bottle-green, then black, and the wide, unshadowed spaces of the marsh melted through citron and violet into a dusky gray-brown, full of inexplicable warmer lights. At last a few stars glimmered forth, and the marshes fell into an aerial, indeterminate blackness, with the unending barrier of the dyke a solid black rampart against the hollow sky. Lights gleamed yellow in scattered windows. Then, from far over the hill, came the faint sound of a church-bell, elusive and sweet as a fading memory, the summons of the little Westcock congregation to that evening service at which every one in the village was expecting to see Luella Warden married to Jim Calder. The sound of the bell pierced to the girl's brain. She rose slowly, noticed how drenched her heavy hair was, and re-coiled it punctiliously. In a flash she pictured the amused wonder that would presently grow on the faces of the congregation, the anxiety with which the kind eyes of the rector would keep glancing at the door, expectant. For a moment, as she thought of his loving interest in her marriage, the concern he had shown for the welfare of herself and Jim, and the way he had helped Jim study to pass his examinations, her mouth quivered and her eyes softened. This was but for a second, however. Then, with lips set hard as stone, she took the dim road homeward.

CHAPTER II.

THE BARQUENTINE *G. G. GOODRIDGE*

THE barquentine *G. G. Goodridge* was a new ship, fresh from Purdy's shipyard and the tarred hands of the riggers. She was of four hundred tons register, and owned in Sackville and Westcock. As she started down the Bay of Fundy on her maiden voyage she was held to be sailing under the special favour of Providence, in that she bore in white letters across her stern, as well as on her starboard bow, the name of the well-loved rector of the parish, the Reverend G. G. Goodridge. She owed her very existence, indeed, to the rector's efficient succour at a crucial moment; and among the seafaring folk, who are always superstitious (as becomes men who live with the great mysteries), it was considered that his name would be her passport to the good-will of fate.

It happened that very late one night, when the barquentine was still on the stocks in Purdy's shipyard, the rector was jogging slowly homeward from the bedside of a sick parishioner in Sackville.

It was a moonless night, the blue-black sky sown thick with stars and the Great Bear wheeling low. Purdy's shipyard is on a short but wide-channelled creek emptying into the Tantramar in that portion of Westcock village which lies on the Sackville road, half a mile south of the Frosty Hollow "Bito." The rector's head was sunk in reverie, the reins hung loose on the horse's neck, and the light "buggy," its top lowered back, jolted at its will over every rut and stone in the rough country road. As he passed Purdy's shipyard, however, the rector raised his eyes, and glanced down at the fine new vessel in which all Westcock was interested. In another week she would be gay with flags; and at high tide, amid the chorus of an enthusiastic throng, she would glide down her greased and smoking "ways" to plunge with an enormous splash into the yellow waters of the creek-basin. The shipyard was a good quarter of a mile from the road, but the great, tarred hull, high on its stocks, was conspicuous against the glimmer of water beyond. But it was not the lofty shadow of the hull that caught the rector's eye and made him sit up, very wide-awake. The next instant he turned the horse's head sharply, drove bumping over the ditch and the roadside hillocks to the fence, sprang out, and threw the reins over a fence stake. Then he vaulted the fence and ran as fast as he could across the fields toward the ship, shouting "Fire! Fire! Fire!" at the top of his great voice.

The flames were just beginning to rise from a heap of rubbish close under the stern, when the rector vaulted the fence. When he reached the ship they were licking high and red upon the fresh-tarred sides. A workman's bucket stood near; and, fortunately for the ship, the tide was at its height, lapping softly almost under the stern-port. The rector was a man of great muscular strength and trained activity. Though his lungs heaved hard from that quarter-mile sprint across the uneven, dusky fields, in a few seconds he had dashed bucket after bucket of water upon the blaze, and upon the little, incipient flames which were beginning to hiss here and there far up the ship's side. By the time the ship-carpenters came running, half-awake, from the big house far at the other side of the yard, the rector had the fire well in hand, and there was only a smouldering, smoking pile of chips and shavings to show what had happened. The rector was hot, and tired, as well as angry at the carelessness which could leave a lot of such inflammable stuff so close beside the ship. His voice was stern as he addressed the staring foreman.

"Did you *want* the ship to be burned," he inquired, pointing to the heap, "that you left all that stuff there?"

The foreman rubbed his head.

"There wasn't no stuff left nigh to her, not a mite, when we knocked off work at sundown," he declared, positively. "No sir-ee, parson. If any one of the hands done a fool trick like that, he'd git the sack right quick."

As he spoke, the rector stooped and picked up an empty kerosene-can. Without a word he held it aloft. One of the hands had brought a lantern from the house. He swung it up, and the smoky light fell upon the circle of bearded, wondering faces gathered about the rector. As they stared at the kerosene-can, understanding kindled, and an angry growl passed swiftly from throat to throat.

"Yes," said the rector, dropping the can with a tinny clang, "it's the work of an incendiary. And he can't be far away."

"We'll git him!" swore the foreman, with an earnest and ingenious oath which the rector did not seem to hear; and in an instant, as if each man in the crowd had received his individual orders, they all scattered, and faded away into the dark. The rector, left once more alone, stood for a few seconds pulling at his beard and glancing after them, an amused smile lurking about the corners

The Barquentine *G. G. Goodridge* 17

of his kindly, tolerant mouth. Then he kicked the pile of embers all apart, drenched them with several more buckets of water till not a spark winked through the gloom, threw down the bucket with a deep breath of satisfaction, and betook himself away across the fields to where he had left the horse and buggy. He had no interest in the catching of the rascal who had set the fire, — and, indeed, they never did catch him. But as a result of that night's adventure the name of the barquentine, which was to have been the *Elmira Etter,* was changed at the eleventh hour to the *G. G. Goodridge,* much to the rector's surprise and boyish gratification. He had always wanted to travel, but had never felt free to gratify the desire. And now, his imagination was keenly stirred by the thought of this ship which bore his name visiting the foreign lands and the strange, peacock-hued seas of which he had wistfully dreamed. It lay close to his heart that this ship should have to do with nought but honest and clean trading, with humaneness and with good works. When he learned that Captain Job Britton, of Wood Point, was to be her master, he felt secure, for he knew Job's sturdy honesty, as well as the real kindness of heart that hid itself, not ineffectually, behind his gnarled and grizzled exterior.

Captain Job was a widower of fifty. When

ashore, — which was seldom, as every ship-owner from Dorchester to the Joggins craved his services, — he lived in a snug white cottage just below the Point, with his one, idolized daughter, Melissa, and Melissa's aunt, a spinster of matured and immitigable acidity. He was rather short, but of an astonishing breadth of shoulder, with short-cut, matted, reddish gray, streaked hair, bushy red and gray beard, and bristling, pale eyebrows over a pair of deep-set, piercing, steel-gray eyes. His massive neck, and all the skin of his face that was not mantled with hair, were mahogany red, and deeply creased with the wrinkles that tell of ceaseless battling with wind and salt and sun.

Melissa, who since babyhood had been well-spoiled, not only by her father, but even by her aunt, was a smallish, thinnish, decidedly pretty blonde of the carroty type, with eyes pale but bright, a skin faintly freckled, and a mouth both full-lipped and firm, which curiously contradicted the softness of the rest of her face. Her voice was a childlike treble, and her whole manner was one of trustful frankness. Nevertheless, for all her softness and trustfulness, no one but her father quite trusted her; and the girls at the Sackville seminary, where she had got her schooling, found that, though she was generous in her way, and anxious to be liked, it was never safe to traverse her purpose in even the most trivial matter. They distrusted her, of course, for her prettiness, among other good reasons; but most of all they distrusted her because, though she seemed so timid, she was not, in reality, afraid of anything, not even of Junebugs and mice, which every nice young lady ought to fear. From all this it would appear that Melissa Britton, behind her small, pale face and under her luxuriant, glossy, light red hair, concealed a personality to be reckoned with. Both she and Luella Warden sang in the parish church choir, her flute-like soprano and Luella's rich contralto being the rector's chief dependence on those rare occasions, such as Christmas, or Easter, or a visit from the bishop, when there was anthem-music to be rendered. Between the two there was a certain natural rivalry in this matter of voice, though neither of them realized it, thanks to the rector's vigilant tact. Melissa admired Luella's voice, but confidently, though in secret, preferred her own. Luella was inclined, as a rule, to agree with her. While the rector, rather preferring Luella's for its sympathetic breadth and cello-like tenderness, never allowed his preference to be guessed.

CHAPTER III.

THE WEDDING THAT WAS NOT

TECHNICALLY, it was a rectory, in that it was the official residence of the rector of the parishes of Westcock and Dorchester; but the old, wide-eaved, brick house where Mr. Goodridge lived was known as Westcock Parsonage. It stood about half-way up the long slope of the hill, presenting its side, with dormer-windowed roof, to the vast, aerial view of the marshes and the bay, while its wide gable-end fronted on the ill-kept road running up and over the ridge. At each end of the house stood a luxuriant thicket of lilacs, and between the lilacs, along below the windows of the view, ran a green terrace studded with pink, yellow, and blue beehives. Below the terrace spread a neat garden of old-fashioned flowers, flanked by old cherry and apple trees; and below that a strip of vegetable garden, showing by its trim prosperity that the rector was a good gardener. Then, a sloping field of upland grass, thick-starred with buttercups and daisies. Then the Wood Point road along the hillside, with its two parallel lines of weather-beaten fence; and below the road a half-mile of fields and rough pasture lots, leading down to the deep-bosomed fertility of the marsh-level. From those high, narrow dormer-windows on the roof, looking southeastward over the solitudes of green, and tawny gold, and blue, all the pageants of the hours and the seasons could be seen radiantly unfolding. Behind the house, to shield it from the fierce north winds, towered groves of ancient, sombre, dark green spruce and fir, their high, serried tops populous with crows. Across the front end of the parsonage ran a low veranda, and about ten paces before the veranda steps stood a lofty, spire-like, blue-green hackmatack-tree, whose feathery and delicate needles sighed to every air. In a circle around the hackmatack ran the red earth driveway, then straight on for about forty paces to the white front gate, leading to the road over the hill. Some fifty or sixty paces below the parsonage gate this road crossed the Wood Point road at right angles, and led away down between pastures on the right and the high fences and trees of Westcock House on the left, till it petered out to a mere cart-track, passed under a set of high bars, and wound away over the marshes toward the creek-mouth and the dyke.

It was up this road that Luella came in the dusk, with the faint sound of the church-bell pulsing intermittently on her ears. She passed the bars without knowing whether she had let them down or climbed over. Mounting the slope, she was poignantly conscious of a sudden waft of perfume from a deep thicket of blossoming lilacs in the back field of Westcock House. The soft, melting, passionate fragrance stabbed her like a knife-thrust. It was memory made palpable, of one wonderful night when she and Jim had sat for hours amid the scented dark of those trees, listening to the soft roar of the ebb down the channels of Tantramar. Her face twisted, and she half-stumbled. Then she pressed on resolutely up the hill.

At the crossroads she halted. To reach her own home, she must turn to the right along the Wood Point road, pass the black groves of Westcock House, with their haunted deeps of silence, skirt the mysterious gully of the Back Lot, descend the water-worn track of Lawrence's Hill, and so along past Purdy's shipyard to the corner store of her uncle, old Abner Baisley, on the bank of the Frosty Hollow " Bito." She did not want to go home. In the dining-room window of the parsonage she saw a light. To her that house stood for every lovingkindness, and understanding, and succour. She wanted to feel the rector's hand, warm and strong, clasp hers for a moment. She wanted Mrs. Goodridge to give her a kiss and a vigorous hug, and

The Wedding That Was Not

murmur at the same time, rather abstractedly, "Well, dear!" Through all the numbness of her despair she was absurdly conscious of the sudden, disconcerting way in which the lady would then take notice, and exclaim — "But where's your sunbonnet, Luella? You'll catch your death of cold, out at night without a thing on your head, and the dew falling!" These things went through her brain, however, like something she had read of long ago, concerning people who perhaps had never existed at all. She knew that the rector and Mrs. Goodridge were both away at church. That pitiless, faint throbbing of the bell had stopped a few moments before, — and the rector was now beginning, "Dearly beloved brethren, the Scripture moveth us in sundry places — " Mrs. Goodridge was in the square, green-lined rectory pew, close under the pulpit, and even now turning to scan the back pews with her bright but near-sighted blue eyes and to wonder what could be keeping Luella and Jim so late. No, there was no help at the parsonage. And if her friends, dear and trusted as they were, *had* been at home, Luella knew that she would not, could not, have let out her cry of anguish even to them. She would have shut her teeth fast, just as she was doing now, till her jaws hurt.

She realized now that she had gone up to the big white gate of the parsonage, and was staring through it, her forehead pressed against the top bar. What her purpose was, or her desire, she did not even try to think. There was nothing to be done, but just wait, wait, wait, every hour an eternity, yet all bearing her with fierce, insidious haste toward a calamity from which there was no escape. With her eyes fixed upon the dim shape of the parsonage veranda, yet seeing nothing, she stood there motionless, she knew not how long. Suddenly she was startled by the sound of footsteps close at her side, and, turning swiftly, she found herself face to face with Mary Dugan, the maid of all work at the parsonage.

Mary Dugan threw up her hands in amazement.

"Well, I never!" she cried. "Be this you, Luelly Warden, or your ghost?"

"It's me, Mary!" answered Luella, in a strained, flat voice.

"But, land's sakes alive, why ain't you down to the church, gittin' married this very minute?" went on Mary, hopelessly bewildered.

"I ain't going to get married," muttered Luella, dully, leaning her forehead once more against the top bar. Her hair had come down again, and seemed to make a pale light in the rich summer gloom.

"You, not git married? What d'you mean?

The Wedding That Was Not 25

What's happened? Where's Jim?" queried Mary, breathlessly.

"We had a falling out. He's gone!" responded Luella, in an even voice, as if it was all no great matter.

Mary Dugan was silent for a moment. She felt herself in the presence of a tragedy, and her simple heart was moved. She had seen a ship go out that afternoon, but had not dreamed it was the *G. G. Goodridge*. She came up close, and threw an arm over Luella's shoulder.

"That wa'n't the *Goodridge* I seen goin' out this afternoon!" she said.

"It was!" replied Luella.

"Poor dear! Poor dear!" whispered Mary, awed by the situation, which her experienced heart was quick to apprehend. "I'd never have thought it of Jim Calder. Of all the Westcock boys, he's the last one I'd 'a' thought it of!"

The infinite pity in her voice smote Luella's slumbering pride to life. She shook off the compassionate arm, and turned upon Mary with eyes that flamed in the dark.

"I did it myself!" she cried, thickly. Her words would hardly form themselves, and her tongue tripped. "Jim ain't to blame. It's every mite my fault. I did it myself!" Thrusting Mary aside, she flung off fiercely down the hill, and turned the corner for home. In her outraged pride she had spoken words which sowed an ill seed of doubt in even the kindly mind of Mary Dugan. For the time, however, Mary had no thought save of compassion for the girl, and of indignation against Jim Calder.

"Poor babe!" she muttered to herself, looking with pity after the dim figure flitting along against the black background of the Westcock House firs. "I'm afeard she's been an' gone an' bit off her nose to spite her face! Lor', how Westcock'll talk! Tss! Tss! I wisht I knowed *jest* what'd happened!" Speculating on this theme Mary let herself through the gate, and strolled contemplatively up the drive between the two rows of little, pointed spruce bushes which the rector had just planted. At the veranda steps she paused, sniffed with deep satisfaction the rich and soft night air, and muttered — "Lor', how sweet them laylocks does smell!" Then, remembering that the front door was locked, she went around to the kitchen and let herself in with the big, back door key.

Meanwhile Luella was speeding on past the haunted groves, and down over Lawrence's Hill. In her sick rage at the pity in Mary Dugan's voice, she quite forgot that she might be cruelly misinterpreted if she took the blame upon herself. All she thought of was that she could not and would

The Wedding That Was Not

not endure to be pitied. She felt that she would strangle with her bare hands any one who should say she had been jilted. At the foot of the hill she paused, and stared for several minutes along the road to her right, where a light gleamed through an apple-tree some three or four hundred yards away. That light came from the window of Mrs. Rebecca Calder, Jim's mother; and Luella said to herself: " She's glad of it. I know she is!" Having muttered this over several times, she seemed to feel Mrs. Calder's uncompromising and inescapable eyes upon her, and grew suddenly aware once more that her hair was down about her shoulders. Hurriedly she coiled it up again, then turned her steps resolutely homeward, with the rush of the ebb tide, as the creek emptied itself tempestuously into the Tantramar, filling the night with soft, indeterminate sound.

When she had come opposite Purdy's shipyard, holding her eyes aloof from the spot where still stood the skeleton poles and scaffoldings, empty as her life, it suddenly occurred to her that by this time church must be coming out. The thought galvanized her into activity. She must not meet any one who had been there, any one who had joined in the buzz of wondering talk in the porch after service. Above all, she could not face her Uncle Abner on his return. He would be furious, and insulted. She could see him stalking back, stiff in his long black broadcloth coat, his raw, high-featured, narrow face both hard and weak, and his thin, grayish-reddish side-whiskers bristling forward. She realized what his petty, intolerable questioning would be, and how his close-set little eyes would be red around the lids as they gimleted into her soul. She must, oh, she *must* be home, and safely locked into her own room over the side porch, before he arrived. She broke into a run, now; and only steadied down again to a swift walk when two "hands" from the shipyard approached. They gave her "Good evenin'," cordially and respectfully, and turned to stare after her in amazement as she went by them with only an inarticulate sound in response to their salutation. Her lips and mouth and throat were as dry as wood. To her infinite relief she reached the "Bito" without passing any more wayfarers. Two teams were hitched to the fence beside the store, and half a dozen men and boys were loitering around outside, waiting for Mr. Baisley to return from service and open up shop again. Not looking at any of them, and merely muttering a collective reply to their various greetings, Luella sped past to the little garden gate, up the narrow path, and in through the tiny latticework porch at the end of the house, which was the private entrance, and served to keep the living-

The Wedding That Was Not

rooms apart from the traffic of the store. Not pausing to light the lamp, she ran up the narrow, crooked, tilted stairs, gained her slant-roofed sanctuary under the eaves, and locked herself in. Till the morrow, at least, she was safe from all torture of tongues.

CHAPTER IV.

HER LOVER AND HIS MOTHER

A PRIM, uncompromising house of two stories, shingled all over, and weather-beaten to a soft, dark gray, was the dwelling of Jim Calder and his mother. In spite of itself, as it were, it had a homey, comfortable air. Big apple-trees, with one white birch and one Lombardy poplar, stood at either end of it. Hop-vines and scarlet-runner beans grew all over its fences; and the little plot between the stoop and the front gate, on either side of the shell-bordered path, was bright with pink and purple sweet peas, orange nasturtiums, scarlet geraniums, pansies, and other old-fashioned blooms. Everything connected with it was aggressively clean. When Luella, standing for that brief moment at the foot of Lawrence's Hill, stared in numb despair at the far-off light in the back window of Mrs. Calder's house, she little guessed that Mrs. Calder was sitting by that light, her austere, faded face bitter with resentment, as she read and re-read an incoherent note of farewell from Jim. The mother, lonely but self-possessed, had expected to hold her son to her heart once again that night, before yielding him up to a wife whom she hated, and before bidding him good-bye for two long years. Now that her boy had left her thus inexplicably, without a kiss, the mother, in her aching and angry heart, laid all the blame upon the girl, whose very existence she had always resented. Over and over, as she sat there by the little oil lamp, rocking fiercely, the open letter in her lap, she told herself that her boy would never have gone off in that mad, cruel fashion, unless he had found out something bad about Luelly Warden. She knew Jim's love for the girl, little as she sympathized with it. And now, forgiving Jim's treatment of herself, she turned all her bitterness against the unhappy Luella. Hour after hour she sat rocking beside the lamp, holding the letter clutched in her worn, big-knuckled fingers, listening to the moaning rush of the ebb as it fled seaward within a furlong of her doors, and picturing to herself the flight of the *G. G. Goodridge* under the starlit night. When the first of the dawn, spreading over Tantramar, began to pale the little yellow flame of her lamp, she got up briskly, pressed out the crumpled paper with care, folded it away under some lace kerchiefs and Sunday bows in her top bureau drawer, turned out the light, and muttered inaudibly a harsh imprecation upon the girl. Then, methodically removing her neckerchief, her stout shoes, and the stiff black silk dress which she had put on in Jim's honour, she threw herself down on the bed without undressing. Such an irregularity was, for her, a mark of the gravest emotional disturbance. So bitter was her heart in its loneliness and resentment that if she could have seen Luella at that hour, white-lipped and dry-eyed with anguish, lying with her face to the wall in the little room overlooking the " Bito," she would have exulted in every fibre over the girl's voiceless despair.

It was just two years ago that very night that Jim Calder, then a sturdy and tan-faced stripling of eighteen, lately home from a voyage to the West Indies, had brought Luella to his mother in a glow of triumph and announced their betrothal. Never till that moment had Mrs. Calder had aught but good-will for Luella. She knew her to be modest, well-mannered, self-respecting, and of good countryside stock, her father having been owner and captain of a two-topmast schooner which traded profitably between the Fundy ports and Boston. Now, however, she saw in this seventeen-year-old girl, with her tall, straight, vigorous form, her mane of burnished flax, like cool, pale gold, her steady, grave, porcelain-blue eyes under deep brows, her broad forehead and clean-cut features of a fairness which all the marsh-winds and unshadowed suns could but touch to cream, her somewhat large and very red mouth under whose childishness was already beginning to show a suggestion of womanly strength, tenderness, and passion, — in this girl she saw a crafty woman, who had succeeded in ensnaring her boy. She looked slowly from Luella to Jim. She studied his frank, young face, with its wholesome, ruddy tan, the mouth ardent and positive, the eyes of light hazel, honest, fearless, kind, — the hair a dark warm brown, thick, elastic, half-curling, and short. She eyed his straight figure, broad in the shoulder, narrow in the hips, of middle stature, and suggesting both strength and alertness. A hot flush of resentment went over her, at the thought that another woman should supersede her, by ever so little, in the heart of her beautiful son. She thought, however, that this emotion was only a proper anger against a designing woman, who had taken advantage of a boy's ignorance. She looked Luella straight in the eyes, and said, coldly:

"I reckon Jim's a leetle young to be thinking about a wife. He's a leetle mite young, too, maybe, to be knowing his own mind."

Jim stared at her in amazement so deep that there was, at first, no room for indignation; but Luella flushed up to the roots of her fair hair. At first her lips quivered childishly, and her blue eyes filled. Then the underlying strength of her nature asserted itself. Her mouth steadied, and her eyes steadied as they answered gravely the elder woman's challenge. She was about to make a severe retort, when a swift glance at Jim's face showed her that some sort of storm was rising through his confusion, and about to break in words which his mother might find it hard to forget. With an inspiration of wisdom beyond her years she intervened.

"I'm so sorry you are not pleased, Mrs Calder," she said, modestly. "But indeed, I'll try to please you and make you like me. I can't help loving Jim."

Mrs. Calder, too, had noted the danger-signal in the boy's face, and fearless though she was, she heeded it. Moreover, she felt suddenly ashamed of herself, and reproachful for having driven the joy from Jim's face. She held out her hand, and forced a smile of frosty welcome to her austere lips.

"Forgive my ugliness, Luelly!" she said. "An' you, too, Jim. I *was* right ugly to talk that way, an' you two young things so happy!"

Luella accepted the proffered hand warmly, with secret triumph. But Jim was not yet conciliated.

"If you've got anything to say agin Luella, mother, out with it, right now!" he demanded, with a little stumbling in his speech from the stress of his wrath. "I know my own mind 'bout as well as most folks, I reckon. An' I'm goin' to marry Luella the day I get to be mate."

"No, Jim, I hain't a word to say agin Luella,— not a word," his mother hastened to protest. "So far's I know, ther' ain't a finer nor a cleverer girl in Westcock parish. I reckon I was jest ugly." And she held out a deprecating hand to Jim.

The boy looked at her in silence for a moment, then at Luella's serene face. The anger died from his mouth and eyes as a cloud melts suddenly to let the sun shine through, and stepping forward impetuously, he flung his arms about his mother's unbending shoulders. As he kissed her she thrust her hands into his thick, warm hair and squeezed his head against her cheek.

"Ye'll have to be powerful good to Jim, Luella," she said, with an attempt at graciousness. "He's awful tender-hearted, but he's got a leetle mite of his old mother's ugly temper. Ye'll have to be nice to him, child!"

Not knowing just what she had better reply to this, Luella smiled her assent, and tied superfluous knots in the strings of the sunbonnet which hung back from her firm white throat. Jim, however, was hugely relieved,— rejoicing more at the clearing of the storm than he could have rejoiced had there been no storm to clear. Seizing the two women, one in each arm, he drew them close to him and to each other, kissed them both laughingly on the neck, and cried, "Oh, I know you two're goin' to git to likin' each other such a lot, *my* nose'll be out of joint with both of you before I git back from my next voyage."

This sanguine dream of his, however, was far from coming true.

For a long time both women tried honestly enough to like each other. But Luella, finding it impossible to quite believe in the elder woman's good-will, was ever ready to suspect covert censure, to interpret the blunders of a self-centred and crude nature as intentional slight. Mrs. Calder, on her part, made what she really believed to be a sincere attempt to discover that charm and goodness in the girl which Jim found in her so abundantly. At every such attempt, however, she would stumble upon something which, to her hopelessly prejudiced eyes, was evidence of the girl's scheming craft. There was little that she could not so twist, in the unhappy perversity of her vision. And thus, in her own teeth, as it were, she forced herself to the unalterable conviction that Luella was unworthy. She had tried her best, she believed. And being in very truth a woman of conscientious scruple, most unwilling to be caught at any time beyond shelter of her own self-commendation, she honestly grieved over what she called Jim's infatuation, and professed to bewail Luella's unworth. Against this attitude Luella could not long contend. When she came to realize it fully, she broke down in girlish anger and misery, wildly resentful of an injustice which she had no power or experience to resist. Pride came presently to her rescue, however, with a certain poise and reticence which acted upon the elder woman like a cutting retort; and before Jim had been three months away his mother and his sweetheart were passing each other, at church or on the country road, without so much as a glance of recognition.

In all this Luella had Westcock on her side, which was a continual balm to her injured heart. Every one knew that she was the victim of the bitter jealousy of a mother, — and of a very unreasoning mother. Luella was not exactly popular, — she was too reserved and too distinguished-looking for that; but she was highly thought of. On the other hand, all the village knew that Mrs. Calder was "hard to get along with," besides being always critical in her attitude toward everything and every one not cut precisely to her own pattern. To be sure, Jim was not cut to her pattern, but rather to the very unlike and very winning one of his long-dead father. Folk said that his mother forgave him that, because she realized she had done the cutting herself and could see no flaw in her own handiwork. When Mary Dugan, at the sewing-circle, declared that if Jim had picked an angel out of heaven, Mrs. Calder would have thought her a Delilah, all Westcock said, "That's so!" And many were the benevolent efforts made to egg Luella on to a proper system of retaliatory back-biting, in the interests of general conversation. But Luella was wise enough to entrench herself in silence, and in thoughts of Jim.

This self-control on the part of a mere child like Luella passed with most of the good Westcock folk as overmeekness, a lack of proper spirit. But in the eyes of the rector, who saw the steadfast stuff that went to her make-up, she found the fullest understanding. He said not a word to her on the subject; but his kind, comprehending glance over and over again came to her reassurance when her courage was near breaking. There was something in that look which always made her not only stronger, but more tolerant and forgiving, and convinced her that things would all come right in the end. Once or twice, having a faith that he could straighten out any difficulty, she thought of begging him to say a word to Mrs. Calder. But she reminded herself that this would be a presumption on her part, and with a flush of shame she forbore. It was clear that the rector knew, and therefore would speak if he thought best.

Being a shrewd as well as a tender watcher of the human heart, the rector did *not* think best to speak to Mrs. Calder about Luella. He was apt to be impatient of self-righteousness beyond other sins; and he thought Mrs. Calder self-righteous. Moreover, she was not of his flock, though Jim was. She was an old-school Presbyterian, who had joined the Calvinist Baptists because there were no other Presbyterians in the Tantramar country. She yielded the rector a rather grudging respect, but at the same time strongly disapproved of his lack of harshness toward sinners. She openly charged him with a readiness to believe that almost any sinner, if not all sinners, might achieve salvation, — a belief which, in her eyes, was nothing less than a damnable and damning heresy. Knowing that she held this attitude toward him, the rector felt that it would only make matters worse if he should attempt to soften her toward Luella. He read accurately the set of that long jaw and positive, long, uncompromising upper lip. Therefore he contented himself with being very kind and cordial toward her, and sympathizing with all her little troubles, in the hope of ultimately softening her heart with the warmth of his own great-hearted, patient humanity.

When Jim came home again, some six months after his betrothal to Luella, he was at first furious, then desperately distressed over the situation. Devoted though he was to his mother, he understood her peculiarities; and it needed only her own statement of her case to convince him how hopelessly she was in the wrong. Luella, on the other hand, refrained from justifying herself to him — and had the reward of seeing herself justified in his eyes without a word. Thereafter, he adopted the rector's tactics of strict non-interference, on the assumption that if time and patience could not soften his mother's heart, nothing could. He resumed his wonted, irresistible sunniness, acted as if nothing was the matter, and managed to keep not only Luella but his mother as well in a state of equanimity throughout his visit.

CHAPTER V.

WHAT MELISSA WANTED

DURING the next eighteen months, — from the hour when she saw that Jim understood her and trusted her in the trouble with his mother, to the day when the *G. G. Goodridge* went out on the yellow tide, — Luella was happy. Mrs. Calder's animosity, acquiring some discretion, held itself in abeyance, — a truce, not a peace. Jim made only short voyages, — none farther than to Key West or Havana or Matanzas, — and managed to spend a good half his time ashore, feverishly studying navigation in order to pass his examinations for mate's certificate. While he was at home Luella had nothing more to desire, and their little world, for the most part, looked kindly upon their young content. Both sang in the choir of the parish church; and on those evenings, once a week, when the rector would give up a couple of hours to the task of helping Jim through the mysteries of latitude and longitude, right ascension and circle-sailing, Mrs. Goodridge would always invite Luella up to tea. The walk home from the parsonage, through the quiet Westcock night, with never a sound but the soft rush of the tide on Tantramar, seemed always a little more wonderful than any of the other walks they took together. Their hopes were gay with all the colours that youth, and the wide imaginations of their seafaring kind, could create; and fulfilment seemed very near.

During Jim's absences, Luella's time was well filled by her duties as housekeeper to her Uncle Abner, and by her devoted attendance on the church and the parsonage. Being the betrothed of Jim Calder, she received no attentions from any of the other young men of the village, except, once in awhile, from her scapegrace cousin, the ne'er-do-well shad-fisherman, Bud Whalley. From their smallest childhood Bud had been like a brother to her; and she loved him all the more resolutely because, as he grew up to a reckless and irresponsible manhood, Westcock turned the cold shoulder upon him. He drank disastrously, at times. He loafed shamelessly all the time, except when the shad were running. He openly jeered at Westcock opinion. So Westcock said he was a reprobate, and drew its skirts aside as he passed. He had no friends in the village but Luella, who tried in vain to reform him, and the rector, who believed there was a lot of good in him which he would some day manage to get at. Bud would sometimes go to church, sitting like a pariah in a dark seat under the gallery. And sometimes, to the scandal of the congregation, Luella would let him walk home with her afterward. When Jim was home, Bud sometimes went walking with him and Luella together, for Jim was determined to be friendly to any relation of Luella's, and had amiable designs for Bud's future. And Bud rewarded Luella's loyalty with a reverent devotion which was altogether the best thing in his futile life.

Abner Baisley's house, the wide-roofed, story-and-a-half, white cottage overlooking the " Bito," was a large domain for Luella to rule unaided. But with the store portion, — which consisted of a large, square room, smelling of molasses, fish, and kerosene, and a little, dark back room subtly scented with tobacco and West Indies rum, — she had nothing whatever to do. Her uncle and the chore-boy attended to that part of the establishment. The rest — the house proper — Luella cared for with no help but that of a scrub-woman at the seasons of spring and fall house-cleaning. She was housemaid, cook, and housekeeper, all at the same time; and having a talent for method combined with a calm, unwasteful energy, she could find time to live a little, and think a little, outside the rut of her daily task. Her chintz-decked bedroom under the eaves, and the cosy, though cluttered, sitting-room, with its outlook upon the changeful channel of the creek, showed that her natural love of beauty had profited by her intimacy at the parsonage. The sleek, flashy-framed chromos and the gaudy green and magenta carpet in the sitting-room she could not change, for her Uncle Abner delighted in both. But in spite of them she managed, somehow, to make the room look pretty and fit, so that it drew frequent compliments not from the rector only, but even from Mrs. Goodridge, who was much harder to please. Through spring, summer, and fall both the sitting-room and her own bedroom were kept bright with all blooms of the season, for the steep-sloped, narrow garden, which seemed likely at any time to slide down into the vast, red, seething basin of the " Bito," rewarded richly the pains she put upon it. It had the earliest blossoms of the year, and the latest. She was a skilful gardener, and under her grave but cunning cajolery the chore-boy, Andy, became almost as interested in the garden as she was herself. In fact, even her Uncle Abner, who would rather have seen the patch blue-green with cabbages for the store, became reconciled to its beauty at last, and ceased to grumble. It was worth quite a number of cabbages to him, to have people talking about his garden. Many, indeed, driving through from Wood Point to Sackville, would stop their horses to look at the steep glory of bloom and green, and end by coming into the store to buy something. Above all, the garden became a pride to Mr. Baisley, when, every Sunday at church, he could look at the fresh flowers on the altar and remember that they were his. There was no other garden in the parish to be depended upon but Luella's, so the rector fell into the way of leaving the matter of the flowers altogether to her.

No one in Westcock begrudged Luella this unprofitable honour, except Melissa Britton. Melissa, at last, as she contemplated the abundant blooms every Sunday from her place in the choir, came to remember that she had a garden of her own. As it stood, to be sure, it was not much of a garden; but she bethought herself that she had both the money and the intelligence to make it something that would far outshine Luella's. Melissa had not a spark of cheap envy in her make-up. If she had not got the idea into her cool and clever head that it would really interest her to attend to the decorations of chancel and pulpit every Sunday, — that it would be a delight to grow such lilies, roses, pinks, stocks, gladioli, dahlias, and then contemplate her handiwork enshrined, Luella might have had all the honour, and welcome. But with Melissa, to want a thing was to set about making ready to get it. She developed a sudden enthusiasm for

Luella's garden. She cultivated Luella, to learn how Luella cultivated flowers. Then she sent away to Boston for several books on horticulture, and to the great advertising seedsmen and florists for their catalogues. Work was begun at once on her own neglected plot, which she astonished with such profusion of fertilizers as warmed it to its impoverished heart. And for several months her imagination was filled with the glowing colour-plates of her catalogues, her memory with an entrancing confusion of unknown names, mostly Latin.

The scheme, which no one but Melissa for a single moment suspected, was making fine progress, when one Sunday morning in church Jim Calder's confident baritone, exulting through the *Te Deum,* caught her ear.

In an indifferent way, Melissa had always recognized that Jim had a good voice. The rector said so, and he knew. But to-day, for the first time, she felt the virile beauty of it, and its vibration started a strange thrill in her nerves and veins. She looked at him with an absolutely new interest, an unwonted brightness and depth of colour coming into her eyes. Jim was just home from a two months' voyage to the West Indies. Melissa, hitherto, had seen him without differentiating him, so to speak. She was amazed, now, at his beauty. All at once he had matured. His boyish mouth had gained mastery. His face of ruddy tan was adorned by a soft little golden brown moustache. His clear, greenish hazel eyes, dancing and fearless, met Melissa's and held them for a moment, and Melissa tingled from her forehead to her toes.

From that moment Melissa's interest in her garden and her seed catalogues entered upon a rapid decline. She no longer wanted to relieve Luella of the duty of supplying the church with flowers. Luella had something else, in Melissa's eyes better worth appropriating.

Melissa knew very well, of course, about Jim's engagement to Luella, but that knowledge troubled her little. Her confidence in her own resources had never been shaken. She was troubled rather more, however, by the knowledge presently thrust upon her, that Jim, who sat directly opposite her in the little choir, was obviously unconscious of her presence. After church she went around, as was usual now, to see Luella's garden, and found an opportunity to compliment Jim, with careless frankness, on his voice, his colour, and his newly achieved moustache. Jim was cordial, in his happy fashion, and appreciative of her compliments, which gained by a certain judicial air with which she conveyed them. Two or three discreet experiments, however, — so discreet that not even Luella's feminine vigilance took alarm, — convinced her that Luella had the young sailor absolutely at her feet. Melissa saw that she would need all her wits in this enterprise. She set herself to consider, at the same time taking care that Jim should happen to see her so often that he could not quite forget her existence. Out of this considering came a gradual, unobtrusive friendliness, which flattered Jim while it troubled no one, not even Luella. Then, by a master-stroke of ingenuity, she made the unsuspicious Luella her ally against herself. She frankly and laughingly challenged Luella to a contest of flowers, vowing that her little garden on the high shoulder of Wood Point should utterly eclipse the steep close of bloom overlooking the "Bito." She got Luella so interested in this contest that she was for ever talking to Jim about it, — and about Melissa. Thus it was Luella herself, more than any one or anything else, that gave Melissa Britton her first importance in Jim's eyes.

When, at last, Melissa announced her sudden resolve to go sailing around the world with her father on his next voyage, of course this stimulating rivalry in gardens came to an end; but it had accomplished its purpose. Melissa was an acknowledged friend and well-wisher of both Jim and Luella. It was not till some months later that Captain Britton took command of the new barquen-

What Melissa Wanted 49

tine, the *G. G. Goodridge,* and gave Jim the berth of second mate aboard her. In this Melissa's hand did not appear; and there was nothing extraordinary in it, anyhow. Every one in Westcock knew that the rector was deeply interested in the ship which bore his name. Every one knew, also, that he was deeply interested in Jim Calder. What more natural than that Captain Britton, who loved the rector, should please him in the appointment of his second mate? Melissa was far too wise to let even Jim know that she had had a hand in the business. She was pleasantly surprised at the news; but not a shade more cordial about it than good compliment required.

So far, all was going well with Melissa's purpose. A weaker girl, however, would have realized with dismay that in furthering Jim Calder's advancement she was hastening the hour of his marriage. Westcock had known for a year that the wedding was to take place " when Jim gits to be mate." But Melissa would not let impatience or oversolicitude force her hand. She had a faith that fate, as usual, would furnish her occasion in good time. If she could not prevent the marriage without betraying herself, — well, it would not be prevented. Jim would have to leave Luella in St. John, a few days after the wedding, — not to see her again for perhaps two years. In those two years would lie her opportunity. It would be strange thing, she thought, setting her mouth hard, if, with two years of unlimited opportunity, she could not triumph over a girl like Luella Warden!

CHAPTER VI.

MELISSA'S MASTER-STROKE

ABOUT two weeks before the *G. G. Goodridge* was to sail, however, Fate quite came up to Melissa's expectations, and played most complacently into her hands. Bud Whalley, coming out to the *G. G. Goodridge* one day when Melissa was on board decorating her cabin, served as fate's instrument. He had brought a half-barrel of " No. 1 Extra " salt Chignecto shad for the use of the captain's cabin; and he was in the genial humour of the three-quarters drunk. Stepping backwards to shout to a friend aloft in the rigging, he fell into the open hold, broke his back across the edge of a balk, and died within fifteen minutes.

Time and again had Melissa held Bud Whalley under the scrutiny of her clear, pale eyes, hoping to detect in him some clue by which to solve her main problem. She knew, of course, the wild young fisherman's devotion to his cousin. And like every one else in Westcock, she was aware of Luella's affection for him, in spite of all his wildness. But she was a shrewd reader of hearts, this country girl, and she saw that nothing could make Bud Whalley a traitor to the one human being who stood by him through thick and thin. Alive, no one could use this harebrained but chivalrous adventurer of the tides. But dead, — however his impetuous spirit may have raged to see it, he was a tool in Melissa's little unrelenting hands.

Several times already Melissa had dropped the germs of doubt into Jim's mind, but so delicately that Jim had never dreamed himself infected. She did not know, at the time, that they would ever spring to life and do her service; but, so long as she was not suspected of planting them, it was well they should be there ready. Now, Luella's unrestrained sorrow over her cousin's death gave Melissa another chance to sow her ill seeds. She gratified Jim by calling every one's attention to Luella's warmth of heart and cousinly devotion.

From that day on, however, her attitude toward Luella changed subtly. She managed so skilfully as to show the change to Jim more than to Luella herself, and the latter hardly noticed it. But Jim could not help noticing it, and wondering about it, and worrying over it; till at last he openly taxed Melissa with it. The girl gazed at him steadily for some seconds, with deep eyes of compassion, and opened trembling lips to reply. All she could say, however, was only "Oh, Jim!" But her voice made it sound like, "Oh, my poor, poor Jim!" Then, as if words choked her, she threw her hands apart, and turned, and ran from him, leaving him half-sick with a sense of imminent calamity. For the next few days, on ship or ashore, she evaded his persistent efforts to have speech with her, till his vague apprehensions became a torture. Nevertheless, he had no faintest suspicion of anything to Luella's discredit, but merely could not endure that the woman whom he loved as his own life should be misunderstood by the woman whom he counted his best friend. He simply would not have it. Melissa *must* "act right" toward Luella, in spite of the fact that Luella, in her innocence of heart and her satisfaction with life and love, was troubling herself not at all as to Melissa Britton's whims.

At last, the very morning before the day set for the wedding, Melissa cleverly allowed herself to be caught. Jim planted himself squarely before her, in triumph, and lost no time beating about the bush.

"What is it now, Melissy," he blurted out, "you think you've got against Luella?"

Melissa dropped her eyes, and tried to get past him. Jim caught her by both arms and held her fast. She thrilled from head to foot under the hard grip of his hands, and from beneath her drooped lids her eyes feasted on their strength. But she pretended to be angry.

"Let me go, right off, Jim Calder!" she commanded, striving to twist away.

"You've got to tell me, Melissy!" he demanded, half-resolute, half-pleading.

"I *won't* tell you, so there! You wouldn't believe me, anyway," she retorted, sharply. Then her face softened. She lifted to his eager eyes a look of infinite tenderness and pity. Under its influence his grip upon her arms relaxed, and she gently freed herself. Then, in a low voice, she continued:

"I just *can't* tell you, Jim! It ain't my business. I think too much of you to risk losing your friendship. I can't have you turn against me. No, no, I can't. Don't ask me! I can't! I can't!" And covering her mouth with both hands she gave a sob and ran away into her father's cabin. Jim gazed after her in amazed consternation, till presently his anxiety turned to annoyance. He wheeled about on his heel and stalked forward to give some orders, muttering as he went:

"Oh, hell! What's the use!" Then he proceeded to restore himself to good-humour by thinking about Luella, who never fretted him thus with the tragical-mysterious. When he went ashore a little later, and walked with Luella in the summer-scented twilight, and talked happily with her about the morrow and the future, and what they would do as soon as he could get a ship of his own, he had forgotten all about "Melissa Britton's whims."

Next morning, Jim's duties on shipboard were many and troublesome. As he hurried hither and thither, a little exultant in his new authority, Melissa suddenly presented herself before him, with a bit of folded paper in her hands. The expression in her face drove the cheer from his. It seemed to freeze his veins with foreboding.

"What — what is it, Melissy?" he stammered.

"Come here, Jim!" she said, in a voice that trembled so that it was hardly articulate.

She led him into the cabin, and faced him, steadying herself with one hand on the cabin table. Her eyes met his directly, and with that same look of pity which had so disturbed him before.

"You are a strong man, Jim!" she said, speaking half in a whisper.

"Yes! yes! what is it? Tell me quick, Melissy." And he half-reached out his hand to take the scrap of paper she held.

She put her hands behind her back, and spoke very sadly.

"I'm going to tell you, Jim! You'll hate me, I know you'll hate me. But I'm your friend, and

I've seen I must tell you, whatever it costs me."

Jim said nothing, but stared at her in bewilderment.

"There," she went on, suddenly. "Read that, Jim! It was in Bud Whalley's pocket. You'll know now why I was different to — her!"

She thrust the paper into Jim's hand, and retreated to the other side of the table, as if she feared him.

Cool, sagacious, merciless with the simplicity of primeval instinct, Melissa had done her work with skilled completeness. An expert might have been deceived in the handwriting. Hours and hours she had spent in copying Luella's rather simple hand, from letters written to her about the garden. She had got the paper Luella always used. She had no faintest flicker of compunction, of pity for the girl whose life she was destroying. She despised Luella for her candour and her trustfulness. In fact, she despised every one a little, except Jim, and her father, and the rector — and him she would have despised also, for his unconquerable faith in humanity, but for her perception of his mental power. She watched Jim now with half-uplifted eyes, feigning herself to shrink from the blow which she had been compelled to deal him. But as she watched the change that came slowly over his face, her feigned fear grew real enough. She did not know what might happen. She feared for him, not at all for herself, — and drew a little nearer. She had never guessed that a face like Jim's, boyish, and sunny, and brave, could change so. It had gone gray, and old, and harder than stone, as she was looking. And because she was in love with him, the sight pierced her heart with such a pang that she cried out under her breath for pity, she who was incapable of pity for any one else.

Well, indeed, had she done her work. When Jim looked at the bit of paper which she thrust convulsively into his hands, he recognized at once the thin, bluish, faint-lined paper, with the ill-formed dove stamped at the top of the sheet. It was part of a bankrupt stock which Abner Baisley had purchased in quantity, at a great bargain. He recognized, too, the careful handwriting which was so unspeakably dear to him. Hitherto he had never seen it without a thrill of joy. Now, before he could even begin to gather the drift of what was written, he trembled with a sick terror. He straightened out the creased page, — but the words swam before his eyes. He thought of hurling the thing from him, unread; but the sardonic humour of fate made his loyalty his undoing. His love for Luella, his faith in her, were too great. He would not insult her by fearing to read what she had written. He read, therefore. And again he read. And yet again, — till the words had burned themselves like vitriol into his astounded brain.

"How *can* you be so hard on me, Bud dear? How *can* you be so cruel — when you think of all that's been between us — when *you know what is between us.* How *could* I *marry* you, no matter how I love you? You know you'd break any girl's heart, that was married to you, in a month, Bud dear. You *know* we'd *hate* each other in a month. And maybe I'd kill you then, — or kill myself, Bud. I *must* marry Jim, — because he's as good and kind as you are bad and cruel. But I'm yours, all yours, always, always, Bud, remember that — just because I can't help it. And I'll be back with you in just a few days. And think how long he'll be away. And oh, Bud, forgive me, and don't be so hard, and love me, love me, Bud dear, always. You *must*, for more sakes than just my sake, Bud.

"Your own
"Luella."

As Jim read the letter over and over the whole meaning of it grew clear moment by moment — clear, eternally immutable, indisputable as naked Truth herself. What had been on Melissa's part but a random shot in the dark proved to Jim the

Melissa's Master-stroke

most conclusive and deadly point of all. The very vagueness of the letter, arising from Melissa's ignorance, testified to Luella's guilty caution. Jim knew well what it was that the letter so dimly hinted at. He would have sworn before all the angels and all the saints of heaven to Luella's unshakable fidelity, — but in the face of these her own deliberate words there was no least room for doubt. His whole world fell in ruin about his ears. His brain was yet too bewildered to fully apprehend what had befallen him — though his body, more instantly understanding, was betraying its anguish in the clenching of fingers, the contraction of eyeballs, the blanching of cheek and lip, the crowding back of the blood into the shocked and reluctant heart. In a far-off way he heard himself asking, "Where did you git this, Melissy?" And vaguely, as if from very far away, he heard her answer, tremulously, "In Bud Whalley's pocket!" Then, as he stared at her without replying, his brain recovered its use, and he knew that life and hope were dead within him. He wished that he could drop dead, then, at that monstrous moment. But he could not. And there was work to do. Slowly his locked fingers relaxed; the letter fell to the cabin floor; and he turned, climbed the steep companionway and hurried "up forrard" blindly.

With a wild thought that he might be going

to jump overboard, Melissa followed close at his heels — after picking up the letter. It was a foolish fear, however. She saw Jim stopped by the first mate, Ezra Boltenhouse, who eyed him curiously, and said:

"Jim, the captain's jest sent word he wants to sail this afternoon's tide, 'stead er to-morrow. Owners has got wind o' some more freight we kin pick up in St. John, fer Matanzas, if we're in time. This 'ere wind's just what we've been a-wishin' fer! Couldn't you pull off the weddin' this mornin', 'stead er to-night, an' git Mrs. Calder aboard in time so's we could go out with the tide? It means dollars an' dollars to the ship — an' this her first trip, too!"

"Ther' ain't a-goin' to be no weddin', Ezra," answered Jim, in a strange voice. "I'm a'ready, right now!"

Mr. Boltenhouse looked deeply troubled. He had a faith that anything could be remedied.

"Now, Jim — " he began.

But Jim cut him short, gave him one terrible look, and strode forward among the men, leaving him astounded. He turned to Melissa for enlightenment.

"Jim Calder ain't the man to leave a nice girl like Luelly in the lurch, surely?" he suggested.

"I reckon he must have good reason, Mr. Boltenhouse!" replied Melissa, gravely. "One don't have to ask. To look at his face is enough."

"But what does it mean? What's it all about? It's nothin' but a pair of young fools they be! Why don't somebody bring 'em to their senses, afore it's too late? I won't never believe a word agin Luelly Warden, anyhow. If Jim lets her slip, he'll lose the finest girl in Westcock."

His sunburnt forehead and sun-bleached, shaggy eyebrows were knotted with solicitude, as he gaped after Jim's retreating form.

A fierce wave of jealousy surged up from Melissa's heart, flooding face and neck; and the note which she clutched in her pocket burned at her fingers. She would show it to this fool who thought the perfection of all womanhood centred in Luella Warden; and it would open his eyes for him. But her wary brain crushed down the rage within her; and amazement at her own madness cooled her with a shock.

"That's just what I'd have thought myself, Mr. Boltenhouse," she answered, sadly. "But from all I can make out, it must be something terrible come between them. I tried to talk to him, till I dasn't say another word, the look in his face was that awful. Oh, I'm glad we're going to sail to-day. I hope he won't go ashore. I'd be afraid something even more dreadful might happen."

"An' couldn't you git any kind of a clue as to what it's all about?" persisted the mate, eying Jim's distant form with resentful bewilderment.

Melissa shook her head hopelessly.

"Well, 'tain't no business of our'n, I suppose!" snapped the mate, turning away.

Jim went about his work like a machine, giving his orders in a voice of iron so unlike his usual brisk and cheerful tones that the men kept watching him furtively. His face, with eyes sunken, yet burning, the mouth gray and dead, effectually prevented questions. When, some four hours later, Captain Britton came hurrying aboard, to find the ship almost ready to sail and no Luella there, he fell into a rage at once.

"What does this mean, Mr. Calder?" he demanded, his face reddening up hotly. "Damn it, man, I sent you word time enough. Do you think I'm goin' to wait over till the nex' tide to suit your convenience?"

"No occasion to wait on my account, captain! I'm ready," answered Jim, in a level voice.

"No occasion? What? — Where's the girl? What d'you mean? What in hell — " stammered the captain, staring about as if he expected to see Luella come over the bulwarks. Getting no reply, he stared angrily into Jim's face. As he did so, his anger paled away. Without repeating his demands

Melissa's Master-stroke 63

for enlightenment he began roaring orders in his great fog-horn voice till he had every man aboard on the run. Then he hurried off to the cabin to look for Melissa, who was his resort in any trouble, and make another vain effort to find out what had happened.

An hour later, the anchor came up, to the rhythm of the swinging chantey; and the *G. G. Goodridge,* under full sail, went out from Tantramar with wind and tide.

CHAPTER VII.

LUELLA'S FRIENDS, AND OTHERS

ON the day after the sailing of the *G. G. Goodridge,* all Westcock stirred with a pleasurable thrill of anticipation. How was Luella going to take it? And how was she going to explain it? A few, however, ventured to suggest that maybe there wouldn't be much information coming.

White and quivering from her night of tearless vigil, Luella came down in the early morning to take up the day's work and face her little world. Her uncle Abner was already in the store, as usual; but when he caught sound of her in the kitchen he came mincing out to the attack, his narrow face sharp with grievance, his sparse side-whiskers bristling forward with resentment because, on his return from church, Luella had disregarded his hammerings at her bedroom door.

"Good morning, Uncle Abner!" said Luella, without looking up. Her supreme effort was to make her voice sound natural. It was not natural; but Abner Baisley was not the man to mark the difference.

"A pretty story, this," he broke out, in his rasping voice. "A pretty talk to make, a pretty scandal to bring on me! I want to know what it means, right straight."

The girl's head drooped a little lower over the kitchen table.

"I ain't got nothin' to tell you, Uncle Abner!" she answered, relapsing into the village vernacular, which much visiting at the parsonage had taught her to avoid.

The old storekeeper had never seen her so meek. His courage rose, and his righteous anger with it.

"You've got to tell me, an' tell me this minute. I command you to tell me!" he cried.

"I tell you, uncle, I haven't got a single thing to say. I just want you to let me be. Oh, I want to be let be!"

Her shoulders sagged forward, till she looked smaller and slighter than he had ever imagined she could look. At the sight his sense of injury and his indignation against her grew yet more fierce.

"You got to tell me! You got to tell me!" he almost shouted, his voice shrilling discordantly. "Think I'm a-goin' to be disgraced this way, made a fool of before the whole neighbourhood, an' not know nothin' about it!"

Luella turned, straightened herself up, and eyed him steadily till he had finished speaking. Something in her gray, cold look pierced his anger and brought him to his senses all at once. This was a woman, not a girl, confronting him, — a woman who had been through the flames of the pit. Her eyes daunted him. But she did not say much. It was only, — after a long pause, —

"You ain't goin' to know a thing about it more'n you know already!"

"But hain't I a right to know, since it teches me so close? Hain't I a *right* to know?" he blustered.

"And if you can't let me be, from this on, Uncle Abner," she continued, unheeding of his interruption, "I'll quit this house right now, an' never set foot in it again!"

This, to the frugal old storekeeper, was a very serious threat. He knew he could get no other housekeeper who could give him so much comfort, and dignity, at so little cost. And much of the furniture of the place, moreover, was Luella's, left to her by her father and mother, who had gone down together with her father's ship when she was a child of ten. He forgot even to save his dignity by keeping up a show of anger, but struck his colours at once, and backed away.

"Well, well, Luella, if you feel that strongly about it, why of course I must be a-mindin' my own business. I jest thought as how it was my duty to you, maybe, to say somethin' — but, there, there, you was always that headstrong. An' it *is* your business, of course. 'Tain't nobody's else's." And with these words he slipped through into the store, softly closing the door behind him. At breakfast, half an hour later, he was genial with conversation about the weather and the crops, seeming to see nothing out of the way in Luella's half-articulate, wholly irrelevant replies.

A little after breakfast the rector came in to see her. His kind eyes were full of trouble, and met hers searchingly as he took her hand. He had heard, of course, Mary Dugan's account of her strange interview with Luella at the parsonage gate, — but his first look into the girl's drawn face told him a different story. Intuitive as a woman, and far more tolerantly tender, he understood how Luella had thought to hide her wound by taking the blame upon herself. Asking no question, he led her into the little sitting-room, sat down beside her on the black haircloth sofa, took her icy hand in both of his, which were warm, and soft, and strong, and looked out of the window across the red creek and green marshes, waiting till her heart should move her to speak.

After a long silence, the spell of his strength and sympathy melted her. She laid her face down on his hands and began to sob convulsively. Then, since he still refrained from questioning her, she tried to tell him.

"Oh, what can it mean?" she gasped. "I can't think what's happened. There was never a hard word passed between us, never, never. I've never wronged him, not even by a thought. Oh, it ain't my fault, it ain't my fault. I don't see how I ever can go on living. I don't see how I ever can."

"I'm very sure it is not your fault, dear," said the rector, releasing one hand to lay it softly on the girl's head. "And you must not tell people it *is* your fault, — as you told Mary Dugan last night. But I cannot easily believe it is Jim's fault, either. Have you had no word, no sign of any kind, from him? It is not like Jim to treat any living creature that way. I won't believe it of him."

At this, which seemed to hint at some hope, Luella's tears came freely, wildly, breaking the deadly tension of her nerves. But what hope could there be? The ship was gone. Jim was gone. But if the rector could think there might be, then, in some mysterious way, surely there might be hope. At last she found her voice enough to murmur — "No, — I ain't — had one — single — word."

"Be brave, dear child," said the rector. "A letter may come from St. John. He may come to his senses before he gets to St. John. And I will write to him. With this wind holding as it does,

Luella's Friends, and Others

my letter would not catch him in St. John, now. I'll write him at Matanzas, where it cannot miss him if the ship calls there."

To Luella this was hope indeed, at least for the moment. She clutched his hand with both of hers, afraid to let go lest she should fall back into the abyss of darkness. Then the rector arose.

"I'll go around and see Mrs. Calder now. She may have had some word."

At this Luella sat up straight, and stared at him with wet, swollen eyes.

"Would *she* get word from him, an' me not?" she demanded. "Oh, how she hates me. How glad she'll be. *Could* it be *her* as got him to do it?"

The rector gave a little sigh of relief. This was more the natural woman, now. He had been afraid, almost, for Luella's reason, when he saw the grayness of her set face, and the eyes gone far back into her head with anguish. Now, he knew that she would get a grip upon herself, and cherish a hope, however frail and far, and front life with that indomitable spirit which she inherited from her blue-eyed viking of a father.

"No!" he declared, positively. "Mrs. Calder could not do that, if she would. She is hard and bitter, I know. But she is not so bad as that. I'll go and speak to her, and let you know."

But from this interview with Mrs. Calder, whose insinuations against Luella he found occasion to rebuke with a sternness that daunted even her unyielding temper, he learned nothing more than that Jim was alive and well, and able to write a letter to his mother. Mrs. Calder would not even say what kind of a letter it was.

Having been thus reanchored, as it were, to sanity and endurance, by the rector's timely understanding and the touch of his inextinguishable trust, Luella held her head up and her tongue still toward all the inquisition of the countryside. Friends and enemies alike found her impenetrable and repellent if her secret was even approached. Otherwise, only by an infrangible gravity of look and speech, through the trying weeks that followed, did she betray what she was passing through. People agreed, with the fine perspicacity which characterizes the human race in general, and the prosperously good in particular, that she was hard and heartless. They chose to believe those wild words of hers which Mary Dugan, innocently enough, had repeated; and they decided that it was indeed, in some way which they could not yet decide upon, all Luella's fault. They resented her incommunicativeness; and called her "stuck up," because she would not bare her heart to the collective village eye. Presently the fickle countryside sentiment went over, almost *en masse*, to the surprised and unresponsive Mrs. Calder, who, indeed, welcomed it but grimly.

Perhaps among all the good people between Frosty Hollow and Wood Point there were not more than two, besides the rector, toward whom Luella could lower her guard for a moment. These were Mrs. Goodridge and old Sis Bembridge. Even the kindly Mary Dugan was somewhat critical and inquisitive. That meeting with Luella at the parsonage gate had been a great thing for Mary in the village. It had given her a sort of proprietary interest in the affair. It had enabled her to speak with a certain authority about it which no one else possessed. Knowing so much, she felt it her right to know more. If Luella could speak to her about it then, why could she not tell her more about it now? In her first elation at finding herself so distinguished, she very generally and confidently undertook to "git it all out of Luella," for the general benefit. And when she found herself confronted by Luella's intimidating reserve, she felt herself injured. In fact, it was largely on her testimony that Luella was adjudged to be "stuck up." Nevertheless, for all this, Mary Dugan was a well-wisher of Luella's in the main, and prompt to take up cudgels in her defence against any serious imputation. It was a childish jealousy, merely, and a childish vanity, which made her seem, just now, something less than loyal.

But with Mrs. Goodridge it was very different. That ardent-hearted lady, always audacious and not always incorrect in her conclusions, had boiled over with generous and instant wrath when she found that Jim had gone. Her fair face reddened slowly to the roots of her gold-brown, abundant hair, and her blue eyes flamed through tears.

"It's all that Melissa Britton," she declared. "The hussy!"

"What nonsense, Jean!" answered the rector. "It's outrageous to accuse people in that reckless fashion. You must not do it!"

Mrs. Goodridge had an overwhelming amount of "feelings" to relieve, at the moment, and no one to relieve them upon except her husband. She turned upon him accusingly.

"You know yourself it's that little red-haired hussy, George! You know it as well as I do. You should never have had her in the choir. You always favoured her over everybody else. If you hadn't insisted on having her in the choir, all this would never have happened. She'd never have got her nasty little eyes on Jim Calder."

The rector threw up his hands in despair and turned away. Then, rashly, he turned back to argue the point.

"Why," he protested in astonishment, "you *know* you've always made a lot of Melissa, yourself, Jean. Much more than I have, always. How can you so turn against the poor child now, merely because your heart is aching for Luella!"

Mrs. Goodridge's eyes got bigger and bluer, and the tears that had been softening them burned dry.

"Made a lot of her!" she cried. "I! That's just the way with you, George! I've tried to be nice to her for *your sake,* just because you would force her on me. *I always* saw through her. I always detested her. And now see what's come of your dragging her forward, and sticking her up there in the choir, and always making her sing solos, when she has no more voice than a frog. And here you stand, defending her, sticking up for her, while that poor, dear child is down there alone with that narrow old hatchet-faced uncle of hers, crying her dear eyes out, eating her heart out with grief. Oh, it drives me mad to think of it! You've always professed to think so much of her. You're ready enough to think of her when you want the flowers stuck around. You ought to be with her now. That's your place. Oh, I've no patience with you!" And bouncing from her chair, she fell to rearranging things furiously on the study table, — books and papers, which, in their seeming disorder, were really just as the rector needed to have them.

Troubled at this, the rector stepped forward to check the disastrous process; but he checked himself instead, and looked on half-ruefully, half-quizzically.

"Of course," said he, "that was the first thing I thought of doing. But I concluded that it was better not to."

"Then *I will!*" retorted his wife, vehemently. "I don't care how late it is, or how dark it is, I'll go alone, since you're so unfeeling."

"No, you must not do anything of the sort," answered her husband, emphatically. "She wouldn't want to see even you to-night. The only kindness we can do the poor child to-night, I know, is to leave her alone. No one knows better than you, Jean, how my heart aches for her. But she must be let alone."

"What do *you* know about what a woman needs? You just don't want to be dragged out at this time of night. And I'd look nice, tramping away down to the aboi-d'eaux by myself in the dark, wouldn't I?"

With this last shot Mrs. Goodridge marched from the room, slammed the study door behind her, and fled up-stairs to her bedroom to cry tumultuously. She knew her husband was absolutely right; and

Luella's Friends, and Others 75

she would not have intruded upon Luella that night for worlds. But if she had not been able to ease her heart a little of its hotness, the dammed-up floods of her indignant compassion would have given her a headache to keep her awake all night. As it was, she had the double satisfaction of knowing that the rector was right, and of thinking that she had made him feel that perhaps he was wrong. She wanted him to feel as miserable as she felt herself; and in the belief that she had done so she began to recover her composure. First, however, she called Mary Dugan to the bedroom, and made the girl repeat her story. Then she asked who else had heard the tale. When she learned that Mary had succeeded in telling the Evanses, and the Purdies, and the Ackerleys, and Mrs. Finnimore, and Mrs. Gandy, the flood of her righteous indignation burst all bounds; and the too garrulous Mary was packed off to bed in tears. This accomplished, the storm cleared apace. One hour later she stole down-stairs again in her crocheted blue bedroom slippers, to mix a creamy egg-nog for the rector, and strictly enjoin him to take it before he went to bed. His habit of working at his desk till the small hours was one which she viewed with anxiety.

Toward Luella herself, however, Mrs. Goodridge displayed none of this rather tempestuous partisanship. At the point of real need, her sympathy and tact were unerring. She waited two days before going to see Luella. Then, when the girl stood gravely and silently before her in the little sitting-room, — which had fresh flowers in it, as usual, — she spared her not only questions but even the searching interrogation of her eyes. Catching her to her heart she held her close, and patted her shoulders, and kissed her pale, bright hair, and crooned over her, — inarticulately, indeed, but to Luella most intelligibly. Under this comforting influence Luella gradually let herself go. She did not say anything, but she slipped back into the child, and began to cry with a child's abandon. Mrs. Goodridge pulled her down brusquely into her strong lap, and let her cry herself out. Then she lifted her up.

"Luella, child," she said, impressively, "I'm not going to bother you with a lot of talk. Talk doesn't do any good. But mark my words. This will come out all right some day. Every man is a fool sometimes. But Jim Calder is not the kind of man to be a fool always. He will come back to you on his knees. I know he will."

"I don't want Jim on his knees!" she declared, loyally; but she lifted, nevertheless, a swift look of gratitude to her comforter's face.

"Tut! Tut! You want him anyway you can get him!" averred Mrs. Goodridge. "And now

Luella's Friends, and Others

wipe your eyes and put on your sunbonnet, and come right along with me, just as you are. You're going to stay at the parsonage for a couple of days. Tell your uncle he'll have to get along alone till Thursday night, the best way he can. You'll kill yourself, drudging for him the way you do!"

Rather hesitatingly Luella obeyed, — but Mrs. Goodridge was a difficult woman to cross. Mr. Baisley, though he hated being left to get his own meals, and was too " nigh " to hire the work done for him, was amazingly cordial in his manner of receiving Luella's announcement of her going. He realized to the full the value of the backing of Mrs. Goodridge at this crisis. He would eat " cold victuals " gladly indeed for two days, to be able to answer prying interrogations about Luella's health and spirits with the careless words —

" Oh, she's well enough, I calculate. She's havin' a gay time, a-stayin' up to the parsonage, an' leavin' her old uncle to do the work."

This formula he used with effect quite satisfactory to his prestige, till he was so misguided as to try it on old Mrs. Bembridge, when she came hobbling heavily into the store for a half-pound of tea, the morning after Mrs. Goodridge had carried Luella away.

CHAPTER VIII.

"OLD SIS"

OLD Mrs. Bembridge — in the familiar speech of Westcock, "Old Sis" — was, according to her lights, a sort of anarch of the countryside. She was a law unto herself; and, what is more unusual, she allowed a like unconfined individualism to others. Generally speaking, she was regarded throughout the neighbourhood as "a bad old woman." Westcock was given to broad and hasty generalizations. As to her age, however, she was scarce fifty, and of a constitution which might well see her through to the hundred mark; and as to her badness, — in the eyes of the rector, at least, and of Mrs. Goodridge, and of Luella Warden, and of certain ever-ailing incompetents who were a burden and discredit to the community, there was room for doubt. She was regarded as peculiarly a widow, having had three husbands. The first had been divorced, the second had died at sea, and the third — whom she had married because he was no earthly use and needed a home — had been considerate enough to run away. So many marital inexperiences — especially when Westcock contained worthy ladies who had never achieved even one — seemed to smack of impropriety. It was immodest, at least. Furthermore, it was commonly hinted that among the superstitious she was held to be a witch; and every one knew that every one else in Westcock, except the person who chanced to be speaking, *was* superstitious. One thing was quite certain, she never, for any consideration, could be induced to go to church, — which looked queer. On the other hand, it was known that the rector was no less attentive in his calls at her little gray, weather-beaten cottage, than at the houses of his most prosperous and most reputable parishioners. There was no question on that point, for whenever he dropped in to see Mrs. Bembridge his hearty, infectious laughter would be heard ringing down across her potato-patch to the road, so that passers-by would smile sympathetically even while they wondered.

But however folk might criticize "Old Sis," it was invariably behind her back they did it. There was something in her penetrating steel-gray eyes that was discouraging to presumption. A few had seen those disconcerting eyes grow kind, but many knew their scorn; and her daring spirit was always ready for battle, no matter what the odds. Moreover, even the clean, invigorating air of Westcock, swept as it was by free winds, and tonic with mingled savours of balsam and salt, did not prevent people from falling sick occasionally; and none could tell when they might need a nurse. There was no nurse in the county to compare with Mrs. Bembridge, whose caustic humour never companioned her into the sickroom. Nothing could daunt her, from a mad bull to the plague; and when the Tantramar country was visited by smallpox, she and she only it was whom the rector and the doctors could rely on. It was obviously impolitic for people to force upon Mrs. Bembridge's attention their righteous disapproval of her.

Except for those deep-set, steady gray eyes of hers, the appearance of Mrs. Bembridge was not altogether prepossessing. On her iron-gray hair she wore a ridiculously small cap of coarse black lace and ribbon, from beneath which, somewhere, a rebellious wisp was always sticking up at a defiant angle. Her face was craggy, high-nosed, and battered, and her great eyebrows were always aggressively at bristle. Her wide mouth, full of big, yellow teeth, was usually grim, but ever ready to relax at the corners with a shrewd, self-contained humour. She was a little under middle height, but very broad and thick in bosom and hip; and being slightly lame, she never walked without a heavy staff to help support her weight. She dressed always in a bluish-gray woollen homespun, the skirt cut so short as to show some inches of her sturdy ankles; and these efficient ankles were clothed in massive, home-knit, white woollen stockings, which had a disposition to come down in rolls over her boat-like, heavy shoes. Over her spacious shoulders and chest, winter and summer alike, was folded a crocheted woollen " sontag " of dingy magenta. In the hottest of the dog-days, in the full blaze of noon, she might be seen limping ponderously along the road in this costume, as indifferent to the heat as to the opinions of her neighbours. Heavy as she was, and lame as she was, she was a mighty pedestrian, and the old magenta sontag was a feature of the road, from Wood Point hill to the " Bito."

The little house where Mrs. Bembridge lived was about fifty paces back from the Wood Point road. It stood something less than a quarter of mile from the parsonage, on the same parallel of the uplands; and like the parsonage it commanded a vast, aerial view of the marshes, the bay, and the winding, copper-red channels of Tantramar. Low, scant-eaved, small-windowed, its shingles storm-worn to an ancient, rock-like gray, it rose naked from the top of a little, rounded swell of tilled land, as if it had been a very growth of the ground. Nothing broke its simple outlines but a small lean-to porch, with a piece of stovepipe sticking up through its clapboarded roof, to show that it was sometimes used as an outer kitchen. Not a tree stood near to break the winds which hummed softly about its lonely corners. Before the porch spread the open chip-strewn dooryard, with a pile of wood at one side, and a sawhorse and chopping-block close by. In the middle of the yard stood the tiny gray well-house, with bucket, chain, and windlass, and mossy water-trough. Some thirty or forty paces beyond the well-house rose the old gray barn, its doors sagging on their hinges, and wisps of hay sticking out through the loose boards enclosing the hay-mow, as the wisps of hair stuck out through the interstices of Mrs. Bembridge's cap. Against one end of the barn, adjoining the stable, was a lean-to shed, once used as a wagon-shelter, but now boarded in and transformed into a hen-house.

Behind the barn the trees began, — a low, dark green, scattered second growth of spruce and fir, diversified with brown stumps and mossy hillocks, little patches of blueberry scrub and the apple-cheeked foxberry. In this spacious pasture-lot roamed Mrs. Bembridge's red and white cow, kept from trespassing on the tilled fields by a straggling and rather dilapidated snake fence which ran close behind the barn. From the end of the barn, and from the bars which admitted the cow, a deeply rutted lane followed the fence down the slope till it met another set of bars and united itself with the Wood Point road. The potato-field came close up to the lane on one side; but the other, along the fence, was bordered by a series of tumbled hillocks, which crowded into the fence corners and were clothed with dense patches of aromatic tansy, or vivid, light green "snake brake," or the modest, purplish-blossomed heal-all, with here and there a tall spike of mullein. At the point where the lane joined the Wood Point road an aggressively spreading bed of tansy, mantled at this season with its dull yellow bloom, had things all its own way and crowded down to the very edges of the highway-bordering ditch. The open fields on the other three sides of the house — they were farmed for Mrs. Bembridge by a neighbour, working "on shares" — were planted in potatoes, turnips, buckwheat, and oats, with a narrow strip of flax; and directly under the two windows facing the road, in a little patch reserved from the potato-field, Mrs. Bembridge had her garden. It was neatly laid off in very small beds; and fully three-quarters of these were devoted to "yarbs," such as summer-savoury, catnip, peppermint, sage, thyme, camomile, rosemary, parsley, and chives. A bed of onions, one of carrots, and one — a specially large one — of cabbages, supplied the owner with all the variety she craved in vegetables, and left her some over to sell. As for flowers, she admitted only two kinds, — a patch of perennial blue "bachelors' buttons," which she loved for their own sakes, and a thicket of splendid, flaunting sunflowers at the other side of the potato-field, down against the fence. The sunflowers she grew because her hens liked the seeds. Across the upper end of the garden, about seven or eight feet from the house, so as to leave space for the banking of the foundations every fall, ran a row of currant bushes, — red, white, and black, — with a bush of wormwood at one end of the row, and another of aromatic southernwood, or "Old Man," as Mrs. Bembridge called it, at the other.

In spite of this rather uncompromising utilitarianism of hers, Mrs. Bembridge had her own ideas of beauty, and loved it fervently in her own way. No other eyes in Westcock revelled more ecstatically than hers in the immeasurable, elusive changes of light and shadow that swept across the vastness of the marsh. Great space, great amplitudes of colour, delighted her. She knew every gradation of tone in the purples of the far Minudie hills, in the blue-gray reflected tints and the golden tawny self-colours of the bay, in the pale greens of the endless grass, in the pink and saffron, flame and rose transparencies of dawn. Sunsets, on the other hand, she took little account of. They always happened behind the house, over a near, uninteresting ridge, and just in the direction of the village of Second Westcock, some six miles away. She despised Second Westcock, and took no interest in anything that seemed to happen there.

Coming nearer home, Mrs. Bembridge's indifference to flowers in her garden by no means meant insensibility to all the achievements of flowering nature. When her potato-field was in bloom, the profusion of white blossoms star-strewn and aerially afloat over the dense green of the leaves seemed to her more wonderful than any garden she had ever seen, — even than Luella's patch of glory on its steep slope over the " Bito." That riband of blue flax-flowers dividing the yellow-green buckwheat from the pea-green oats thrilled her as the sunrise sometimes did. And the buckwheat, when it bloomed, — that sudden lavish outpouring of pink-white foam, honey-scented, and drowsily musical with bees,— seemed to her too miraculously lovely to speak of. Her delight in all these things she regarded as a sort of stolen joy, on which her own grotesque appearance was a kind of jarring comment.

To her way of thinking, however, there was nothing incongruous in her finding beauty in her homely, necessary hens. Without apology, she prided herself on having the prettiest flock of hens in Westmoreland County, — and all prime layers, too. They were of an uncommon breed known in that neighbourhood as "Creepies." Their legs were so ridiculously short that they seemed to creep rather than walk; and scratching, even in the most seductive of garden-beds, was so difficult that they seldom yielded to the temptation. These plump, exemplary little fowls were to be found throughout Westcock in all the varied minglings of feather which characterize the common dunghill tribe, — but not in Mrs. Bembridge's flock, which consisted of fifteen hens and two cocks. Once upon a time a sea-captain, returning probably direct from a Spanish port, had brought in his hen-coops some thoroughbred "Blue Andalusians," and given them to certain of his housekeeping neighbours. From this persistent strain its peculiar and very beautiful colouring had spread, till specimens might be found in every Westcock barn-yard. In the hens it was a uniform, unmarked, clear dove-blue, all over, with blue legs, white ear-lobes, and long, overhanging, vivid red comb. In the cocks the body colour was this same lovely gray-blue, but the flowing neck-hackles, saddle, and tail-feathers, were glossy black, and the thin, high, scarlet comb stood proudly erect. By careful crossing and strict selection throughout a number of seasons, Mrs. Bembridge had succeeded in bringing her flock of "Creepies" to the

"Blue Andalusian" colour; and now they were the envy of all who saw them. Of course, every clutch of chickens would throw a number of "sports," or variations, of black, white, red, brown, or speckled; but these were all severely weeded out as they grew up. She would sell no eggs for hatching; and during the hatching season she would sell no eggs at all, but rather put them down in salt and chaff against the season when eggs are high.

Next to a sunrise over the Minudie hills, or a buckwheat-field in bloom under the blue of noon, Mrs. Bembridge was inclined to rank the picture of her trim and beautiful flock crowding about her feet at feeding time. They were tame and friendly, all of them. With these, and her red and white cow, and her big, moon-faced gray cat who ignored her socially but was always somewhere around at meal-times and milkings, she really felt small need of human companionship in her bleak gray house on the windy upland.

CHAPTER IX.

LUELLA AND THE BLUE HEN

ON that morning when Mrs. Bembridge, in her magenta sontag and perky little cap, limped laboriously down to the "Bito," to make her purchases of Mr. Baisley, — and, if fortune should favour her, to learn something of Luella, — her temper was by no means less crisp than usual. Her heart was aching heavily for the girl; and at the same time she was fretted with a curiosity which she would have scorned to confess. Added to this, it was one of those days when, without any rhyme or reason that she could perceive, her "rheumatiz" was "actin' out." Hers was the mood in which the wise are wont to resent most indignantly the foolishness of fools. She hated to be gracious to Mr. Baisley (in her thoughts she called him "Old Baisley"), while making her purchases, but she constrained herself to a fair imitation of geniality, as a means of hearing something about Luella. To her eyes that morning the storekeeper had never before looked so hatchet-faced and mean. She had never before so disliked the fashion in which his stiff and meagre whiskers were brushed straight forward to balance, as it were, the manner in which his hair was "slicked" straight back.

When she had very slowly dug out her battered wallet from the secret depths of her pocket, and fumblingly counted out the change, and with great deliberation restored the wallet to its hiding-place, she gathered up her parcels and turned to go. She had not found words to make any inquiry about Luella. To mention the poor child's name, she felt, would be something like an intrusion upon her sorrow. But this very silence was so unusual in itself that Mr. Baisley could not refrain from commenting upon it.

"You hain't inquired for Luelly, Mrs. Bembridge!" (Behind her back he called her "Old Sis;" but a customer is a customer!) "I reckon it's the first time in ten year you've come into the store, an' not spoke of her first thing. You've always seemed to think a sight of Luelly."

Mrs. Bembridge turned back to the counter with alacrity.

"Y'ain't fur wrong on that pint, Mr. Baisley," she responded. "I jest do think a sight of Luelly Warden. How be she these days?"

Mr. Baisley leaned across the counter, and scanned her weather-beaten old face.

"'Tain't possible you hain't *heard!*" he ejaculated. Then he drew back, as if impatient at his own folly. "Tut! Tut! of course you've heard. They've got hold of it from the Joggins to Shemogue by this time, I calculate."

"Oh, mebbe I've hearn, an' mebbe I hain't hearn!" she answered, non-committally. "An' what one hears in Westcock — mebbe it's true an' mebbe it ain't true! How *is* Luelly?"

"Oh, she's well enough, I calculate," chuckled Mr. Baisley. "She's havin' a gay enough time, I know that, a-stoppin' up to the parsonage, an' leavin' her old uncle to do her work 'round the house!"

The old woman glared at him. Since Luella was not at home, there was nothing to be gained by holding herself under an unnatural restraint. The speech was harmless, but it gave her overwrought feelings their opportunity.

"Abner Baisley," she exclaimed, in a voice that grated in her throat, "you'd oughter be ashamed of yerself, you'd ought, to talk that way of the child. An' you her own uncle. Y'ain't got no more heart in you'n a pig's foot." And bringing down her heavy stick with a bang on the floor, she limped heavily and haughtily forth, to do battle with valiant tongue against any enemies of Luella whom she might encounter.

This undertaking gave her a busy day, and when,

Luella and the Blue Hen 91

toward milking-time, she hobbled back to the little gray house, her cap awry and her hair bristling beyond its wont, she left a trail of cowed antagonists behind her.

It was not till the following morning, however, that she was rewarded with the sight of Luella. The girl came over to see her. It was at Mrs. Goodridge's suggestion; for it was Mrs. Goodridge who always thought of these timely and fitting little things for people to do. After breakfast, when the rector had started away alone on one of his long drives through the woods to Dorchester, and Luella had helped Mary Dugan wash up the breakfast dishes and get the vegetables ready to be cooked for dinner, Mrs. Goodridge said:

"Why don't you run across the fields, dear, and see Old Sis? She's just devoted to you. And there's no one who will stick up for you more loyally. She'll be so pleased at your coming to her of your own accord!"

Luella shrank for a moment. She could not yet bear to meet questioning eyes — which all seemed to her either hostile or derisive. But Mrs. Goodridge — who wanted to get her out among the fields and trees which she knew she loved — answered her unspoken thought.

"Across the fields, and through the pasture, dear! You won't meet anybody, going that way.

You know the path back of the barn, there. It'll bring you straight to her place."

"Yes, ma'am," replied Luella. "I'll go an' see if she's got any more of those pretty blue chickens hatched out. I recollect she had two hens setting awhile ago."

"And give her this tea, with my love, Luella," continued Mrs. Goodridge, getting out from the cupboard a little square package, covered with tin foil and red and black hieroglyphics. "Tell her it is something very special, just sent to me from Fredericton; and I'm not giving away any of it, except this package to her. And, oh, be sure and tell her not to use more than *half* as much as she uses of your uncle's tea, for it's more than twice as strong."

"Yes, ma'am!" said Luella; and set out to find the path behind the barn.

There was no mistaking it, worn as it was by the passing of many feet, — for the country folk love a short cut, as much as they hate walking the dusty highroad. Skirting widely the straw-littered space behind the stable, where the manure-heaps had been, the path went between two huge fir-trees, then out across a field of red clover to the fence that bounded the young fir-woods and Mrs. Bembridge's pasture. So narrow was the path that the heavy purple clover-heads, swaying under the embraces of innumerable great black and gold

Luella and the Blue Hen

bumblebees, brushed thickly against Luella's knees as she passed. Scents of bloom and honey steamed up warmly about her, and the humming of the bees was curiously comforting to her. She was beginning to feel more like herself, and so was able to notice these things — even to be glad of them in a numb sort of way. The hopeful cheer of the parsonage, with Mrs. Goodridge's oracular declarations that "it will all come out all right," and the rector's sanguine confidence that Jim would send some word to her from St. John, had for the moment lightened the load of her despair. They could not know, of course, — no one but herself and Jim could know, — what cause there was for despair. But even so, even now, a letter from Jim *might* make things all right, except for the weary waiting till his return. Surely, surely, that letter would come. There was nothing conceivable to her that would make Jim such a monster of cruelty as to leave her without that letter. Yes, it *must* come, in a few days now. The rector plainly expected it. And Mrs. Goodridge, too. And though it would not ease her aching loss, it would set her right before her friends and neighbours. Staying herself to courage with this hope, she drew in deep breaths of the scented air, forced down the terror in her heart, and tried to take some pleasure in the sunlit world.

Having crossed the field, she found a pile of stones on each side of the fence, forming a sort of rude stile; and here, too, she found Mrs. Bembridge's red and white cow, gazing longingly over the fence at the clover, discontented with the sweet but scanty grasses which grew among the young firs. Luella murmured, "Co' Bossy! Co' Bossy!" and tried to pat the mild-eyed animal on the nose. But the cow tossed her horns with a resentful snort, and pranced away as if Luella had insulted her.

"Queer!" mused the girl as she walked on. "The critters don't seem to like any one that's unhappy! I wonder how they know!"

The little path, trodden deeply into the turf, wound this way and that to avoid clumps of green fir saplings or hillocks of moss and vine. Not heavy-scented like the clover-field, this woody pasture had nevertheless a perfume of its own, — clean, elusively pungent, with subtle balsamic tang which thrilled the girl's sensitive nostrils. Once a fragrance more pronounced, though still most delicate, caught her notice; and she knelt beside a pink-dotted hillock to gather a bunch of the frail, twin-flowered *Linnæa* for Mrs. Bembridge. But remembering in a flash how Jim had once picked these blossoms for her on Westcock Hill, she crushed them violently to her mouth, flung them far into the bushes, and hurried on, seeing no

Luella and the Blue Hen 95

more of the beauty of the day. It was all she could do to keep from turning and fleeing back to shut herself up in her room at the parsonage.

Mastering herself with strong resolution, however, she went on swiftly, seeing nothing till she found herself confronted by the blank back of Mrs. Bembridge's barn. Then, pulling herself together violently and trying to assume a defensive face of unconcern, she followed around the corner of the barn; and there was the old magenta sontag at the well.

At the sight of Luella Mrs. Bembridge dropped her bucket and came stumping toward the bars. But Luella sprang nimbly over the fence at the nearest point.

"Why, if 'tain't Luelly! My very Luelly!" exclaimed the old woman, cheerily. "Where you ben this long time? I hain't seed you for weeks."

"Been home!" replied Luella, obviously avoiding her keen eyes. "Visiting at the parsonage since day before yesterday, — and here's some extra special kind of tea Mrs. Goodridge sent over to you. She said to give you her love, Mrs. Bembridge, an' tell you not to use *half* as much of this tea as you would of Uncle Abner's, seeing as how it's more than twice as strong."

She had rattled on with a volubility altogether unlike her usual deliberation of speech; and with a fierce pang of compassion the old woman had noted the change in her face, — the aging lines, the pallor, the sunken shadows beneath the eyes.

"Bless yer dear heart," said Mrs Bembridge, taking the package and sniffing at it with critical approval before consigning it to her deep pocket, "Bless yer sweet heart, but it's a sight for sore eyes ye be! I was down to the 'Bito' yesterday in the hopes of seein' you; an' yer uncle told me as how ye was right smart. But ye don't *eg*zactly look *right* smart this mornin', Sweetie!"

With a brave determination that she *would* look "right smart," — that she would *not* wear her heart on her sleeve, — Luella lifted the troubled deeps of her blue eyes squarely to the speaker's face, and answered, "Oh, it's just headache." The next instant she clenched her hands, and half-turned as if to run away. Informed by wide experience and untrammelled sympathies, the wise old eyes of Mrs. Bembridge had looked straight into her soul. They had surprised her secret. Loving the girl as she did, the old woman was startled, and shrank at a sudden vision of the misery heaping up for her ahead. But she removed instantly from Luella's face the inquisition of her gaze, and looked away with a quick affectation of having seen nothing. With a caressing hand on the girl's arm she led her toward the barn.

Luella and the Blue Hen 97

"Come, Sweetie," she said, "I've got somethin' to show you!"

Luella was trembling. She opened her mouth to speak, but no sound came. However, Mrs. Bembridge was not looking at her; and in a moment she regained some self-control.

"I was just wondering," she managed to say, in a small, hard voice, "if any of those hens you had setting had come off yet!"

"Ye've hit it, Luelly!" cried Mrs. Bembridge, with a forced chuckle. "I've got the purtiest brood here, jest hatched, that ever I seen, — eleven out o' thirteen eggs, an' all blue but three. They was pretty nigh all hatched last night, so by now they must be " — but here she stopped speaking, and stepped ahead hastily to fumble with the big wooden latch of the barn door. In reality, she could not let Luella see her face just then; and she could not utter another word. She had suddenly found herself choking with rage at thought of the man who could desert the girl he loved at such a time. Her big, rugged hands shook with a craving to get their grip on Jim Calder's throat; and for some seconds her difficulty in working the latch was not feigned. Then, as the door opened, she trusted her voice again.

"By now," she continued, "they must be 'bout ready to come off. I'll git you to help me, Sweetie, if ye'll be so kind. I know ye're a right smart hand with chickens. Look out for yer fingers, though. Old Lady'll peck some."

"Oh, I don't mind that," said Luella.

"She's the crossest old thing ever," went on Mrs. Bembridge, talking hard. "But she's the best setter and mother in the flock. Them Spanish Blues ain't much good as setters nor mothers. They're jest all for layin', an' if they *do* set, they like as not gits tired of it in a week, and quits jest when the eggs is spiled, an' goes to work layin' agin. The Creepies on the other hand, — as you know well, Sweetie, — they're jest *the* setters an' mothers, bein' quiet dispositioned, an' so short in the legs it's most the same thing to 'em whether they stand up or set down. 'Tain't no strain on 'em to keep on settin'. Now, this new breed o' mine, of course, — the 'Creepy Blues,' I calls 'em, — they've got the natures of the two breeds so mixed up like ye can't never tell which is goin' to crop out. Mostly, they're great layers, but kinder flighty when it comes to the question of raisin' a family. Seems like mebbe the strength of the Creepy blood had been all took up in the job of shortenin' down them long Spanish legs. Well, they done it!"

During this chatter they had entered the pleasant gloom of the barn, which was crossed with long, dusty-golden bars of sunlight streaming through

Luella and the Blue Hen   99

the cracks between the boards. At the inmost corner of the barn floor, against the front of the unused manger, stood a half-barrel, filled with hay to within a few inches of the top. As they came to this snug nest a harsh, scolding squawl issued from it, and Luella saw a small blue hen, which ruffled up its feathers and threatened her savagely with open beak. Squatting down cross-legged beside the nest, Luella offered the palm of her left hand, half-opened, for the angry hen to peck at. Her right hand she slipped gently under the fowl's hot, denuded breast, among the warm little balls of down which she felt huddling there. Lifting one softly forth, she held it up to the light, cherishing it in both hands. It was all a tender Maltese blue, softer than velvet, with tiny glossy dark beak and feet. It snuggled its body against her warm palm, and its round, dark, liquid eyes gazed forth trustfully from between her finger and thumb, taking a first look upon the world beyond the egg-shell wall.

"Oh," murmured Luella, with a long sigh, "ain't they the sweetest things?" And after holding it to her cheek for a moment she deposited it in the hollow of her apron.

"You bring the chicks, an' I'll lug along Old Lady under my arm. The pen's all ready," said Mrs. Bembridge, anxious to give the girl something to do. One after one, ignoring the strokes of the furiously protesting mother, Luella drew forth the chickens and gathered them in her lap, — a warm, huddling, peeping, helpless but unterrified little group, the most winsome of younglings. As Luella's head bent low above them, hot tears began to drop on her cherishing hands. Mrs. Bembridge saw the tears. She dropped the indignant hen back on to the nest, and in spite of her rheumatism plumped right down on her knees at Luella's side.

"There, there!" she murmured, with the same formula of soothing that had come to Mrs. Goodridge's lips. She pulled the girl's head and shoulders down upon her broad bosom, and crooned over her. "There! there! Don't be scairt, Sweetie. There's them as is your friends whatever happens. There's them as is your friends, an' nothin' ain't agoin' to turn them agin you, whatever happens. Remember that, Sweetie, — *whatever happens!*"

Luella, for a moment, closed her eyes, and leaned against this sturdy support. It was now an unspeakable relief to her to feel that Mrs. Bembridge understood. With one hand she covered tenderly the huddling little ones in her lap, while with the other she groped for the old woman's hand and gave it a grateful squeeze. Then, not being of the

Luella and the Blue Hen

kind that leans long on any one, she straightened up, and resolutely shook the hair back from her face.

"You are so good to me, *so* good to me. I just can't tell you how I feel about it. But, oh, Mrs. Bembridge, — *do* you think there's any chance of me gittin' a letter from St. John? The rector appears to think there's sure to be some kind of word from St. John!"

Mrs. Bembridge had not hitherto thought of this as a probability at all. Now, her opinion was that if Jim Calder could go off as he did, he wasn't likely to repent, or come to his senses, at St. John. She knew of no special virtue in St. John to cause such a reformation. She picked up the scolding hen again and tucked it safely under her arm before answering. Then she said:

"Why, surely, Sweetie! The ship must be in there by this time. Like as not there's a letter on the way now. But let me tell you, whether you git a letter or don't git no letter, don't you go fer to break your little heart an' cry your sweet eyes out over a man, not over the best that ever lived, — an' that ain't no Jim Calder. They ain't none of 'em worth it, Sweetie, — nary a one of 'em. Bring along the chickens, now." And shaking her grizzled head reminiscently she lead the way out into the sunlight, the squirming, hysterical hen held inflexibly under her left arm. As for Luella, as usual when she had nothing very definite to say, she held her tongue, and followed obediently with her lapful of peeping chickens.

CHAPTER X.

THE INTERVIEWING OF JIM'S MOTHER

THREE days later, after Luella had returned to her home above the "Bito," a letter did come with the St. John postmark on its envelope. Moreover, it was in Jim Calder's handwriting, — with which the village postmaster, old Mr. Smith, was quite familiar. But it was not for Luella. It was for Mrs. Calder. Within an hour its coming was known from the Bito to Wood Point; and it was known, also, that no word had come to Luella. To her, so had she set her hope upon it, this was almost like a second desertion. But now the blow hardened her. She held her head high, and forced herself to smile, and eyed her world of scrutinizers defiantly.

Immediately, of course, Jim's mother had callers. She was the proud possessor of exclusive information, which it was hoped she would be liberal to divulge. The callers were all rudely disappointed. Beyond the two facts that she had received a letter, and that the letter was from Jim, she would tell nothing. When asked, — as she was, brazenly, by certain of the bolder sort, — if Jim said anything about Luella Warden, her only answer was a snort of indignant scorn and an abrupt termination of the interview. In the course of the day, therefore, public sentiment veered back somewhat toward Luella's side. As Mrs. Calder's stock went down, Jim's, to some extent, depreciated with it; and folk were found to suggest that, if Jim were anything like his mother, maybe it wasn't Luella that was in the wrong.

Next to Luella herself, it was, perhaps, Mrs. Goodridge who was most upset over the absence of news from St. John. The rector, for his part, was more grieved than surprised. He wrote a letter of stinging rebuke and stern demand, addressed it to Jim in care of Captain Britton, and sent it to the chief owners to be forwarded so that it would catch the *G. G. Goodridge* at the first port where she should stop to discharge cargo, Matanzas or another. This done, he confined himself to befriending Luella by showing in every possible way his unshaken confidence in her. But the impetuous heart of his wife could not rest content with this. She craved immediate information. When she learned of Mrs. Calder's letter, and that stony-tempered lady's refusal to say anything about what was in the letter, she put bit and bridle on her indignation, smoothed her countenance to gracious-

The Interviewing of Jim's Mother

ness, and set out, without consulting the rector, to see what she could do.

The garden in front of Mrs. Calder's house was all one summer smile with blossoms. The red geraniums in the windows, glowing through the snowy curtains, welcomed her auspiciously; and the incoming tide clamoured musically in the red channel of Tantramar, a hundred yards away, across the field. But not at all auspicious was the welcome of Mrs. Calder. Forbiddingly civil, she ushered Mrs. Goodridge into the cluttered and stuffy stiffness of the front parlour, grudgingly throwing up one blind to admit the unaccustomed sunlight. All Mrs. Goodridge's honeyed praises of the room and its art treasures — its flowers of wax and paper, its wool-worked, framed texts on the wall, its gorgeous-blossomed wall-paper and the stupendous purple roses on its rag-carpet — could not soften Mrs. Calder's long upper lip into complacency. She was aggressively on her guard. Mrs. Goodridge talked on safe topics, and managed to make each topic convey some more or less veiled compliment to her hearer, or to Jim. As a rule, she was the most impatiently direct of women. But she believed herself something of a diplomat. At last, however, Mrs. Calder's unresponsiveness began to fatigue her. She had no taste for coldly monosyllabic replies. That unyielding granitic upper lip exasperated her. A faint flush began to steal up over her fair, smooth face, faint gleams of anger to gather into her fearless blue eyes. All at once she dropped her diplomatic manner, as it were, with a slam.

"Mrs. Calder," she said, sitting up very straight, and just the faintest tinge of superiority filtering into her tones, "I've come to ask you if your son has said anything in his letter which can throw any light on the unhappy affair which we all know about. Your son, as you know, has been very dear to both Mr. Goodridge and myself; and Mr. Goodridge has done everything he could to forward his career, — as I need not remind you, I am sure. That good and sweet girl, Luella Warden, is also very dear to us, and we cannot see her suffer as she does without making every effort to help her. She does not know why this blow has fallen upon her. The suspense is simply killing her. And not a word of any kind has reached her. She is all in the dark. I have come to Jim's mother in the hope that I may learn something to help her. Can you tell me if Jim has said anything to you that would explain his jilting of the poor child the way he did?"

Mrs. Calder set her lips, and answered, coldly:

"If my son'd wanted that Luelly Warden should git any word, likely he'd have writ to her himself.

The Interviewing of Jim's Mother

I've had two letters from him, — shows he kin write!"

Mrs. Goodridge held her wrath in hand, but her eyes flamed disconcertingly. She was silent for perhaps a full minute, looking her hostess through and through. It had always been a matter of private pride with Mrs. Calder that she was "jest as good as anybody." But now, in some unaccountable way, she was being made to feel herself distinctly inferior to Mrs. Goodridge. Her determination was not in the least shaken. But her pride was wilting badly. She was shrinking back into the sullen obstinacy of an inferior. Presently Mrs. Goodridge spoke again. Her tone was stern, but her words were persuasive.

"But, surely, Mrs. Calder, — I know you are a good, a Christian woman, — surely, you cannot wish that a poor, hurt child like Luella should suffer any more bitterly than she has been made to suffer already, if you have it in your power to do anything for her. Just think of it, Mrs. Calder. Why, to look at her face you would say she had aged ten years, — since Jim went off and deserted her!"

Mrs. Calder did not weaken, — not in the least; but she felt uncomfortable. She looked uneasily at the coarse, gnarled hands awkwardly folded in her lap, gave them a twist in her apron, and glanced out of the window with an assumption of indifference. Then she turned and forced herself to meet Mrs. Goodridge's eye.

"I don't need nobody to learn me my duty, ma'am!" she answered, loftily; then looked away again through the window. She regretted that "ma'am," as soon as she had uttered it.

"Of course not, Mrs. Calder," — and Mrs. Goodridge's tone was as if she said "My good woman." "Of course you do not need to be taught your duty. That's why I am so confident that you will do it. It is all a dreadful mystery, this affair. I'm quite sure there has been some terrible mistake. It is not at all like Jim. If he has told you anything, I beg you to be frank with me, that we may try to save these two children from ruining their lives."

"What Jim's writ to me," answered Mrs. Calder, sullenly, "ain't nobody's business but his'n an' mine. You may as well understand that right off, first as last."

Mrs. Goodridge stood up, to the full height of her stately figure, and her voice rang sternly:

"At least, you are a mother, Mrs. Calder. Would you like a daughter of yours to be treated as Luella Warden is being treated?"

Mrs. Calder felt that she was by no means cutting the figure she had planned to cut in this interview.

The Interviewing of Jim's Mother

She began to grow abashed, and so took refuge in anger.

"That hussy!" she cried. "That tow-haired, deceitful hussy, what's stole my boy's heart away from his old mother, and stole his sense out of his head with them innocent-lookin' chaney-blue eyes of hern! Let her git what she desarves! Let her git what she desarves! I'm glad ther's some justice in this world. She'll git nothin' out of me, to my dyin' day. The hussy!" And her voice shrilled to a hiss.

"Shame on you! Shame on you! You are a wicked and malignant old woman," said Mrs. Goodridge. She spoke slowly, and in a quiet voice, but the indignant scorn suppressed behind her voice propelled every word into her hearer's very heart. "I am filled with astonishment that Jim Calder should have a mother like you. I'm sorry I have been so misguided as to look for anything better in you. Good afternoon, Mrs. Calder!"

Her face was calm with apparent self-possession, and the flush had faded out of it. She would not condescend to show her anger. She would not let this wretched old woman think herself capable of upsetting her. But in the folds of her ample skirt her hands were clenched till the nails went white. She strode to the closed front door, then stopped, and turned and eyed the stolid figure in the rocking-chair.

"Good afternoon, Mrs. Calder!" she repeated, with a penetrating emphasis.

The angry woman understood that emphasis very well, and would have liked to ignore it. But she could not. After a moment's struggle she got up, and came and opened the front door, and held it open respectfully, but in sullen silence.

"Thank you, Mrs. Calder. I trust that your hard heart may some day soften! May no one ever be so cruel to you as you are to that unhappy child! Good-bye!"

The very flow of her skirts, as she walked away along the path by the roadside, was a weighty and unanswerable rebuke to the bitter old woman in the doorway.

CHAPTER XI.

THE SEWING-CIRCLE

AFTER the shattering of the one hope to which she had clung, Luella sank into a kind of numbness of slow terror. To all but the parsonage folk and Mrs. Bembridge, however, she kept a brave face, — a face of forced but almost cheerful unconcern, yet with a veiled defiance. This attitude won her little sympathy, but it pretty well secured her from prying curiosity. She did her work as thoroughly as ever; and with apparently all her old enthusiasm, she cultivated her glowing garden above the yellow turmoil of the Bito. She went to church; and in the choir her rich contralto thrilled as full and firm and cello-toned as ever. But never for one instant could she forget. Every moment, waking or asleep, that formless weight of fear and pain bore down upon her heart. It tortured her dreams, yet made her afraid to wake and face a new day. Only her strength of will and her vigorous health of body saved her from breaking down under the unrelenting strain.

In this way, the summer dragged on, each bright, windy day seeming longer than the one before it, till every beauty that she had loved — the marshes, and the shad-boats beating in, and the yellow tides, and the shining red channels when the tide was out — came to hold a daunting menace for her. It was during storms, or when the countryside was drenched with rain, that she felt least overwhelmed. Storm seemed, in some way, to strengthen and stay her, and heavy rain, she fancied, in some way fenced and covered her against the oncoming dread. But when haying time had passed, and the aftermath had sprung up thick and green, and the marshes were everywhere dotted with the cattle turned out to feed on the rich pasturage, then her fear grew so hideous that she began almost to long for the relief of discovery. Then at last, one sultry afternoon in mid-August, it came.

The sewing-circle met that afternoon at Miss Evans's, a low, wide-winged white cottage, with a bright red front door, on the road between the Bito and Westcock church. Mrs. Ben Ackerley was there, and Mrs. Finnimore, and the Widow Gandy, and Miss Hopkins, and Mitty Smith, and half a dozen others, old and young, rich and poor, all working together in the high democracy of the church, and all eagerly occupied in making things to be sold, three weeks later, at the church bazaar.

The Sewing-circle

The object of the bazaar was to raise funds for the purchase of a new organ for Westcock church; and on that account, of course, the members of the choir were particularly interested in it. Luella had always been diligent in church work, and she was a member of the sewing-circle, but to-day she shrank nervously from the ordeal of facing the group of searching eyes and busy tongues. She went up to the parsonage very early in the afternoon, with the idea of going to Miss Evans's in the protecting company of Mrs. Goodridge. But to her disappointment Mrs. Goodridge had already gone. Luella was afraid to go alone, — but she was still more afraid to stay away.

The moment she entered the room, however, she realized that she had made a mistake in coming. The buzz of conversation stopped, and all eyes turned upon her, — some with indifference, some with curiosity, but some with a sudden, penetrating, pitiless comprehension. She went deathly pale on the instant, — and stood for a second or two visibly trembling. Then she almost ran across the room to Mrs. Goodridge. She had seen Mrs. Finnimore, with a lift of the eyebrows, flash a look of malicious comprehension at Mrs. Ackerley, — and she knew that her secret was discovered. Without speech, it thrilled electrically from one to another, till all the married women in the room but Mrs. Goodridge felt the signal, looked, and knew. Most of the girls, too, received a dim communication that made them open their eyes in a pleased expectation of some excitement. Only good-natured Mitty Smith, who sat bending, with parted lips, over her task of embroidering a white baby-cap, was unconscious of the sinister thrill in the air.

Mrs. Goodridge, affable and accessible to all, but inwardly aloof, received none of these signals that were flashed about the room. She saw only that Luella was white and tremulous; and tactfully she seemed not to see it. Making room for the girl to sit beside her, she said, with careless cordiality:

"Here, Luella dear, I wish you'd go on with this hemstitching for me. I hate such fussy work, and you do it so much better than I do. I'd rather darn or sew on buttons." And passing a fine handkerchief over to Luella, she turned and began talking to Miss Hopkins — who was a notable cook — over her plans for the refreshment table at the bazaar.

In a few moments, however, she became conscious that something was wrong. Speaking into Miss Hopkins's sympathetic ear, she was saying:

"As for pies, Miss Hopkins, I should think we'd need about three dozen apple, and a dozen and a half lemon meringue, at least, and as many — " but at this point she noticed that whispering had taken the place of the customary open conversation. All about the room, heads were together, in twos and threes. Mitty Smith sat alone, mouth open intently, unconscious of everything but her work on the little white cap. And Luella sat alone, half crouching behind a tall, three-decker wickerwork sewing-basket, her drooped face no longer white, but crimson. Mrs. Goodridge's eyes began to blaze. She swept them once more all over the company, keenly noting the countenance of each individual. She did not understand anything but the fact that in some feminine way the whole herd of women was bullying Luella. Miss Hopkins saw the expression that came into her face, and coughed nervously, as a prairie-dog whistles a note of warning to his fellows at the approach of danger. But the signal was unheeded, or unheard. Every one was absorbed in the sensation of the moment. Suddenly came the harshly self-righteous voice of Mrs. Ben Ackerley, trampling down the restraint of the whisper, in reply to something Mrs. Finnimore had said.

"Yes, some folks is that brazen there ain't *nothin'* that could shame them into —"

And just here Mrs. Goodridge thought well to finish her sentence.

"And as many more of mince, Miss Hopkins," she concluded, in a voice which rang loud and sharp, like a command. It made every one except Luella sit up very straight, and every one who sat up straight — except Mitty Smith — look guilty.

There was a moment of dead silence, while Mrs. Goodridge's gaze pierced to Mrs. Ben Ackerley's stiff backbone. Then a strangled sob burst from Luella's throat. Warm-hearted Mitty Smith jumped up, dropping her work on the floor, and ran and threw her arms over Luella's shoulders.

"Don't cry, Luelly!" she murmured, coaxingly. "What's wrong, dear?"

Her one thought was that Luella must have made some dreadful mistake in her work, and ruined that beautiful handkerchief.

Mrs. Goodridge's first impulse was to gather Luella to her side, comfort her, give expression to certain definite opinions in regard to the rest of the company, and bid them good afternoon. But she realized her responsibility to the rector, the parish, and, above all, the bazaar. She could not allow herself to be too frankly a partisan. To be compelled to compromise in this way was a trial to her unconforming spirit; but she consoled herself in part with the sudden reflection that if she were to go away then the tongues of the circle would wag all unrestrained. She would stay, and put a curb upon them.

Smoothing the frown from her forehead and the

indignation from her voice, she said sweetly to Luella:

"You're all overwrought, dear. It was thoughtless of me to set you at that fussy work when you're not well. Now, I want you and Mitty to do some errands for me, up Sackville. I drove down here from the parsonage, instead of walking, because it's so hot. Old Jerry's out in Miss Evans's stable, and the carriage is in the yard. You and Mitty go and hitch up. Here are two lists, of things for the Circle and things for myself. And here are some pieces of ribbon I want you to match. Get everything at Smith & McElvey's, be sure. And see Mr. McElvey himself. Have him make out the two bills separate, and remind him he promised me a special extra discount on everything we wanted for the sewing-circle. And don't drive old Jerry too hard in this heat — you couldn't do it, though, if you wanted to, for he goes just as he likes, and that's the reason the rector won't drive him any more. And come back here for me, so you can drive me home."

During this long speech, — purposely drawn out to give every one a chance to think a little, — Luella had recovered her outward composure somewhat, and was once more as pale as her collar. In a voice that was faint but fairly steady she asked for some directions about the ribbons. Then she left the room, followed by Mitty; and she felt as if all the other women were hissing shame and denunciation after her. Once outside, however, she forced herself to a spasmodic cheerfulness, in order to protect herself from Mitty's amiable but troublesome interrogations.

As soon as the two girls were gone, Mrs. Goodridge resumed her work as if it were the only thing of importance to her in Westcock; and for several minutes there was a tense, expectant stillness in the room, broken only by the rustle of stuffs and the occasional faint click of thimble on needle. Then, contemplatively, without looking at any one, she remarked in a gentle voice:

"There's one thing sometimes fills me with amazement. When a number of really nice women — women naturally kind and good and full of Christian charity — get together, how often a queer change seems to come over them! It would almost seem as if Christian charity thought a sewing-circle was no place for it, and therefore stayed outside."

There was a moment of pregnant silence. Then pretty little feather-headed Mrs. McMinn spoke up from the other side of the room.

"Land's sakes, Mrs. Goodridge," she piped, glibly, "you ain't surely goin' to ask us to associate with a girl like Luelly Warden. It ain't pos-

The Sewing-circle 119

sible. It's as plain as the nose on her face what's the matter with *her*. Land's sakes, John wouldn't *let* me associate with her. My, but he'd be mad!"

During this speech the truth had struck Mrs. Goodridge for the first time. It had struck her in the face. For half a second her courage almost failed her, so weak had her position become. Then her dauntless spirit rose to the greater difficulty, and the light, which had flickered for a moment, glowed again in her eyes. Like a flash she recalled every detail of the personal history of each one of the women before her. As for Luella's own case, she knew that the girl, influenced by tradition and example, had held herself as sacredly the wife of her lover as if all the bishops, priests, and deacons of the diocese had performed the ceremony. It was an attitude which Mrs. Goodridge fervently deplored, — but she understood it, and could judge it fairly. She was determined that the Westcock people should judge it fairly, too.

"Of course, Mrs. McMinn," she answered in polite agreement, "I can quite understand your position in such a matter!" and Mrs. McMinn, whose wedding-day, thanks to the firm insistence of the rector, had preceded the christening of her first baby by nearly six weeks, flushed uncomfortably, and glanced about the room to see if any one seemed to think the rector's wife meant anything.

For once she had no answer ready. But Mrs. Finnimore stepped into the breach. She was a fat lady; and as she spoke she rocked her chair gently, her knees wide apart and her hands resting on her stomach.

"'Pears to me as how Mrs. McMinn's about right, Mrs. Goodridge, with all respect to your opinion. We can't, in justice to ourselves, have nothin' to do with a girl like Luelly, — more's the pity, too, for afore this happened I'd always thought she was such an exceptional fine girl. Of course, it's different with you, Mrs. Goodridge. Bein' the parson's wife, you can afford to do as you please, — an' maybe it's *right*, too, that you should stand by the weak an' erring sister. But us respectable folk, we got to think of our own reputations. An' we jest can't associate with Luelly Warden — with all respect to you, Mrs. Goodridge."

Having thus delivered herself, she leaned back, and rocked harder, and half-closed her little fat eyes complacently. She had only lived in Westcock five years; and having come from a remote place somewhere in the State of Maine, there was no one present who knew anything whatever of the first forty years of her life.

Mrs. Goodridge hesitated before replying to Mrs. Finnimore, whom she particularly disliked. She cast her eyes about once more, to select the best point of attack. The majority of the women present were securely entrenched, having taken no open liberties with the conventions. But two of the leaders Mrs. Goodridge knew to be so vulnerable that she wondered if they would have the audacity to contend. She hoped they would frankly take Luella's part, if only as a measure of personal precaution. There was the ever-censorious Mrs. Ben Ackerley, whose only daughter, as honest and faithful a little soul as ever lived, had presented her lover with two fine boys before she could get around to the fuss and formality of a wedding. And there was the village gossip *par excellence,* the Widow Gandy. She was indisputably a widow by her second husband — but as to her first, whether he was dead, or divorced, or both, or neither, nobody could tell but the Widow Gandy herself, and her testimony had always lain under some suspicion of prejudice. She let it be generally understood that she had been compelled to divorce him, and that he had died of grief in consequence. Then, there was Miss Hopkins, of the pies. She was the pink of inviolate spinsterhood, but of distinctly indeterminate fatherhood. It was through no fault of hers, however, that she bore a mother's rather than a father's name. She was a kindly soul, a lover of concord, innocent in thought and act, given to going with the crowd for the sake of peace, and incapable of wishing ill to any one unless it were a decrier of her pie-crusts. Mrs. Goodridge dismissed Miss Hopkins from her thoughts at once. But she felt herself in something of a dilemma.

"It seems to me," she said at length, striving to keep her heart's heat out of her voice, "that some of us could afford to make allowance for poor Luella and sympathize with her, and even associate with her, much better than we can afford to criticize her. She is to be blamed, of course. She has done wrong, of course. But who of us can throw stones at her?"

"She's a shameless hussy!" came the prompt and pious response of Mrs. Ackerley, who was lacking in imagination as well as in perception. From somewhere across the room some one of quicker intellect snickered. Mrs. Goodridge did not see who it was, but she felt herself less alone for that snicker. There was at least one person present who could appreciate her points.

"It seems to me," she continued, ignoring Mrs. Ackerley's interruption, "that some of you ladies draw extremely fine distinctions in these matters, — quite too fine for me to perceive them. She's done very wrong, of course. *I* regard such things as sinful. But there are others in Westcock who have done wrong in exactly the same way. *They* have not been punished. *They* have not been treated like

The Sewing-circle 123

outcasts. I can't understand such inconsistencies. Mind, I'm not finding fault with the others, whoever they are. But I claim the same consideration for this unhappy, brutally deserted girl, Luella Warden, in her hour of need, that has been given to these others, whoever they may be."

Had it not been for Mrs. Ackerley, it is quite possible that this plea might have won the whole company over to Luella's side. Mrs. Gandy, who, for all the perils of her tongue, was not at heart malevolent, was already smiling acquiescence. Little Mrs. McMinn, thoroughly daunted, was eager to capitulate. Mrs. Finnimore, with nothing at stake, was open to conviction. The hostess of the day, Miss Evans, a small, gentle old maid with silver hair brushed lustrously down over her ears in a Madonna curve, was just opening her mouth in support of all Mrs. Goodridge had said. But Mrs. Ackerley broke in.

"*I* say as how Luelly Warden's nothin' more nor less than a wanton hussy," she cried, facing Mrs. Goodridge defiantly. "Girls that gives their word to a lover, an' sticks to him faithful, an' marries him when the time comes, — it may be soon, or it may be a mite late in some folks's opinion, — but it's all right, an' them girls is jest as good an' jest as honest as anybody. You hain't named no names, but I know as how it's my girl you're a-hittin' at,

Mrs. Goodridge. But you know, jest as well as I do, 'tain't the same thing at all. My Annie's a good, honest girl, an' I won't have *nobody* speak of her in the same breath with that hussy, Luelly Warden."

"I'm sorry you've been so ready to fit the cap on your own daughter's head, Mrs. Ackerley!" answered Mrs. Goodridge. "I've nothing but respect and regard for your good daughter. But I want you to have a little decent humanity for another girl who is in just exactly the position your daughter was in for a long time, and who is, moreover, suffering under a cruel wrong!"

"My Annie jest like Luelly Warden?" almost shouted Mrs. Ackerley. "Was my Annie ever jilted by her man, I'd like to know? I dare anybody to say it! Would any man in Westcock desert his girl when she was 'that way,' 'less he know'd 'twas some other man as done it? Would Jim Calder 'a' done it? You know well enough what Jim's own mother'll say! An' you talk about that hussy bein' jest like my Annie!"

Mrs. Goodridge did know very well indeed what "Jim's own mother" would say; and the knowledge did not tend to conciliate her.

"*I* say, Mrs. Ackerley," she retorted in a cutting voice, leaning forward in her chair, "*I* say that Luella Warden is a good girl, an honest girl,

The Sewing-circle

just exactly as your Annie was. I say that Luella Warden is in her own eyes, — and, I do truly believe, in God's eyes, also, — the *wife* of Jim Calder, — the hideously wronged wife of Jim Calder. And I expect *my friends* to treat her as such!"

"Like my Annie, indeed! Listen to that! She's a common hussy!" almost shrieked Mrs. Ackerley. jumping to her feet in her excitement, and clutching at her sewing-bag, as if she were about to throw it at her opponent's head.

Mrs. Goodridge was past all diplomacy, now. She sat up very straight, and eyed Mrs. Ackerley with biting scorn.

"I understand," she said, sternly. "The enormity of Luella's sin appears to lie in the fact that her lover — her *husband, I* call him — has basely deserted her, — left her to face alone her shame, and her anguish, and the persecution of such women as you. She has no *man* to protect *her* — and that is the opportunity of such as you. From such 'good' women as you, Mrs. Ackerley, may we all be saved!"

Mrs. Ackerley looked around the room for an ally, but found none so bold as to come to her defence.

"Umph!" she snorted. "Ye're all cowards. Ye're all scairt o' *her!*" She started for the door. Then she turned about. "I'll never set foot insider

Westcock church agin, if I live to a hunderd. I'll jine the Baptis' church to-morrow!" Then she strode away hurriedly, not waiting to observe the result of this awful threat. And in a sweet voice Mrs. Goodridge called after her:

"I'm sure, I hope you will be very happy in the change, Mrs. Ackerley. But from what I hear of good Mr. Sawyer, their minister, you won't find any more encouragement to malice and slander over there than among us."

When Mrs. Ackerley's outraged black-alpaca shoulders had disappeared, Mrs. Goodridge cast an approving glance around the room. It seemed best to take it for granted, now, that every one had been on her side in the tilt with her vanquished adversary. And it suited every one, just then, to let it appear so. Nearly every one present liked Mrs. Goodridge, and quite every one present dreaded to cross her imperious will. As victor, she could well be generous. So, with the air of dismissing a matter unpleasant but also unimportant, she said, thoughtfully:

"I'm sure we all feel that the good lady who has left us does herself, in reality, a great injustice. She is not really so heartless and merciless as she would have us think. I have known her to be most self-sacrificingly generous, when her prejudices were not aroused. But there is no getting over the fact that she will never listen to reason, — and she is a little bit too impetuous for comfort. We will try our best to get along without her."

There was a faint, rather inarticulate murmur of assent; and then an industrious peace settled down upon the circle. Later in the afternoon, when the members had scattered to their homes, all had made up their minds to a compromise. They would run no risk of a falling-out with Mrs. Goodridge by openly snubbing Luella; but they would gently "freeze her out." They knew the process would be easy, and safe; for Luella's sensitive pride would notice things that Mrs. Goodridge would never think of heeding.

CHAPTER XII.

ABNER BAISLEY'S BILL

IN spite of Mrs. Goodridge's substantial triumph in the sewing-circle, the news about Luella, of course, went over the village like wild-fire. Some spread it with laughter, some with pretence of tears; but no one failed to spread it. Even Mrs. Goodridge herself had to tell it that very evening — to the rector, after Luella had gone home; and she was hotly indignant when the rector, without any surprise whatever, simply said, " Poor, deluded child! That's just what I've been afraid of all along!"

"Afraid of all along!" she echoed, sharply. "Then I'd like to know why you didn't say so, George! You ought to be ashamed of yourself, leaving me to find out such a thing as that from an impertinent little whipper-snapper like that Jinnie McMinn!"

"Why, Jean," protested the rector, in astonishment (he had not even yet got over being astonished at his wife's unexpectedness), "I merely

Abner Baisley's Bill

feared it, as I told you. Of course I didn't *know* it, any more than you did. So how could I tell you?"

"I should think you might have told me what you thought!" pursued Mrs. Goodridge, obstinately. But the rector, changing the subject a little, asked such an interesting question about Mrs. Ackerley's outbreak that his wife at once forgot her grievance in the retailing of her triumph.

It was not till the following morning that Mrs. Calder heard the news. Her house was off the direct road between Wood Point and the "Bito." But one of the Martin girls went out of her way to go and tell Mrs. Calder, just as that good lady was clearing the kitchen table after her frugal breakfast. Sallie Martin was in a hurry. She came into the back yard, stuck her head in the kitchen window, and delivered a terse statement of the situation. To her amazement, Mrs. Calder's stony countenance thawed at once, even to an unmistakable smile of welcome. Then she laughed aloud.

"Ye don't tell me! Be ye sartin sure it's so? Come right inside an' have a cup o' tea, Sallie Martin, and tell me all about it," exclaimed the good lady, with enthusiasm. But Miss Martin had no time to lose.

"Ain't got a minnit to spare!" she responded. "I hadn't ought to've took the time to come way 'round, only I thought as how *you'd* mebbe like to know, Mrs. Calder. Now I must run, for I've got to git saleratus, an' molasses, an' a lot o' things, down to the Bito, an' be back home afore half-pas' nine. Mother's bakin' to-day." She turned away, resolutely, a little disconcerted by that loud laugh which had greeted her tidings.

"But be ye *sure* it's so?" persisted Mrs. Calder, eagerly, drying her hands on her apron as she hastened out into the yard in the hope of gathering more such news.

"Sartain! No mistake about it! Ask Mrs. Ackerley! Good day. I *must* be goin'!" answered the girl, almost running from the yard.

All the morning Mrs. Calder went about her work with a cheerful smile, such as she had not worn since the day Jim sailed. Her satisfaction worked upon her mightily. In the afternoon, when she went, in her best cap and shawl, to have a good talk with Mrs. Ackerley, the latter greeted her with the exclamation:

"Well, I never seen the like of ye, Mrs. Calder! If you don't look *ten year* younger'n when I seen you last!"

On the following morning, when every one else in Westcock had heard about it, and thrashed it all well over, the matter came to the ears of Luella's uncle. As ill luck would have it, from the bitter tongue of Mrs. Ackerley it came,

Abner Baisley's Bill

Mrs. Ackerley was walking down to the Bito, to visit Mrs. Finnimore across the Creek. As she passed the dingy window of the store, — cluttered with fly-specked card-board boxes and bottles, strings of woollen socks and coloured glass beads, and soiled but brilliant advertisements of patent medicines, — she hastened her steps and averted her eyes. It was just the wrong moment for her to remember that she was owing Mr. Baisley, this long time, the sum of seven dollars and sixty-three cents; and that Mr. Baisley had more than once anxiously interrogated her on the subject.

To Mr. Baisley, on the contrary, as he caught sight of the passing form, this seemed to be just the right moment for him to remember his little bill. But it was not. He was distinctly unfortunate in having such a memory at that moment.

Hopping nimbly around the end of his counter, he ran out into the road, and confronted Mrs. Ackerley with a face of mingled protest and persuasion. The lady stopped, bridling resentfully.

"Good morning, Mrs. Ackerley," he said, politely. "I hope I see you well!"

"Thank ye, Mr. Baisley," she answered. "I can't rightly complain. Fer though I'm fur from well, there's others so much worse off that, when I consider, I'm bound to feel thankful to the Lord!"

"Excellent, Mrs. Ackerley," agreed the storekeeper, rubbing his lean and freckled hands. "A thankful sperrit is a blessed thing. Seein' you pass by, I jest thought as how I'd remind ye about that little bill. I'm a leetle mite hard put to it, this week. The bill's nothin', ye might say, to the likes of you, Mrs. Ackerley. *Only* seven sixty-three! But to me, it's these little things as mounts up. An' I'd be obliged if you could help me out this morning!"

Mrs. Ackerley knew that she couldn't, — not even to the extent of the odd sixty-three cents. But she did not want to say so, after the tribute Mr. Baisley had paid to her opulence. She was not unwilling he should think that seven sixty-three was nothing to her. She would try to turn his flank and escape revealing her weakness.

"I'm surprised, I declare I'm surprised, Mr. Baisley, that *you* should be thinkin' about a few cents on a day like this, when you'd oughter be a-hidin' yer head in shame in the back o' yer store! You, to be stoppin' respectable ladies on the street an' talkin' to them about money!"

She made as if to pass; but Mr. Baisley, dumfounded and indignant at this unexpected assault, put out a detaining hand, — and she suffered herself to be detained.

"Hidin' my head? — Me? What fur, I'd like to know? Shame? I'd have ye understand, Mary Jane Ackerley, *I* hain't done nothin' to be ashamed of! I'll be obleeged to you if you'll kindly explain!"

A bricky flush was stealing up through his thin whiskers, and the pupils of his eyes narrowed to pin points. He had always despised Mrs. Ackerley, anyway, — and now, for her to presume to "talk up" to him, — and owing him seven sixty-three, — was rather too much!

"If 'tain't you, Abner Baisley, it's yer house, — an' that's the same thing!" retorted Mrs. Ackerley.

Now it was one of Mr. Baisley's none too abundant virtues that he was not overquick in suspicion. He took it that Mrs. Ackerley was referring to the fact that Luella had been notoriously jilted, — which would have been cause for shame, indeed, had the stain not been clean wiped out by the open support of the rector and Mrs. Goodridge. Feeling quite secure on that point, it was with a certain exultation that he struck back at his insolent assailant.

"Ho!" he crowed. "It's my house ye're hissin' at, be it? Well, all I kin say is, look to yer own house, Mary Jane Ackerley, look to yer own house!"

Knowing how unanswerable her retort to this thrust would be, Mrs. Ackerley was not greatly enraged. She was too interested, she was getting too much solid satisfaction out of the encounter, to be really angry.

"Ye'll be singin' another tune, Mr. Baisley, when ye come to know what everybody else in Westcock knows," she sneered. "That fine niece o' yourn, she's fooled some of us these two months, sence Jim Calder found her out an' quit her, — but everybody knows her now fer the common hussy she be!"

Mr. Baisley shrank back in dismay as her meaning struck him. It never occurred to him to doubt the charge. Mrs. Ackerley passed on loftily. Then, turning with a harsh laugh, she cried, brutally, "Don't you care, Mr. Baisley! A girl like that'll draw customers!"

Almost choking with fury at this gross insult, Mr. Baisley turned and rushed into the store. His rage burned most fiercely against Luella, for having brought this shame upon him. But through it all he kept a firm grip upon one consoling thought. What a blessing that he had not succeeded in collecting that seven sixty-three from Mrs. Ackerley. She should be sued for it at once. He would swear out a *capias* that very afternoon.

CHAPTER XIII.

TURNED OUT

LUELLA was dusting in the sitting-room when her uncle burst in upon her. One look at his flushed face and furious, fishy eyes told her what had happened. Well, she was glad it had come. Nothing could be worse than the suspense. She braced herself for the storm of his shrill rage, and faced him steadily.

"It's true, is it?" he demanded, clutching a chair-back and steadying himself.

"Is what true?" asked Luella, quietly.

"You know what!" he almost screamed. "Don't ye go tryin' to wriggle out of it. Mrs. Ackerley's jest been tellin' me. Be it true, I say?"

"I don't know what Mrs. Ackerley's been saying, Uncle Abner!" answered Luella, with dignity. "She's a foul-mouthed old gossip."

Mr. Baisley jerked his arms as if he were going to strike her with the chair. But Luella's blue eyes met his unquailing.

"I want a straight answer!" he shouted. "Be it

true? She sez as how ye're jest no better'n a common hussy, — an' everybody in Westcock knows now what's wrong with you, — an' there ain't nobody you've fooled but me!"

"I know I've counted myself Jim Calder's wife! I've trusted him!" answered Luella, in a low voice, dropping her eyes, and going suddenly scarlet.

The moment her eyes fell Mr. Baisley sprang forward, fairly beside himself. He had courage when she seemed to shrink. He grabbed her by the arm and almost flung her from the room, toward the foot of the staircase. "Then out of my house ye go, this minnit!" he shrieked.

Taken by surprise, Luella had yielded to the suddenness of this attack. But she wrenched herself free, and drew herself to her full height, her eyes flaming upon him. She was a good two inches taller than he, and had no fear of his violence.

"Don't you lay a finger on me agin, Uncle Abner!" she panted. "Don't you *dare* lay a finger on me agin! It will go hard with you if you do, — mind, I warn you!"

Mr. Baisley drew back a couple of steps.

"She sez a girl like you'll draw custom! That's what she sez. I won't be shamed by the likes of you. I won't have you around my house a day longer. Out ye go this minnit, afore I chuck ye out!"

Turned Out 137

"No, you won't chuck me out!" replied the girl, coldly. "An' I won't go till I get a team to take my box. And I'll send for my things to-morrow, Uncle Abner."

In his excitement Mr. Baisley had forgotten that most of the furniture in his house belonged to Luella.

"You won't tech a stick o' that furniture. If 'twas ten times as much, it wouldn't pay me fer your board all these years I've kept ye. You won't tech a stick of it, I tell ye!" And again he advanced upon her, threateningly.

Luella's lips curled with contempt. Could this pitiful thing be her mother's brother? She knew that he could never make good his threat, for her services if set against her board would leave a very stiff balance in her favour, and she was not the stuff to be trampled upon. But she scorned to advance this argument at present. She could not stand any more wrangling. If there should be any more, she feared she might lose her head and do something she would be sorry for.

"Keep off!" she ordered. "Keep away from me! Don't say another word to me! I'll go to-day, when I'm ready. And you, — you better keep clear of me." As she spoke the long-pent wrath, injury, fear, anguish, all together flamed to her brain in something like a madness. Her eyes grew big, and dark, — and Mr. Baisley backed away before the dangerous look in them. As he backed, she followed, without realizing what she did. "You better keep right there in the store till I get away, —so's I won't shame you any more! But don't you dare to speak one word to me again, long's you live!"

When she came to the sitting-room door, Mr. Baisley had retreated as far as the table. She chanced to lay her hand on the door-knob. Instantly she slammed the door to, and locked it. Then, she darted up-stairs to her room, and flung herself down on the bed to think what she had better do.

It never for an instant occurred to her that she might go away from Westcock, — go somewhere where she was not known, and escape the bitter tongues. She belonged to Westcock, — and in case Jim should return, in Westcock he should find her. But her first thought was of the parsonage. Within those old brick walls she knew there was a safe haven for the present, with unfailing help and counsel for the future. For a little while she let herself be comforted with the idea that she was going to the parsonage. Then, when her heart had ceased to choke her with its poundings, she allowed herself to face the fact that she had no right to go there. She had no right to make any such demands upon the friendship of the rector and Mrs. Goodridge. Her common sense, and a certain native good taste, came to her rescue. She would go to Mrs. Bembridge, and pray to be allowed to make her home there. She knew well enough the answer she would get.

This decision made, Luella sprang up from the bed and set herself hurriedly to packing her big brass-studded box with such things as she would need at once, and with the trinkets and knick-knacks which she most intimately valued. Then there were other boxes to pack, in readiness for to-morrow's moving. Dinner-hour went by, but Mr. Baisley did not interrupt her. As far as she knew, he did not leave the store even to enter the kitchen. As she moved about, she chanced to pause for a moment to look out of her window. Her eyes fell upon her garden, now a riot of colour with its flaunting August blooms, — dahlias, hollyhocks, tiger-lilies, asters, marigolds, coxcombs, crowding out the green, bending over the little paths, blotting the trim outlines of the beds to a semi-tropic jungle. At the sight a huge wave of homesickness flowed over her, drowning her courage. She burst into a wild fit of weeping, — and the work of packing up was delayed for an hour.

Along about the middle of the afternoon, as she was looking out again upon the garden, schooling herself to the thought of leaving it, she saw her uncle drive by, descending the Bito hill. He had the Richardsons' wagon, the one he always borrowed when he went up to Sackville. He was on his way to swear out the *capias* against Mrs. Ackerley. But this, of course, Luella could not suspect. She was a little surprised at his going on this particular day; but the chief thing she thought of was the fact that his absence suited her plans. Andy, the boy, was probably left in charge of the store. Hastily washing her face to remove the traces of her tears, she ran down-stairs, opened the door leading into the back store a little way, and called Andy into the kitchen.

From the boy's beaming face Luella saw at once, to her unspeakable relief, that he had heard nothing.

"Andy," she said, with a cheerful smile, "what time will you be getting away to-night?"

"'Bout seven, I guess, Luelly," was the answer.

"Well, then, I want you to do something for me, right after you get your supper," she went on. "An' I don't want you to say a word about it to *any one.*"

The boy's eyes sparkled agreement, and he nodded his shock-haired, brown head.

"I want you to get Lawrence's express wagon for me, — or Tate's, if you can't get Lawrence's,

Turned Out 141

— *hire* it, you know, — don't borrow it, — and bring it round here to the gate for me about eight o'clock. I'm taking a box of things up to old Mrs. Bembridge's. I'll drive up with you myself, and you can leave me there, for I'll be going over to the parsonage afterward and so I won't be back home to-night."

"Co-rect!" said Andy, and started back hurriedly into the store, thinking he had heard a customer come in. He was devoted to Luella; but he was at the age when it pleased him to be laconic and undemonstrative.

"And, oh! say! Andy!" she added, stopping him, "don't go bringing anybody else with you. We can handle the box, me an' you, perfectly well. I know how strong you are!"

"*Co*-rect!" repeated Andy, departing with a gratified smile.

That night about eight o'clock, in the scented twilight, with the rushing of the tide in her ears and tears in her heart, Luella bade good-bye to her garden. When she and Andy had carried down the box and deposited it in the wagon, she had the boy help her pick two huge armfuls of flowers, which she truthfully told him were for Mrs. Goodridge and Mrs. Bembridge. He had never before seen her quite so lavish of the precious blooms, and he marvelled somewhat; but whatever Luella did he considered "jest about right," so he made no comment. Surreptitiously, Luella kissed many of the lovely, nodding blossom-faces which she had to leave behind her, — and she left them wet with a salter wet than dew. But outwardly she was just as cheerful as Andy had a right to expect; and as the laughter of the two rang from the garden to the store, Mr. Baisley snarled savagely. He could hardly contain himself at this proof that Luella was treating his punishment so lightly. He even felt a faint qualm of misgiving. A vision of what the house would be without her flashed across his mind. As for her, she must have something pretty good ahead of her, he thought, or she could never laugh like that when she'd just been turned plumb out of doors! "The ongrateful hussy!" he snarled, under his breath; and retiring to the gloom of the back store he served himself with a frugal dram of old West Indies rum to calm his feelings.

During the drive from her uncle's house to Mrs. Bembridge's, Luella was grateful beyond words for the uncomprehending companionship of Andy. He believed in her, admired her, was half in love with her in his boyish way, — and having not yet reached the stage of self-conscious diffidence in his passion, he was boyishly joyous over his triumph in "gittin' to take Luelly fer a drive." His simplicity and his happiness kept Luella from feeling

Turned Out 143

too terribly the overwhelming nature of what she was doing. This drive through the sweet night air, with the noise of the ebbing waters in her ears, was the most momentous move of her life. But with Andy's help she fenced her brain from the full realization of its import.

There was light in Mrs. Bembridge's windows. At the unwonted sound of wheels turning into her lane Mrs. Bembridge came out and stood in the kitchen door, holding a candle, which she shaded with her hand against the night wind. The flaring little flame lit up only her rugged face, and the magenta sontag crossing her broad bosom. The face looked grim, almost forbidding, as it peered forth into the darkness. Luella kept silence, with a hand of restraint on Andy's arm, till the wagon reached the middle of the yard. Mrs. Bembridge's hand, before the candle, cast a huge shadow over the chips, all the way to the barn. The picture of the lonely cottage, naked in its fields and black against the open, glimmering sky, the tiny patch of light in the narrow doorway, and the sombre, inquiring face sharp lit by the wavering flame, bit into her memory so that no detail of it ever faded. It seemed to her to symbolize in a vague way what her own life was become, — so small and uncertain a light in so great a darkness.

"Who be it?" demanded Mrs. Bembridge, in

a voice abrupt and peremptory. Her efforts to throw the light upon the visitors were being foiled by the caprices of the wind.

"Just me, Mrs. Bembridge! Me an' Andy. I've brought up those things, you know, — and some flowers!"

Luella's voice was too cheerful to be true, and the old woman's sensitive sympathies perceived at once that something had happened. She had no idea what Luella meant by "those things," but she was too wise to show her ignorance.

"Bless yer heart, Sweetie. Fancy ye rememberin' about it!" she cried, her face glowing with swift welcome. "Come right along in, both of yez, an I'll make yez a pot o' tea."

Luella had sprung lightly from the wagon, and was now helping Andy lift out the box. Carrying it between them, each with free arm extended to balance the effort, they staggered into the house and set it down in the only vacant corner. Then, breathing hard and wiping his wet forehead on his sleeve, Andy made answer.

"No tea fer me, thank ye kindly, Mrs. Bembridge! But I'd thank ye fer a pint o' water. I'm kind o' dry!"

His thirst quenched from the bright tin dipper which Mrs. Bembridge handed him, he turned to bring in an armful of flowers. Luella followed him close, to avoid the necessity of explanation. And Mrs. Bembridge, showing no sign of her bewilderment, hobbled at their heels with the candle.

When Andy had gathered up a full armful of dahlias, hollyhocks, asters, and meadowsweet from the bottom of the wagon, Luella took them from him.

"Give me those!" she said. "And take all the rest around to the parsonage. But don't tell Mrs. Goodridge I'm coming over! Be sure an' don't tell her, Andy. Just say I sent the flowers!"

"*Co*-rect, Luelly!" answered the boy, jumping into the wagon. The word "co-rect" was one which had but recently come to Westcock; and Andy refused to use any other when this could be made to serve.

"Good night!" he called, as the wagon went bumping dimly down the lane.

"Good-bye!" answered Luella, with a sudden catch in her throat. It was not Andy, but her youth, her old life, to which she was bidding farewell. She watched the team fairly out of sight, — the horse was white, and she could see it for some distance down the road. Then, her arms filled with the great bundle of bloom, she turned to Mrs. Bembridge, whose candle had been blown out.

"Hain't ye ben a-robbin' yer garden?" asked

the old woman, as a roundabout expression of her wonder.

"Oh!" cried the girl, with a shaking voice, "it ain't my garden any more. My uncle has turned me out. I've only you to come to!"

"An' you done jest right, a-comin' to me, Sweetie!" was the unequivocal response. "It's a proud an' glad woman I be this night, that ye've understood me so. Fer I couldn't love me own darter, if I had one, better'n I love you, Luelly Warden. An' that's God's truth!"

She put a sturdy arm around the girl's waist, and led her into the house.

A few months later, when the country was buried in snow, and the tides chafed harshly through tumbled and mud-stained ice, the child was born. It was a boy, dark and dark-haired, like certain of Jim's forebears; and when it was eight days old the rector christened it Seth, which had been the name of Luella's father.

CHAPTER XIV.

JIM AND MELISSA

As the *G. G. Goodridge* went sailing down the bay, that blowing summer afternoon, Jim Calder had no power to think. The conviction of Luella's unfaithfulness had numbed his brain. He went about his duties efficiently, but without seeming to be conscious that the men obeying his orders were alive. The ship's company, from the captain — and Melissa — down to the cabin-boy, appeared to him like so many automata. His look was a safeguard against interrogation. No one was daring enough to infringe upon his reserve. He saw the last of Westcock village, the tall poplars of Westcock House, the dykes of Tantramar Mouth, disappear behind the oak groves of Wood Point, — but did not realize what he saw. Beauséjour faded behind him, and the Minudie hills; and toward sunset, after passing the Joggins and Grindstone Island, the waters of Fundy grew less turbid. The yellow Tantramar silt was being left behind. Happening to notice this small matter, as he stared over the ship's rail, a conviction took form in Jim's mind that this was his last farewell to Tantramar. Yet not his, surely, but some other's, — for he could not believe that this man looking over the rail was himself.

Late that night, during his watch, as he walked the deck under clear stars and a moderating wind, the faculty of thought came back to Jim's brain, and in agony of spirit he went over and over what had happened. As to what he had done in leaving Luella without a word, he had, strange to say, no misgivings. It was for her own sake; — he felt that he would surely have killed her, if he had gone to her there where she waited for him on the dyke. To his absolutely sincere mind the evidence of her baseness and treachery was so conclusive that it was inconceivable to question it. Yet, he loved her, — though with a sort of horror, — and he would not have any one know what she had done. He would not ever, as long as he lived, make any explanation. *She* would need none. She would understand only too well. She would have to hold her tongue, for her own sake; and he would bear the blame, to save her. He knew what Westcock would think of him, for deserting her under such circumstances. When the child came, they would take it for granted it was his. What a scoundrel the rector would think him. What would Captain Britton think; and honest Ezra Boltenhouse! He would leave the ship before *they* could hear of *that*. He would leave the ship, and change his name, and cut himself off for ever from his own people. Never again would he see the dear green marshes, the winding creeks and uplands of Westcock, the red flats and yellow tides of his unstable Tantramar. But Luella would be saved. Her treachery would never be known. And she would know, — she would understand, — that he had spared her. Between these thoughts, and sudden recurring bursts of inward fury that found expression only in convulsive workings of his face, he wore out his strength as the night wore out. In the first ghost-pallor of dawn he leaned against the mast, quivering with weakness. He was on the brink of collapse. Never before had he been so near it. Never after was he to come so near it again, till the time of passing over the great and final brink. But he was only a boy, — and called upon to bear far more than a man's portion of calamity. His knees trembled, the steady-sloping deck seemed to reel, and he clutched at the mast for support. Then, up through the failing confusion of his brain a sharp memory thrust itself. That note — that fatal note of Luella's! What had he done with it? If any one else should see it, she would be ruined irrevocably. He must destroy it. The cloud passed off his brain;

and his strength returned, as he feverishly searched every pocket.

It was not to be found. He could not remember anything that had happened for some time after reading that note. But he must have left it on the cabin table. He almost ran to see, — but one glance down the companion, where the table was in full view under the swinging lamp, showed him it was not there. Surely, he told himself, Melissa must have picked it up.

It would be two or three hours yet before he could see Melissa, — but he was no longer weak. When his watch was ended he could not go to his bunk, but kept pacing tirelessly up and down in the growing light. The dawn came in lavender and rose, then gold, then blue, — and with the blue of full day came Melissa up to the deck, her face bright with morning.

As Jim hurried toward her, his eyes haggard and his mouth white and set, she turned pale. She had expected that at this hour of the morning he would be in his bunk, after his watch. For one instant she almost imagined that he had found her out, so unnatural and almost savage was his look. But her courage never failed her.

"Good morning, Jim — my poor friend, Jim!" she said, softly, in a voice of tender understanding.

Jim and Melissa 151

"That letter!" he demanded, under his breath.
"I can't find it!"

"You dropped it on the floor, poor boy!" answered the girl.

"You never left it there!" he panted, his eyes widening with sudden terror.

"Of course not, Jim!" she answered, reprovingly. "Do you think I'd leave it for some one else to see? Do you think I could be so horrid as that?"

"No, of course not, Melissy!" he responded, suddenly humble, now that he knew the letter was safe. "I know how good you are! Best give the — best give it to me, Melissy!"

"What for, Jim? It wouldn't be good for you to keep such a dreadful thing as that. It'ld be bad for you. It's just morbid, Jim, for you to want it!"

"I want to tear it up!" he answered, heavily. "Do you suppose I'd keep — that? Give it to me, M'lissy!"

"I did tear it up, right off, Jim!" answered Melissa. "Do you suppose I'd want to keep a thing like that? I tore it up into little, teeny bits, right off, and threw it overboard! It fairly burned in my pocket, every minute since I got it! I was that glad I can't tell you, Jim, when it was all gone!"

"It can't never be all gone, Melissy, — never so

long's I live, it can't!" said Jim, his eyes wandering away from her face and out over the morning waves.

A pang of savage jealousy surprised the girl's heart.

"But why were you so terribly anxious about it, Jim?" she demanded, as it were in spite of herself. "You looked as if you were ready to kill some one if you didn't get it that very minute!"

She knew she was foolish to talk this way, but she could not help it. For the moment her self-control had weakened. Jim, however, was now too dull, from the long stress, to notice anything very clearly. The simple question was all he heeded. It called for a simple answer.

"It would 'a' ruined her, if anybody but you'd 'a' found it!" And turning away abruptly he went down to his bunk, to escape Melissa and every one else for a time. His head felt light, and he was not very sure of his steps, and he knew his bunk was the place for him.

CHAPTER XV.

TO SOUTHERN SEAS

UNHINDERED by any caprice of wind, or tide, or fog, the *G. G. Goodridge* arrived at the busy wharves of St. John, where she added to her cargo a small but valuable consignment of manufactured goods for Matanzas, Cuba. The stuff was hurried aboard, and the ship cleared again at once. Jim's duties as second mate kept him toiling through almost every hour of the twenty-four; and though he could not have told afterward what he did or how he did it, his work was well done. Time he stole to write a letter to his mother, — a little letter of love and farewell, merely, declaring that he was well, but making not the remotest reference to Luella or to the abruptness of his leaving. That letter had worried Mrs. Calder, not by reason of its conspicuous omissions, but because of an unwonted indecision in the handwriting, which gave her an impression of sickness.

This impression was not misleading. As Jim

wrote, he was holding his brain to the task with difficulty. Strange whims of spelling strove to express themselves through his pen. As he glanced about the cabin everything seemed unreal to him, — and he himself the most curiously unreal of all. Till the ship was once more under way, however, — till the steeple-crowned rocks, the dark heights of Partridge Island, and the last faint smoke of the city had sunk below the horizon, — he held himself in hand. Then the terrifying unreality got the better of him, — and the last vague remembrance he had was of strong hands jerking him back violently from the bulwarks.

The captain — who was the only doctor the *G. G. Goodridge* could boast — pronounced Jim's case brain fever. It certainly seemed to be a fever; and unquestionably it attacked the brain. Jim was either delirious or in a stupor for nearly three weeks. With the aid of two large volumes called "The Home Physician," and a well-stocked medicine chest, Captain Britton doctored Jim solicitously; while Melissa nursed him intelligently night and day, and probably saved his life by omitting to give him most of her father's doses. Matanzas was reached; and passing the little fort at the Canimar mouth, the ship cast anchor at the head of the beautiful blue and beryl bay, where the bright opal-hued city basks in the sun between the windings of the

San Juan and the Yumuri. This was in the heat of early September; — and Jim, in his hot bunk, babbled of the cool, red rush of Tantramar. He knew nothing of where he was, — or of the rector's letter, which caught him here the day after the ship got in. Melissa, as his nurse, took charge of it, — and took also the precaution to read it. She found it so convincing that she could not run the risk of letting it ever reach Jim's eyes. She tore it up, and dropped it over the side for the pelicans to consider.

It was not till Cuba had long been dropped behind into the wastes of the purple Caribbean that Jim came to himself. His sanity returned all at once, — but his strength so slowly that for long it seemed as if his life might flicker out on any one of the puffs of hot air which came spasmodically from the torrid coasts. Not till the turbid mouths of the Orinoco were passed did life once more take hold upon him, and give him once more the semblance of a man. When he was again on deck, he seemed, outwardly, to have put by all remembrance of Tantramar and the tragedy that had gone before his sailing. He was deeply grateful to Melissa for her devoted nursing, — but in a subtle way he made her feel that he was not grateful for the life which she had saved. When the old tan, at last, came back to his face, the vigour to his voice and form, his attitude toward Melissa was always chastened, as it were, by a sort of distant reverence which she did not dare to assail. At times she came near to losing her self-possession and betraying her passion to him, as she saw herself drawing no nearer to the goal for which she had so desperately striven. A jealousy which she had never known before, and which she despised with all her heart, took hold upon her at times, as she saw that Jim was more than ever unconscious of her womanhood. She even began to have a misgiving, perhaps for the first time in her life. Was it possible that defeat might lurk in her victory, that after all her triumph might prove barren? As she writhed through the nights of heat, thinking this thought over and over, she would make up her mind to a bolder policy with Jim; but always, when she looked into his eyes, she became afraid. The novelty of this fear daunted her own judgment. And she concluded, at last, to wait. Time, she felt, must fight on her side. She would wait, no matter how long, till the unquestionable hour should come.

When the *G. G. Goodridge* made harbour at Montevideo, Melissa was all eagerness to get ashore; so Captain Britton took her with him when he went to present his papers to the consignee. Here he got the ship's mail, — which Melissa gaily took charge of, while he occupied himself with the business of his cargo. There proved to be a letter for Melissa herself, from her aunt, telling of the talk in Westcock about Luella, and effectively eviscerating Jim for his action in forsaking the girl. Over this Melissa smiled sourly. What most concerned her, however, were two letters for Jim. One she knew to be from his mother. With her usual cool sagacity and foresight, she had taken pains to note Mrs. Calder's handwriting in the past. That letter went back into the pile. But the other was from Luella. That disappeared smoothly into Melissa's pocket.

Not till hours later, in the seclusion of her own cabin, did Melissa bring this letter forth to really examine it. It was a thick missive, bearing double postage, and stamped with a date just ten days after the sailing of the *G. G. Goodridge*. Melissa fingered it with a curiosity less cool and triumphant than she would have evinced a month ago. Doubt and failure had at last succeeded in fretting a tiny flaw in the armour of her heartlessness, and she was conscious of a sense of shame. She had intended to read the letter, to glut her jealousy upon its grief and its vain pleadings. But to her astonishment she could not do it. Instead, she violently ripped it up and tore it to tiny pieces, altogether unread. These fragments she tied up securely with two iron spikes, and then dropped the package into the sea. When it had vanished she drew a long breath, and realized what a strain it had been to her, — the possibility of that letter, and the possibility of her failing to intercept it. Now that the strain was over she felt sick, and almost hysterical. Coming on deck a half-hour later she saw Jim approaching, and with an inspiration of weakness allowed herself to trip over a coil of rope. As she fell she gave a little, suppressed cry of pain, and clutched at her side. Jim, of course, sprang instantly to pick her up, and for a moment she leaned upon him. He inquired, with a fitting solicitude, if she were hurt; but when she assured him she was not (while cleverly making it apparent that she was), she found him quite too easily reassured upon the subject. In a sudden flash of anger, of a kind of weary, disappointed rage, she tore herself from his indifferent arms and fled back to her cabin. That evening she kept to her bunk, pleading a headache; but next morning, heartily ashamed of her weakness, she was about the deck again with her usual careless cheer. She had caught Jim's look of impatient wonder, and was resolved that she would make no such mistake again.

CHAPTER XVI.

MELISSA'S TRIUMPH

AT Montevideo there came a change of plans. Instead of sailing for a Chilean or Peruvian port, the *G. G. Goodridge* got a charter for Barcelona, Spain, with a rather unsavoury cargo which made Melissa carry her little nose high in air for some time. It was chiefly hides, with a lot of dried beef, and a miscellaneous assortment of boxes, barrels, and bales, into the mystery of which she made no attempt to penetrate. During a long, sweltering calm in mid-ocean, near the equator, the smells which fumed up from the packed hold sickened her, and it took weeks of buffeting with a clean norther off Cape Blanco to bring back the colour to her white cheeks. By the time Barcelona was reached her nose was acclimatized to smells.

At Barcelona there was unexpected delay in the matter of discharging cargo. For a time there was some mystery about it, which the captain, deficient in his knowledge of Spanish, could not fathom; and every one on board the *G. G. Goodridge* was getting into a very bad humour. Then a lot of wharf hands were got to work at the unloading, — but they were a scurvy-looking, incompetent crew, very unlike the nimble, sinewy fellows Captain Britton had been wont to find at this busy port. Presently it came out that there was a strike on, among the longshoremen and stevedores of the port. The men at work on the *G. G. Goodridge,* it seemed, were some of a gang who had been drummed up in Marseilles and Genoa, and brought over to help in breaking the strike. They were nervous and suspicious, as well as ugly-tempered; and they had an exasperating fashion of glancing back over their shoulders every other minute as they worked. The mate said it gave him the creeps to see them; and it got on Jim's overstrained nerves till he felt himself growing hungry for an excuse to smash some one, merely as a relief to his feelings. His irritation was not directed against any of these suspicious wharfingers, but against the striking longshoremen who made them suspicious and caused all the ruinous, nerve-racking delay. Strikes were unneeded and unknown in Westcock; and Jim could not see what they were good for under any circumstances.

There were two other vessels — an American full-rigged ship and a Norwegian bark — unloading at the same pier with the *G. G. Goodridge;* and

Melissa's Triumph

this pier suddenly became a sort of storm-centre. There would be a fight, either between strikers and police or strikers and workers, every morning when the men came aboard; and Captain Britton had to issue very stringent orders, to keep his crew of Fundy men from sallying ashore to take a hand in the fray. Law-abiding but belligerent in their instincts, they burned to rush to the assistance of the hard-pressed police and beat some sense into the troublesome strikers' heads. In this desire they had the ill-disguised sympathy of both Mr. Boltenhouse and Jim. But Captain Job Britton was not a man to trifle with, and his word was enough.

The dangerous excitement, the sense of struggle, were like wine in Melissa's veins. They brought back the colour to her cheeks, the dancing fire to her eyes, and filled her with a kind of exaltation. Under the menace of impending battle she regained her self-confidence. She even got a mysterious impression — an intuition, she called it to herself — that her own long-delayed triumph was at last drawing near. It was impossible to keep her out of danger, for she was the only person on the ship who dared to disobey her father. She was all over the ship, wherever the most was going on; and frequently she was out on the pier, pretending to scrutinize the work, if Mr. Boltenhouse or Jim chanced to be there. She was always on the pier, indeed, if Jim was there, — and with Mr. Boltenhouse often enough to avoid any appearance of favouritism. There was a difference, however. When with the mate she was always close at his side, — "under his wing," as he put it, bothering him with questions and amazing him with her cleverness and insight. When on the pier with Jim, on the other hand, she usually held somewhat aloof, not obtruding herself upon him, but furtively noting all that went on about him. The true significance of this attitude she hardly acknowledged to herself, pretending it was a mere part of her policy. In reality, however, she had an uneasy feeling that Jim was in danger, that some sudden peril was about to strike at him without warning.

Intuitions, as a rule, are like the answers of the Delphic Oracle. It is hard to get them. And when you have them, it is still harder to interpret them aright. Melissa's prescience was a true prescience; but a portion of its truth was little like her expectation of it. Her faith in a speedy victory was moving to a strange fulfilment.

There came a morning when the strikers were so violent that few workers dared come to the pier. Every one was angry; and Jim the most angry of all. There were not enough workmen to keep things properly moving, and the wharf beside the *G. G. Goodridge* was getting clogged. The gang on the pier was working under its own foreman, superintended by Jim, who had picked up a smattering of Spanish during his visits to Havana, Matanzas, and other Cuban ports. At the head of the pier there was a noise of ceaseless bickering between the strikers and the little cordon of police who held them in check.

Suddenly the excitement at the pier-head quieted down, as if by magic. The strikers had grown so numerous and so belligerent that the worried police had consented to a truce and a compromise. On condition that the strikers should refrain from forcing the line and attacking the non-union workmen, it was permitted that three of their delegates should come out on the pier and talk to the gangs who were unloading the three ships. The purpose of these delegates, of course, was to either persuade or frighten the new men into joining them.

As soon as the delegates were let through, and started down the pier, unhindered, the workmen understood what they were coming for, and work began to lag. Some were for yielding at once. Others, of more strenuous mettle, were for standing by their terms with the bosses and fighting the thing through at any cost. These buckled down to their job with redoubled energy, casting black looks over their shoulders at the rest, and muttering curses upon any who should attempt to interfere with them. The foremen, of course, straightway set themselves to the task of stiffening the waverers. Meanwhile, for a minute or two, Jim stood glancing from one group to another in bewilderment. He knew nothing of the machinery and methods of a strike; and with his limited Spanish he failed to catch, at first, the phrases that would have enlightened him. He felt, however, that there was new trouble abroad, and that the strikers were making it. His jaw set, and an ugly light flashed into his eyes. Melissa thrilled exultantly as she noted the change in his face, — and moved a little nearer, without thinking what she was doing. Apparently, she was absorbed in the investigation of a basket of coarse laces which an old woman was displaying to her. The old woman followed her movement, surprised; and Melissa, forgetting to bargain, reseated herself on the edge of a box, and concluded a hasty purchase at a price which made the old woman's eyes sparkle with triumph. As for Jim, he had not even noticed that the girl was on the pier.

The delegate who came to the *G. G. Goodridge* was a big, swarthy, Spanish fellow, with glittering black eyes that showed a great deal of the white, and a confident, bullying manner. The first wharf-hand he encountered was carrying a box of dried fish. In an undertone he spoke a few words; whereupon the wharf-hand, after a moment's hesitation, dropped the box with a crash that split it open, grinned deprecatingly, and started off up the pier. Jim waited for the foreman of the unloading gang to interfere; but the latter, with an angry yet anxious face, pretended not to see what had happened.

The next man to whom the visitor addressed himself was a wiry little, surly-faced Italian, with a red handkerchief tied around his head. The Italian went on with his work without showing any sign that he heard what the striker was saying to him. Jim heard, being only a few feet away; but could not catch the drift of the unfamiliar vocabulary and hurried, slipshod pronunciation. He could see, however, that the delegate was getting enraged at his hearer's aggravating unresponsiveness. At this sight, Jim's own wrath boiled higher, and he had to keep a firm grip on himself to avoid interfering. He knew that in this matter it was his business to keep his hands off and leave things to the foreman to settle. That was the counsel of wisdom, — but to his unhappy and bitter spirit it was a hard counsel. He imagined his fury was all against the insolent strikers; but in reality it was against life, — it was upon the throat of life itself that his fingers were itching to clutch. The rest of the workmen on the wharf, his own men busy on the deck, the tall spars and rigging, the other ships crowding in port, the hot, pale sky, the green-blue water of the harbour, and the bright-coloured buildings jostling down to it, — all was unreal to him, of as little significance as a scene on a theatre curtain. Reality was right there ahead of him, where the big striker was now threatening the unconcerned little workman.

Suddenly the striker's voice rose and he made a savage grab for the Italian's collar. The physical action worked on Jim's overstrained nerves quicker than thought itself. Almost in the same instant he was over a pile of deals and face to face with the aggressor. The Italian, jerked violently backwards, was writhing in the effort to turn and grapple with his assailant. Then Jim's fist shot out, — and the Spaniard went sprawling, while his furious victim staggered free.

As the fellow dropped, Jim caught him with both hands by the back of his shirt collar, and dragged him to his feet. Then, shifting his right hand to a grip at the seat of his trousers, he ran him ignominiously some ten or twelve feet up the pier, between the bales of hides, and with a well-placed kick projected him forth into a clear space, where his discomfiture proclaimed itself to every one within eye-shot. A roar of laughter went up all over the pier.

"Get out now, you hound, and go mind your own

business!" commanded Jim, in awkward but very intelligible Spanish. Then he turned on his heel and strode coolly back to where he had dropped his tally-sheet.

If Jim had been more experienced he would not have been so unconcerned in his confidence that the affair was settled. The Spaniard, half-dazed by a method of handling which was so novel to him, picked himself up slowly, at first. Then the full ignominy of his defeat rushed over him, the public shame of it. His rage blazed into madness. He was no longer the swaggering bully. Half-crouching, silent, deadly, he darted between the barrels like a running weasel. His long knife flashed out, and he leaped straight at Jim's back, stabbing. It was all so swift that not a man moved, not a voice cried out in warning. But Melissa's instinct had been even swifter than the Spaniard's hate. She had seemed to see everything just a thought before it happened, — and even as the knife flashed downwards she had slipped between, with a gasp. The blade went into her side, right to the hilt.

Jim whirled about, amazed, and caught her in his arms. A savage cry went up from the pier and ships. Jim forgot to defend himself; but before the madman could strike again, the little Italian, leaping upon him nimbly, had stabbed him clean to the heart. Even in that moment the picture that stamped itself whimsically on Jim's mind was the radiance on the face of the little Italian as he sprang and stabbed home.

Jim looked down at the white face upon his shoulder, the small form drooping in his arms, the crimson spreading quickly upon the bosom of the soft white frock. For a second he stood motionless, astounded, while pier and ships hummed with coming battle. As he stared down upon Melissa's face, her half-closed, already darkening eyes opened wide to his. From their depths her great and longing passion declared itself. A shock of overwhelming surprise set him trembling; and into that intense look, which strove to search his very soul, came instantly an eager demand. A rush of emotion — not love at all, but immeasurable tenderness and pity — went over him. He bent and kissed her on the lips. But even at that moment, his thought fled with an unutterable anguish of desire back to the green countryside of Tantramar, and the lips of the woman he loved; and a sob strangled in his throat. To the girl, however, dying in his arms, it seemed that that sob was for her. The ebbing life surged back, for a second, into heart and brain. Her lips clung to his, and she whispered:

"*Did* I save your life, Jim? Twice, now, I've saved you. Tell me I've saved you, Jim."

"Yes, M'lissy, dear, you've saved my worthless

life," he answered. " But you shall not go — you must not go — we *mus*t save you! " — he went on, picking her up and rushing up the gangway with her, in a sudden terror at the grayness spreading upon her white face. Even he, for all his inexperience, could not misunderstand that look.

But into Melissa's eyes came a passion of triumph and of utter gladness. Not for one instant did it enter her strange, unswerving, unrelenting brain to confess her crime and make restitution for the ruin she had wrought. Instead of that, her darkening consciousness held only the exultant thought that at last Jim was hers. Feeling his arms about her, she hardly noticed the fierce agony in her side. In her brain she kept repeating: " I have saved him — I have saved him — I have the right to him — he is mine — " till suddenly all stopped.

As he reached the head of the gangway, Jim felt a shudder pass through the light form. All at once it seemed to slacken and grow heavier. And he knew that she was dead.

The next moment Captain Britton met him, his ruddy face white as chalk, his eyes terrible with horror and reproach. He snatched Jim's burden from him with a hoarse cry of " Give her to me! " But as the lifeless weight sank inertly against his bosom he staggered, stared about him wildly, then fixed Jim with a dreadful look.

"She's dead! It's your fault! Get out of my sight!" he said. Then he turned and carried her to the cabin.

These wild words Jim hardly heard, and heeded not at all. In a daze he followed to the very foot of the companion. But there he stopped, with a realization that he had no right to intrude upon the father's grief. For a second or two he hesitated, with a bitter and desolate thought of Luella. He knew that he was shocked, but in no way profoundly grieved, at Melissa's death. He resented in himself, dully, the lack of this deep grief. He wondered why he could not have loved this girl, so true and so unselfish, — who had almost joyously given her life for him, — instead of that other who had so vilely betrayed him.

As he stood there, heavily pondering, a noise of shouts and trampling feet went over his head with a rush, bringing him back to his surroundings. It was Ezra Boltenhouse leading out the crew of the *G. G. Goodridge* to take vengeance on the longshoremen. Sharply Jim remembered that things were happening on the pier. He sprang up the companion, and followed as fast as he could run.

Things had already been happening on the pier. The body of the murderer had been pitched over

Melissa's Triumph

into the harbour. The mob of strikers about the pier-head had broken through the police-line with a yell and were now surging down the pier. Half a dozen of the feebler spirits among the wharf-hands, in a panic, had run to meet and join them. The rest, drawing their knives or snatching up whatever might be made to serve as a weapon, awaited the clash in a sullen fury. The death of Melissa, whose pale, unusual beauty they had extravagantly admired, had made them eager for vengeance.

As the crew of the *G. G. Goodridge* charged up the pier the crew of the American ship came tumbling out with a cheer and joined them. The mob, seeing now that they had undertaken too much, paused irresolutely. Those who turned their heads saw that the little line of police was coming down behind them. The next moment the men of the *Goodridge* were upon them.

Ezra Boltenhouse was in front, swinging a capstan-bar which he used like a flail, his great strokes clearing a path before him. But Jim, who was a swift runner, came up the next instant, and thrust his way to Ezra's side. In his haste, not to be left behind, he had forgotten to snatch up a weapon of any kind. But with his naked hands he darted straight at the man before him, a tall fellow whose eyes had scowled for a second into his. Jim made good his hold upon the fellow's throat with such a grip that his chin went up, his eyes bulged, and he fell backwards, with Jim on top of him; and the knife dropped from his fingers. As the two lay grappling, the American sailors came up on the run, cursing joyously, and trampling them under foot, — being in too much of a hurry to look where they were stepping, and very much afraid lest they should be cheated out of their fair share of the fight. Before their onset the mob was hurled back upon the police, and the whole yelling, grappling, struggling mass was swept up the pier.

When the storm had passed over him, Jim found himself dazed and battered, but fervently concentrated, through it all, on the task of throttling his enemy. The fellow's face was purple already, his mouth open in an unpleasant way; and with a swift revulsion Jim realized that he did not at all want to kill him. Loosening his vindictive clutch he sprang to his feet. The man got up slowly, and drew deep breaths.

"Git!" commanded Jim.

The fellow did not understand Jim's English, but the gesture that went with it was intelligible. He looked around furiously. His companions — those of them who were not lying wounded further up the pier or being dragged off in the hands of the police — were now scattering and running for their lives. He looked again, anxiously, at Jim. Then,

Melissa's Triumph 173

having regained his breath, he ran to the pier-edge and dived into the tide. Jim stared, wondering if he would have to plunge in to the rescue. But a second later the fellow came up, and struck out toward a fishing-craft near by. Seeing that he was a good swimmer, Jim turned away, and straightway forgot all about him. The fight was over. The men, sailors and wharf-hands all together, were returning noisily down the pier. Jim turned his back on them all, sat down on a barrel close to the edge, and got out his pipe. The look upon his face effectually forbade intrusion.

CHAPTER XVII.

THE SPELL OF THE EAST

As Jim sat there, smoking and staring out seaward, he felt that Fate had crushed him again to earth. It was not grief for Melissa's death, — he was surprised to find how little that bore upon him as a personal loss, — but it was the sense that he had caused her death, that overwhelmed him. He felt it intolerable that she should have sacrificed herself for him, when he could give nothing in return. He had never dreamed of her loving him; and even now, as he marvelled at the revelation, his whole heart went back to Luella with a rush of longing which so wrenched him that his pipe fell, unheeded, into the water. His eyes closed, and he felt her eyes burning into them, terrible with love, and pain, and reproach. Her hands seemed to draw him close, her lips seemed to touch his own, — and a groan forced itself from his throat. The sound of it brought him to himself, and he looked around uneasily. No one had heard it. No one was near. And he drifted back miserably to the thought of the heart-broken man in the cabin, bending over the body of his only child. He pictured the little white-frocked figure, darkly blood-stained, the abundant, ruddy hair thrown far back from the small, dead face, — and he saw the strong face of Job Britton distorted with grief. It was that look on Job Britton's face that turned the knife in his heart. He repeated to himself the words, " Get out of my sight! "— and he told himself they were just. The *G. G. Goodridge* was no longer any place for him. Nor did he want to have anything more to do with her. Upon this thought came a sudden vision of what he would do. He would cut himself off for ever from his ship, and his own people. He would sail to the China seas, shipping only for voyages in Eastern waters, and return no more to the waters of Fundy. And he would try his best to hide himself from the search of memory, by taking a new name.

This resolve was sudden, but clear and final. Under the impulse of it he sprang up, hurried on board, and sought out Ezra Boltenhouse.

" Mr. Boltenhouse," said he, abruptly, " I'm going to quit this ship. Would you kindly git my papers from the captain? "

" Why — but — Jim, my lad! " stammered the mate, half-comprehending, and nevertheless bewildered. "What d'ye mean? Ye can't quit the ship that way. We need you, right here!"

"I know the captain'll give me my papers, an' let me go, glad enough," said Jim, heavily. "This ship ain't no place for me, Ezra. He'd always be remembering it was me that killed her, so to speak. An' I want to git away. The *G. G. Goodridge* is only a bit o' Westcock, anyways, Ezra. She talks to me, nights, of Purdy's shipyard, — and oftentimes when the wind roars in her ropes I hear the 'Bito' rushing, — an' I just can't stand it. Let me git out, Ezra!"

The mate laid a massive hand on Jim's shoulder.

"Well, lad," said he, slowly, considering as he spoke, "I reckon as how you'd ought to know best. I hain't got no idee what was wrong with you afore this awful day. But any one could see there was *somethin'* wrong, terrible wrong. An' the poor little girl yonder seen it, too. But another thing I seen, that you didn't see, Jim, — an' nobody seen, not even her own father, but only me, — that she was jest eatin' her little heart out fer you, Jim."

"I never knew she cared, — not till to-day!" answered Jim, hanging his head. "Because she cared — that's another reason I'm goin'. *He* knows it now! He said to me, 'Git out o' my sight!'"

"Oh!" exclaimed Mr. Boltenhouse, "he told

you that, did he? Well, but he's a just man, Jim, an' he'll never hold it agin you after he comes to himself a bit. He didn't know what he was sayin', he was that crazy. But I'll git your papers for you, Jim, jest as soon's it's decent to bother him about it."

"Thank you, Ezra! An' the sooner you can fix it, the better for me. An' with your leave, I'd like to go ashore soon's I get my chest packed up."

"I wish you didn't take it so hard, lad!" said the mate, kindly. "But I know you'll come out all right. It's sorry I'll be to lose you. An' if ever I kin be of use to you, Jim, jest you count on me!"

The two gripped hands, and Jim turned away to his cabin to get his few belongings stowed. He could not endure to look again on Melissa's dead face. And he shrunk from seeing Melissa's father again. At dusk that evening he went ashore, with two of the crew carrying his chest between them. He would not turn his head for a last look at the *G. G. Goodridge;* and he took lodgings overnight on a street away from the water-front, that his eyes might not fall upon her again. Next day he went by train down the coast to Gibraltar, to seek an English ship on which to work his way to London. He left Barcelona Jim Calder. When he reached Gibraltar he was Jim Callahan. When he wrote to his mother, and told her what he had done, he gave no explanation whatever. But he said she was not to tell a living soul, nor talk of his affairs in Westcock; and he knew well that no force and no persuasion would ever drag his barren secret past her teeth.

For a week Jim wandered aimlessly about the City of the Rock, so sunk in his own darkness that he saw nothing of the interest and the wonder of the place. Then, saying nothing of his mate's certificate because he had changed his name, he shipped before the mast on a homeward bound Bristol brig. From Bristol he went as passenger on a channel sloop around to London, and had not been about the docks of the East India Company three days before he had signed for the voyage to Singapore. The ship was a brand-new one, full-rigged and of twice the tonnage of the *G. G. Goodridge*. She carried under her bowsprit a richly gilded, billowy-breasted figure of a woman, and was named the *Belle Eliza*.

The crew of the *Belle Eliza* was made up of Swedes, Finns, and Lascars, with only four British; and Jim found the isolation which he craved. Throughout the voyage, which was uneventful, he made no friends. At Singapore the *Belle Eliza* got a charter for Sidney, New South Wales, and as this was going still farther away from home, Jim signed again with her. By this time the East was getting into his veins, and beginning to drug his memory. From Sidney his ship went to Shanghai, and thence back to Singapore. The waters of Fundy sank back into the realm of dark and bitter dream. The pale green marshes, the fir-clad uplands, the yellow flats, and winding channels of Tantramar, all were resolutely and vigilantly forgotten. With stern lines about his mouth, — yet lines which softened into something of the old sunny cheer when he smiled, — Jim took grip again upon life.

CHAPTER XVIII.

AT MRS. BEMBRIDGE'S

MRS. BEMBRIDGE'S bleak gray house in the fields began to grow more gracious-looking soon after Luella came to it. Mrs. Bembridge herself, owning as she did a bit of "marsh" which could be depended on to cut three tons of prime hay to the acre, was not destitute. Luella was, pecuniarily, what the country folk called "pretty well-fixed." There was comfort, therefore, in the lone gray house; and Luella saw to it that, little by little, and with no violence of innovation, there should be some simple beauty, also. Her time and energy were largely absorbed by her baby; but in the spring, as soon as the frost was out of the ground, she managed to get some lilacs, snowballs, and roses set out around the house, with half a dozen young apple-trees at the south end, along the edge of the buckwheat-field. Then she started a garden that should in time come to surpass the old one overhanging the "Bito." Between the garden and the baby, who was rather a busy baby for his months, she found herself so occupied that there was little time for repining, and the delicate colour by and by crept back to her pale cheeks. She went nowhere except to church, to the parsonage, or berry-picking down in the "back lot;" and therefore the prim-lipped would-be aloofness of the Westcock ladies hardly touched her. By temperament self-contained and inhospitable to gossip, she escaped a million petty stings. Mrs. Bembridge strove all the time to enclose her in such an atmosphere of love as might gradually heal her grief. By the path through the fir-pasture came the rector frequently to see her, and Mrs. Goodridge to bring some trifle of baby adornment for little Seth. The baby, always under Mrs. Bembridge's initiated eye, throve to a marvel. So it came about that Luella's first summer in the new life passed in a peace that gave her time to gather her strength. The sleepless, bitter hour just after dawn would darken her face with shame and loss; but before the morning was through the shadow would be almost gone, chased away by the little tender offices of motherhood. The dark-haired, sturdy boy that smiled at her breast was her heart's unmatched physician.

But there was another influence which contributed to Luella's mastery of her sorrow. For months she had clung to a feeble hope that her letter to Jim at Montevideo would elicit a response.

All her love, her faith, her loyalty, her amazement, her longing, her terror, and her grief had gone into that letter. She could not believe that it would leave him untouched. Throughout the tender Tantramar spring she kept half-expecting a reply. Then, at last, the frail hope faded. A scornful indignation began to take its place. One hot, hay-scented July morning, toward noon, when Mrs. Bembridge, still in her magenta sontag, came limping hurriedly home to get dinner, Luella saw in her eyes the glint of news. She paled, and her heart quivered sickly.

"What is it?" she asked, snatching up the baby from his cradle, and holding him to her heart as a shelter.

"I've jest been down to the post-office!" answered Mrs. Bembridge.

"You — *haven't* got — a letter for me?" stammered Luella, catching her breath.

"No — no — no — Sweetie. Nothin' fer you! No, indeed!" replied the old woman. "But Mr. Smith tells me as how there was a letter come yistidy for Mrs. Calder, an' it had on it the Montevideo stamp. So — ye see jest how 'tis, Sweetie. 'Taint fer any girl as keers fer her own self-respect to let herself go on frettin' fer a man like that, sez I."

Luella had put the baby down again into his

cradle, where he lay soberly sucking his thumb. Now she stood up very straight. Her face reddened slowly and darkly, and a hot light came into her eyes. She walked up and down the room several times, clenching her strong, slim hands fiercely. Then she stopped short, and faced about. Mrs. Bembridge waited, expecting the wild outbreak which was struggling behind those hard-set lips. But it never broke through. Luella glanced down at the baby. Then she went aimlessly across the room, and sat down by the window, as if tired by the storm which had raged unheard within her. At last, very quietly, she said:

"I won't. He ain't worth it!"

For half an hour she sat perfectly still, while Mrs. Bembridge was getting the dinner. She went over and over in her aching memory the devotion and the passionate outpourings of her unanswered letter, and the fiery humiliation which raged within her proved to be a bitter but wholesome medicine. From that day she taught herself to smile more frequently, and to make herself less of a kill-joy in the house.

With no great events to arrest it, time at the gray cottage slipped by with a soundless speed that was almost startling to Luella. Each day was long enough, each night too long; but, being all of so like a complexion, the sequence of them speedily ran into one, and a month seemed the same as a week. The day's unchanging routine was enough to keep brain and hand occupied. The seasons stole softly upon one another's heels. Little Seth's first tooth, his first creeping (which was in pursuit of the unsympathetic cat), his first unaided step on his own strong baby feet, — these were huge events in this secluded life. And as for small events, they were numerous enough to keep the air from stagnating. These were of various kinds. Visits from the rector, or Mrs. Goodridge, or Mary Dugan, or good-natured Mitty Smith; the hatching of a brood of chickens; the coming up of the seeds in hotbed or garden; the first sailing of the shad-boats from the mouth of the far-off creek; the first ripe strawberry; the harvesting of the golden oats in the upper field; the fall assembling of the swallows; the first small white egg, usually blood-streaked, of the most precocious of Mrs. Bembridge's blue pullets; the high and hollow honking of the first southward flight of the wild geese; the sudden whiteness of the first snow. With these the days made themselves different; yet not so different but that Luella was seized with a kind of trembling amazement one lilac-scented evening in June, when some mingling of scent, and far-off sound, and sunset colour, reminded her that it was now five years since Jim had gone away. Since that day she had

At Mrs. Bembridge's

never been down to the dyke beside the creek mouth; but now, putting a white sunbonnet over her heavy, flax-blond hair, she set off without a word to Mrs. Bembridge, and hastened down across the marshes through the dying sunset. Out by Tantramar, in the great spaces, nothing had changed. There loomed the gaunt net-reels, across the mouth of the creek. The same sparse grasses flickered along the dyke-top. The tide was ebbing, with its lonely, sighing roar. Only there was not, to-night, that long wind drumming in her ears. That wind, how strangely she remembered it, and the confusion of it in her brain. To-night the air was still, and her memory clear as glass. Could it be five years? Her long control melted in an anguish of self-pity, of pity for Jim, of longing for the love so inexplicably slain. Once more she threw herself face downward in the grass beside the road; and when, hours later, she went home to the gray house in the fields, Mrs. Bembridge looked at her heavy eyes and troubled her with no questions. Luella sank down upon her bed without undressing, buried her face in little Seth's thick brown curls, and cried there softly, so softly that the child was not disturbed. When she had cried herself to sleep, the old woman stole in and lightly spread a shawl over her. And so she slept till morning, when Seth, according to his wont, awoke with the birds.

The following day Mrs. Bembridge came limping in hurriedly with news. The *G. G. Goodridge* was in the lower bay, and would be up with the next tide.

Luella turned pale, but showed no excitement. She had nothing to hope from the return of the *G. G. Goodridge*. All Westcock knew that Jim Calder had left the ship at the time of Melissa Britton's death, and betaken himself no one knew whither. All that could be said of him was that once or twice a year a letter with strange, outlandish postmarks, and stamps of the other side of the world, would come to Mrs. Calder. But what was in them Mrs. Calder would not say.

For some minutes after Mrs. Bembridge had made her announcement there was silence in the room, broken only by the loud ticking of the clock, and the voice of little Seth playing and talking to himself out in the yard. The old woman stood it as long as she could. Then, giving her cap a twist that made her short gray wisps of hair stick out excitedly, she followed up the subject.

"It's five year now since Job Britton's sot eyes on his own home, an' more'n four since Melissy was killed. That girl was the apple of his eyes, — everybody knowed that. An' Miss Tingley sez,

At Mrs. Bembridge's

sez she, as how the captain ain't never been able to face the idee of comin' home an' not findin' Melissy there to welcome him. One must respect feelin's like that, o' course. But now, after all these year, seems to me like somebody might speak to him, — somebody'd *oughter* speak to him, — an' find out if he knows anythin'."

Here she paused, looking at Luella expectantly. But still Luella had nothing to say.

"Seems to me," went on the old woman, "like as how the rector might speak to him, bein' an old friend of hisn, an' so specially interested in the ship, an' in you, Sweetie, — an' in Jim!"

At the mention of Jim's name, which had not been spoken between them once since the birth of little Seth, Luella began to tremble. She turned red, then white again, laid down her sewing, got up, and went out in the yard to speak to the child. When she returned, two or three minutes later, she had regained her composure.

"I'll go and see Captain Britton myself," said she, "the minute he gets home. If he knows anything I know he'll tell me." Then she took down her sunbonnet from its peg.

"That's right, Sweetie!" answered the old woman with warm approval. "But where be you a-goin' to now? Captain Job can't be to his house afore to-morrow forenoon, nohow!"

"I'm going over to the parsonage," said Luella, "to ask Mr. Goodridge to find out for me, an' let me know, the minute I can see the captain. Oh, you don't know, Granny, what it is to just think of doing *something, anything,* after all these years when there was *nothing* one could do! I *know* it's no use, no earthly use, — but it's wonderful just to be able to try!" And she hurried out eagerly, while the old woman looked after her with wet eyes.

During the long five years since she left her Uncle Abner's house, Luella had not once been down to the "Bito." All her little shopping had been done for her in Sackville, by Mrs. Goodridge, or at the little Wood Point store by Mrs. Bembridge, who had scornfully withdrawn her custom from Abner Baisley. Luella had been regular, as of old, in her attendance at the little Westcock church, but she managed, in an unobtrusive way, to avoid exposing herself to snubs. She had left the choir at the first of the trouble; and gentle old Miss Evans, at the secret suggestion of Mrs. Goodridge, had offered her a seat in her pew, which was close up to the front, immediately behind the parsonage pew. By always staying in after service, in order to walk home with Mrs. Goodridge over Westcock hill, Luella avoided meeting those who were unwilling to meet her. Those

At Mrs. Bembridge's

others who stayed had to meet her under Mrs. Goodridge's challenging eyes, or in the shelter of the rector's loving-kindness. They were civil enough, therefore; and Luella took care not to test their civility too severely. Once, on her way to church, Mrs. Ben Ackerley had met her, and passed her with a snort of lofty scorn; and once, Mrs. Finnimore, jogging along in her rattle-trap of a wagon, had stopped with an air of infinite condescension, and inquired after the health of little Seth. Her manner was trying, but Luella responded pleasantly, which encouraged the good lady to prolong the interview.

"Let me tell you, Luelly Warden," she said, bending down with fat importance from the high seat of the unwashed old wagon, "let me tell you, you've got a friend as is a friend, in Mrs. Goodridge. You can't never know how faithful she sticks up for you, amongst them of the parish as is inclined to be censorious. That counts more for you, I kin tell you, than all the rector sez an' does for you, because everybody knows *he'd* stand by you, anyways, he's that kind-hearted, an' never so happy as when he's tryin' to help them as has fallen."

At this Luella, her face aflame, turned away abruptly.

"Well, I never! Such impudence, the hussy!

After me takin' the trouble to stop an' speak to her!" muttered Mrs. Finnimore, indignantly, twisting around in her seat to glare after Luella's tall retreating form. Then, with a succulent *tzlk-tzlk* and a slap of the reins, she started up her old sorrel again, and jogged on to tell her gossips of Luella's insolent impenitence.

"It's spiled she is, the hussy!" was her ultimate verdict. "The dear soft-hearted rector, an' Mrs. Goodridge, who jest does it to spite the rest of us, has cleaned spiled her, till she thinks she's a white-souled martyr, the impudent hussy!"

It was the possibility of such interviews as this, rather than the dread of frank hostility like Mrs. Ackerley's, that led Luella to guard her seclusion. She had no need of going down to the "Bito." And for her outings she had all the room she wanted, in the woods, the flowering pastures, and the sun-steeped scented berry-fields.

With the news of the return of the *G. G. Goodridge,* however, a change came over Luella's attitude. It occurred to her that her strict seclusion had seemed like an acknowledgment of guilt. It was a wrong to little Seth, — and at the thought of the possible implications she grew hot all over, and suddenly sick. What right had she to shelter herself at the cost of imputations upon her baby.

At Mrs. Bembridge's

Passionately she pledged herself to be more brave in the future, for the boy's sake.

By the time she had come to this resolution she had reached the parsonage yard. Mary Dugan, in a bright pink calico dress pinned up half-way to her stout knees, was at the well, about to lower the bucket. She dropped the well-crank, and came forward smiling to greet the visitor.

"Land sakes, Luelly," she cried, heartily, "but you're lookin' spry an' fine. I never seen you with a finer colour, — an' your eyes is bright as two chaney buttons."

"I guess you're flatterin' me, Mary," answered Luella, laughing excitedly. "Is the rector in? Or Mrs. Goodridge?"

"Mrs. Goodridge, she's gone up Sackville, an' won't be back afore tea-time," answered Mary Dugan. "But you'll find Mr. Goodridge in the study."

Luella started eagerly for the kitchen door.

"But what's the hurry?" demanded Mary, who had been working all the morning, and now ached for a bit of a gossip. "He ain't goin' to run away. I hain't set eyes on you for a week. Hain't you got time to stop an' tell me the news? How's Seth?"

Luella was already at the door-step, but she paused reluctantly.

"How would *I* have news to tell, Mary? And I can't stop, anyways. The *G. G. Goodridge* is in the lower bay, — an' she's comin' up to-night, — an' I've got to see the rector right off."

As the last words left her lips she vanished into the house. Mary Dugan gazed after her, shaking her head.

"I'd like to know if that ain't news," she muttered to herself. "Biggest kind o' news, *I'd* call it. Poor Luelly! Wonder if she thinks Jim Calder'll be aboard!"

Luella, meanwhile, was speeding in through the outer kitchen and the inner kitchen, to the narrow, dark hall, at the further end of which, just beyond the big hall stove, she could see the rector's study door half-open.

Mr. Goodridge, in a black alpaca house-coat which sat awkwardly on his powerful shoulders, was writing at his much littered study-table, with a range of pigeon-holes and piles of books before him. At Luella's light tap on the door, his strong soft voice responded absent-mindedly, "Come in." Not till the girl stood close beside his table did he look up. Instantly his eyes brightened, with sunny little wrinkles gathering about them. He dropped his pen, whirled his chair half-around, and held out his hand without getting up. He regarded Luella less as a guest than as a child of the house.

At Mrs. Bembridge's

"Hello, Luella, where did *you* spring from, so noiselessly? How did you know you wouldn't scare me out of my wits?"

Luella laughed, and grasped his hand. It was a hand whose clasp — strong, warm, straightforward, and tender — ever heightened the devotion of his friends, and disarmed the hostility of his few enemies. The sick, in body or in spirit, clung to it. The well rejoiced in it. And no one who once knew it could withhold from its possessor the utmost of faith and trust.

"I just wanted to ask you something, Mr. Goodridge," said Luella, hesitating as to how she should tell her errand.

"Ask away, child! Anything the matter?" responded the rector, brushing away the thick brown moustache and beard from his mouth with a characteristic gesture.

"The *G. G. Goodridge* has come back. She's in the bay," said Luella.

"You don't say so!" exclaimed the rector, jumping up as if he would go aboard at once. Then he bethought him, and sat down again.

"When did she arrive?" he asked.

"She ain't in yet, sir!" answered Luella, in her excitement dropping back into the vernacular. "She's in the lower bay, — an' comin' up with nex' tide."

The rector had been thinking as she spoke, and biting thoughtfuly at one end of his moustache, as was his way in any uncertainty of mind. What did Luella think that the return of the *Goodridge* could signify to her? He looked at her doubtfully.

"There's Captain Britton, you know, sir," said Luella, answering the inquiry of his eyes. "And there's Ezra Boltenhouse. One or the other of them *might* know something, might say something, that would — that would help me to understand."

The rector had a swift vision of Luella's years of waiting without a word, of her long sorrow and humiliation, of her quiet, enduring patience, — and his quick sympathy brought a lump into his throat. He took the girl's hand again, into both of his, and said, gently: "Yes, dear child, of course. They might be able to tell us something. I promise you I'll see them both the moment they come ashore." Then, because tears had come into his eyes, and he did not want to encourage Luella to any outbreak of emotion, he smiled cheerfully, and added:

"I must see my ship, you know, the first moment possible, and find out how she has been behaving herself. I'll go aboard, in fact, the very first thing to-morrow morning."

"Oh, thank you, sir, so much!" breathed the girl. "But" — she went on diffidently — "I've been thinking that I'd ought to see them both myself, too! There's things I want to ask Captain Britton, specially. Don't you think I might, Mr. Goodridge?"

"Assuredly!" he agreed. "It's your right, Luella, to make every kind of inquiry. I'm sure Captain Britton would feel so."

"Then, oh, please, sir, won't you find out the first minute he'll be home, and will see me. That's what I came to ask you. Captain Britton was always kind of friendly to me, — he knew my father well, — and I don't believe he'll mind me bothering him. And I can see Ezra later."

"Yes, I'll see to it for you, Luella," replied the rector, still musingly biting his moustache. "I'll send you word by Mary Dugan, as soon as I have seen the captain. But don't build too much on this, child!" he added, taking note of her unwonted colour and air of suppressed excitement.

"No, sir, I'm not expecting anything," said she. "But I'm *doing* something; and so I can kind of pretend I'm expecting something."

When Luella had left the rector to continue, amid the seeming confusion of his papers, his interrupted writing, she went out by the front door, to avoid the delay of further talk with Mary Dugan. She did not turn back through the yard, to seek the homeward path through the fir-pasture, but continued straight on, beneath the great hackmatack, down the drive to the white gate, and down the hill to the Wood Point road. Here, for an irresolute moment, she paused. Her impulse was to turn to the right, homeward, to the gray house in the fields, where security and little Seth awaited her. Then her face flushed with a daring resolve. She turned to the left, along the road past the black spruce groves, — the road that led to the " Bito."

CHAPTER XIX.

DOWN TO THE "BITO"

LUELLA had no definite, concrete aim in view, when she set out for the "Bito." Her going was simply a sort of decree of emancipation, issued by herself to herself. She did not care much — in fact, at the time, she considered not at all — what other people might think of it. She was concerned only to register her resolve, and to do it with some unmistakable emphasis.

As she passed down Lawrence's Hill, it seemed to her that she had been absent half a lifetime from these old familiar scenes, — yet it had meant but the turning of a corner to look upon them again. It was with a homesick pang she noticed how the young firs on the hillside had grown to goodly trees. Where she had formerly looked out over their tops to the red windings of Tantramar in his green levels, now patches of dense wood walled off the view. At the foot of the hill to the left a company of ancient white birches had been cut down, leaving a raw scar on the landscape. She felt their destruction like a loss, and hurried on with face averted.

When she came opposite Purdy's shipyard she forced herself to stop and look, — to go up deliberately, and lean upon the old snake fence and look. There was a ship on the stocks now, a high, black ship nearly ready for the launching. It looked to her just like the *G. G. Goodridge*. And though she had felt quite secure in her self-control, she now began to shake so violently that — after glancing around to see that no one was in sight — she sat down on the side of the road to recover her calm.

Hitherto, to her great relief, she had met no one on the road. Now, however, just when she felt least ready for an encounter, she saw a fluttering red and white figure in the distance, coming from the direction of the " Bito." She sprang to her feet and continued her journey. The chances were that anything in petticoats was a foe; and she would meet her standing up.

The red and white figure, however, presently proved to be that of a little barefoot girl in a short red frock, swinging her white sunbonnet by the strings. When she came nearer, Luella recognized her by the big, round black eyes and gipsy-dark skin as little Sadie Babcock, from just across the

"Bito." Luella had often admired her, in the days gone by, and given her flowers from the garden over the "Bito;" and now, at ten years old, the child's wild beauty was more piquant and insistent than ever. Luella's heart warmed to her. It was such a relief, moreover, to meet a child like this, toward whom she need not stand on guard.

"Why, hello, Sadie!" she cried, joyously, advancing with a bright smile, and both hands outstretched. "My goodness sakes alive, how you've grown!"

But to this cordial greeting the child made no response. Her round black eyes fixed blankly on Luella's face, she stuck a string of her sunbonnet into her red little mouth, and sheered off to one side of the road.

"Why, Sadie, don't you know me?" continued Luella, gaily, still advancing. "Don't you remember Luella, that used to give you flowers?"

The child knew her very well, this tall, fair-skinned, blue-eyed young woman, with the heavy, flax-blond hair. She remembered her flowers. She thought of the way she was pointed out to her in church. She remembered the things that were said of her by the pious backbiters who came in to drink tea with Mrs. Babcock. She swerved right up upon the hillocky side of the road, by the fence, to give as wide a berth as possible to this enticing monster.

"Ma sez, I mustn't speak to the likes o' you!" she announced, bluntly, with no change in the blank stare of her black eyes. Then she darted past, and went on loiteringly, chewing her sunbonnet string and looking back.

Luella stopped as if she had been struck in the face. The sunny fields, and the bright, dry ribbon of road, reeled about her for a moment. The insult, coming from an innocent child, overwhelmed her. She had no thought of anger, but only crushing pain and humiliation. With her head down she walked onwards. And presently the idea came to her of what was in store for her boy when, two or three years later, he should begin school. She had not realized that her unhappiness had become a byword among the Westcock children. Thinking of Seth and what he would be made to suffer, she forgot herself and grew strong again. For Seth's sake she would face everybody, and face them down if necessary, and take the place that was her due among others who had taken just as much liberty with conventions as she had. In her own eyes, and, as she truly believed, in the eyes of Heaven, also, she was Jim Calder's wife. And she would no longer seem, by shamefaced seclusion, to confess herself merely his cast-off mistress. Her ex-

Down to the "Bito" 201

pedition to the "Bito" had ceased to be either a daring adventure or a declaration of rights. It had taken on something of a consecration. It was the beginning of a struggle for the honour and the happiness of little Seth.

Luella was looking well that morning, with her excited colour, and her trim, blue and white gingham frock with spotless white collar and cuffs. She remembered, with satisfaction, that she "looked all right," when she saw little Mrs. McMinn approaching. She had not seen Jinnie McMinn, except at church, under Mrs. Goodridge's eye, since the dreadful day of the sewing-circle at Miss Evans's, five years ago. On the church porch Mrs. McMinn had always nodded to her, civilly enough, and she had returned the salutation in like spirit. But she wondered how it would be now.

Mrs. McMinn had just come out of Abner Baisley's store, and had fairly started up the road before she realized that Luella was before her. She stopped in a sort of confusion, and for a moment seemed on the point of fleeing back to the store, which she imagined would prove a safe refuge. Then, with a slight heightening of her colour, she came on, and met Luella's eyes with a pleasant smile.

"How are you this mornin', Luella?" she inquired, politely, holding out her hand. As it was done in a public place, almost in front of the store, and with the windows of three cottages inquisitively agape, Luella appreciated the little matron's courage, and responded cordially.

"I'm well, thank you, Jinnie," she answered.

Mrs. McMinn was at heart a kindly and honest little woman; and now, under the spell of Luella's clear eyes, grave with suffering, she yielded to a sudden womanly impulse.

"Luella," she said, reddening deeply, "I was thinkin' in church, only last Sunday, when Mr. Goodridge was preachin' about how we deceive ourselves more'n we deceive other folks, that I hadn't been actin' right by you, all these years. *I'd* oughter have stood by you, whoever else didn't. We both took the same resks, fer the sakes of the men we loved. An' Lord knows, *you* never deserved to suffer, no more'n me. Sez I to myself, 'It's jest luck, I'm not in her place now!' I've been jest plain skeered, Luella; an' I wish't you'd forgive me, an' let's be friends!"

Tears came into Luella's eyes. This was medicine to the bitter wound which little Sadie Babcock had inflicted.

"Yes, indeed, Jinnie," she answered, rather faintly, controlling a foolish impulse to cry. "I think it's fine and brave of you, very brave. Because you know what Mrs. Ackerley will say, behind your back, — and Mrs. Gandy, and the rest of them. Like as not, Mrs. Gandy's sayin' it to herself about you right now, for I see her face glued to the window over yonder."

"Let her look!" cried Jinnie, tossing her head. "I ain't goin' to be bossed by them old cats no longer. Let her say what she likes. An' say, Luella, can I come up presently an' see little Seth?"

"I wish you'd drop in and see us this afternoon!" responded Luella, with a choking laugh which saved her from tears. "You don't know what a lot of good you've done me, Jinnie. I was feeling pretty bad, when you came up. God bless you for it, Jinnie!"

"Well, I'll be in this afternoon!" said Mrs. McMinn, tripping on contentedly. She had been feeling ashamed of herself for some time, and now she had the rich delight of feeling proud of herself, instead. There was something about Luella which made her appreciation and her gratitude precious, whatever the cloud she was under. And there would be, too, the approval of the rector, and of Mrs. Goodridge. "What do I keer fer what Mrs. Ackerley'll say to my face, or what Mrs. Gandy'll say behind my back? Tschut! I'll snap my fingers at 'em all!" said the little matron to herself, tossing her fluffy head and snapping her small red fingers as she went.

Mrs. Gandy, staring from her window just across the field, was already sufficiently surprised by the interview she had been watching. What was her amazement, however, when she saw Luella now march on, and turn deliberately into her Uncle Abner's store. This was too much. Throwing dignity to the winds, she clapped on her hat, and hurried around to purchase a can of kerosene. She had hopes of being witness to a most interesting interview. For all her shameless haste, however, she was too late. She had had some little distance to travel around by the road, and Luella was already coming out of the store, with a serene countenance, and a brown paper parcel under her arm.

When Luella entered the store Mr. Baisley was weighing out an order of tea, for a customer whom Luella did not know. At the sight of her the old shopkeeper was so startled that he dropped the tea scoop on the floor, and stood speechless, his thin, gray mouth half-open.

"Good morning, Uncle Abner!" said Luella, civil and cool. "I want half a pound of your best tea, and a package of corn-starch, and a crock of preserved ginger. You might put it all into one parcel for me, please, so's it will be handier to carry." And she laid a crisp note on the counter.

Mr. Baisley could think of absolutely nothing to

say in this most unlooked-for situation. For divers reasons, but mostly, perhaps, because he had turned her out of his house, he felt very bitter against Luella. Moreover, she had cost him all the parsonage trade, which was a heavy item, to say nothing of Mrs. Bembridge's modest custom. He thought, now, of refusing to serve her, of ordering her from the store, of rebuking, in scathing phrases, her effrontery in coming to him in this way. But her steady blue eyes were upon him, moving him to discretion. And the instinct of his calling conquered. Methodically he finished doing up the package of tea for the other customer. Then turning to Luella and speaking with quite his customary counter deference, he said:

"Good morning, Luella. Preserved ginger, did you say? Sixty-cent size?"

"Yes, please, Uncle Abner," answered Luella, sweetly. "And a half-pound of your best *mixed* tea, and a package of corn-starch. That's just the even dollar, is it not?" And she pushed the crisp bill over to him.

"Well," thought Mr. Baisley, as he tied the purchases into one neat parcel, "after all, a customer's a customer, — an' cash is cash." So, as he handed over the package, he said, suavely: "You'll find that tea good, the best I've ever handled at the price. I hope you'll call agin."

Luella restrained severely a hysterical impulse to shriek with laughter.

"Thank you, Uncle Abner, I likely will," she answered, and departed with a casual nod, as if she were doing this same thing every day.

Just outside, she ran into Mrs. Gandy. Disappointed that the interview had been so brief, and herself so late, the good lady pursed her mouth rather primly and made ready to patronize Luella. But Luella, not liking her expression, went by her with merely a bow of chilly recognition. It was right, for she knew that Mrs. Gandy was a backbiter and a hypocrite. But it was not wise policy, for Mrs. Gandy had influence and a busy tongue.

On her homeward walk Luella met no one but Mr. Sawyer, the Baptist parson, driving at leisurely pace, in his battered old "buggy," toward Sackville. He smiled kindly upon her, touching his hat with his whip. As she turned into the home lane, past the warm-smelling tansy bed, she felt that her expedition had been, on the whole, a step toward freedom for Seth.

CHAPTER XX.

THE RECTOR SPEAKS OUT

WHEN the next sunrise came streaming, in long rays of pinky gold, over Minudie, and Beauséjour, and the pale, vapourous levels of the Tantramar Marsh, there was the *G. G. Goodridge,* swinging at the old anchorage off the Ram Pasture. The winds which, throughout the summer months, are wont to sweep the green marshes steadily all day long, were not yet awake, and the brimming tide, in bay, and river, and every many-looped creek, was like glass, reflecting the streamers of light, the tinted clouds, and a flock of crows flying seaward from the parsonage groves.

Before the sun was an hour high the wind was up, bending the grasses, and ruffling the smooth waters to a tawny yellow tone flecked and barred with white foam. Through this bright tumult a boat put off from the little creek-mouth where the fishing sloops were harboured. It was driven by two strong rowers, — the rector, with his black coat thrown aside and his sleeves rolled up, showing his white, huge-muscled arms, and big Chris Godine, a fisherman farmer, the owner of the boat.

The rector was in a hurry. He was one of those men whose energetic bodies are spurred to ceaseless activity by a still more energetic brain and imagination. To these men no day is ever quite long enough for the accomplishment of all that they plan to do. One lifetime seems ridiculously inadequate to them, for great as is their reach, their aim is incalculably greater.

With boyish delight in the exercise of his strength the rector, who was rowing stroke, surged upon his oar, whipping the heavy blade through the water like a toothpick. Chris Godine, though a seasoned oarsman and pulling the easy oar, was fairly tugging his heart out in the effort to hold the boat's head up against him. For half a mile he kept it up, watching for some sign of fatigue in the tirelessly heaving shoulders before him. Then, with a windy grunt, he yielded, and drew in his oar.

"Give it up, parson!" he panted, drawing his shirt-sleeve across his dripping forehead and letting the boat swing round into the trough. "I can't hold her up agin that stroke o' yourn. Ye'll have to let up on me a bit. Even at stroke you kin pull me round."

The Rector Speaks Out 209

"Nonsense, Chris!" exclaimed the rector, gleefully looking back over his shoulder. "Why, I wasn't pulling very hard. I was just beginning to get warmed up."

"Well, parson, you got me warmed up all right enough," said Chris. "I reckon ye'll have to pull jest about half what ye're a-pullin', 'f we're to make a straight course for the ship."

"Any way you like, Chris!" he answered, cheerfully, with a frank delight in having forced the hardened boatman to cry quits. "I'll go slow as you like. But you're a bigger man than I am, Chris. You ought to be able to hold me."

The fisherman laughed, with a sort of respectful derision. He knew that the rector's chief foible — if not, indeed, his only one — was his boyish pride in his remarkable athletic prowess. The rector could run, jump, spar, put the stone, lift weights, better than any other man in a parish of strong and athletic men.

"You know well enough, parson, you kin lick any other man in the parish, big or little," said Chris. "I ain't ashamed, not a mite, to have ye pull me round."

"What nonsense!" protested the rector, modestly, but smiling in spite of himself. "But I'll pull easier, if you're not feeling quite up to the mark this morning."

When the rector went up the ship's side, he was met by Ezra Boltenhouse, who greeted him warmly and led him straight to the cabin, where Captain Job was making up his papers preparatory to going ashore. Captain Job looked up and came forward eagerly, gratified at the unexpected visit. In the five years of his absence he had grown a good ten years older, and his once ruddy, cheerful face had a haggard look. To the rector's quick sympathies it was plain at once that the one great, dominant fact in Captain Job's life was Melissa's death, which to him still seemed to have taken place but yesterday. The rector's heart responded understandingly to this long, engrossing sorrow. His words were all of tenderness, of indirect condolence. Then he spoke directly of Melissa's death, and of the story of her heroism as it had come to Westcock; and presently Captain Job was telling the whole story at fullest length, as he had pieced it together from various eye-witnesses, he himself having chanced to be in his cabin at the time. The recital evidently did him good. Never before, in all the weary years that he had dragged through since that dreadful day at the Barcelona pier, had he been able to talk to one whose sympathy was in every way complete and understanding. When he had quite talked himself out on the subject, and dried his deep-set, far-looking eyes, the rector

The Rector Speaks Out 211

gently led him away from it, to accounts of the *G. G. Goodridge* and her behaviour in a gale, of the purple, alien waters her keel had ploughed, of the strange-jargoned, strange-coloured, strange-scented foreign cities whose wharves had given her hospitality. In these accounts the rector had so ardent an interest, — feeling himself almost a part of them by reason of that part of him which had gone into the life of the ship, — that poor Captain Job caught some warmth from his ardour, and talked till a long unwonted light came back into his eyes. The rector had put new strength and cheer into his desolated spirit.

When the rector started to go, Captain Job followed him to the ship's side, where, far down, the little tethered boat was tossing and stemming the tawny rush of the tide. As he was about to go over the rail, the rector turned, and said, in a low voice:

"Captain Job, I want you to do something for that unhappy child, Luella Warden. Through all her terrible trials she has borne herself with a patience and a steadfastness that have commanded our sympathy. She has never been vouchsafed the slightest clue to Jim Calder's treatment of her. She is desperately anxious to have a little talk with you, as soon as possible. Will you do me the favour to make an appointment with her, through me, either at your own home, or at the parsonage?"

To his amazement, as he spoke, he saw that the captain was getting excited.

"I won't see her!" he cried, harshly. Then, remembering himself, he went on more quietly. "Forgive my bluntness, parson! But I jest *can't* see that girl. I couldn't speak civil to her, nohow. *I* know what she is!"

The rector's smiling face had grown very grave. "You astonish me, Job!" said he, soberly. "I really think it is your duty to see the poor child, though I asked it as a favour to myself. *If* you know what she is, you must know that she is an unfortunate but honest and pure-minded girl, led away by wretched traditions, and the victim of a misplaced trust in the man who was to have been her husband."

Captain Britton was now red in the face with anger. Under the rector's steady gaze, however, he controlled himself.

"I'm right sorry to differ with you, parson!" he said, after a moment's struggle. "But I know what I know. I know what kind of a girl she is. I've got it all, straight enough, from one as had the proofs, an' whose word I'd take before any other livin' being's. If that girl's pulled the wool over your eyes, you ain't the first she's done it to. I won't see her, that's flat. If, as I hear tell, she's got a boy, 'tain't none o' Jim Calder's, that's all I can say!"

The rector's face was grave indeed, now, his high white forehead white still, and wrinkled with indignation. At the same time, there was a certain shade of embarrassment, of doubt, in his indignant eyes. Something fanatical in Captain Job's tone and attitude convinced him that the unknown informant, whose word was so far above question, was none other than Melissa herself, who had, for some inexplicable reason, poisoned her father's mind against Luella. Melissa was dead, beyond reach of reproach; and the rector could not bring himself to imply to her sorrowing father that she might have lied. For the moment, he avoided seeking an explanation of the captain's words.

"You are not yourself, Job Britton!" he answered, in a tone of stern rebuke. "Your grief over your child has warped your judgment, and somehow perverted your good heart. So I make allowance, this time, for the wicked and brutal slander you have just spoken. Your own conscience, I believe, will some day convict you of the lie. But don't dare to speak that way again to me, or in my hearing, of that wronged and defenceless girl. From the tongues of women, my own parishioners here in Westcock, I am unable to protect the poor child. From the slander of men I can, and I will, Job." And he eyed the captain in a way he had, which never failed to convince any one that he meant just what he said. It had instant effect on the overexcited man before him.

"I'm sorry we can't see the same way in this matter, parson," said Captain Job, quieting down. "But, of course, I'm bound to respect your wishes as regards the girl, since you stand up for her. Only, don't ask me to see her, fer I won't do it, an' that's all there is to it!"

"No, it's not all there is to it, Job!" retorted the rector, sharply. "You stated that you had proofs. I want you to make that good to me, now, or take it back." He had grown hot during the captain's speech. He knew, beyond the reach of question, that Luella was innocent of the vile charge just uttered against her. But he knew, too, that it was whispered in Westcock, in some quarters. In rebutting that wicked and dangerous slander, the truth might strike whom it would.

Captain Britton found himself in an awkward situation. He had no proofs. He had merely been told by Melissa that *she* had had proofs. Moreover, she had pledged him, cleverly justifying the pledge as she did so, never to let any one know that she had told him, — never to let her name "be dragged into it," as she put it. He believed her, naturally. But he could not support his statement without betraying her. He wished that he had held a better guard upon his tongue.

"I didn't say as how *I* had the proofs, parson!" he protested, awkwardly. "I said I'd got it straight from one as *did* have the proofs, — an' whose word was as good as proof. Same time, there's circumstances I can't explain, which make it impossible for me to go into it more fully."

The scorn in the rector's eyes was not pleasant to face.

"And it's *you,* Job Britton," he said, slowly, "the father of a girl who was Luella's friend, whom I have heard stabbing a defenceless girl in the back, with the foulest slander that you could utter. I little thought it would ever be you, who would be the one to call such words from me. But whoever it was that told you he had 'proofs' of that disgraceful slander," — and here the rector spoke very slowly, holding his hearer with an eye that was as cold and dangerous as steel, — "whoever it was, he lied to you; and whoever repeats it, he lies."

He paused for a reply; but the captain, too much abashed and too bitterly conscious of the false position in which he had placed himself, looked away in uneasy silence.

"And furthermore, Job," he went on, "I demand that you tell me who that person was, that

I may deal with him as he deserves. In repeating the lie as you did, you made yourself in a measure responsible for it. But I know you are honest, just as I know Luella Warden is honest. I want to get at the real liar. I have been aching, these five years, to get at the real author of all this misery and devilish wrong."

There was absolutely nothing for the captain to do but strive to squirm out of his dilemma. He had no defence that would not involve Melissa. He could not resent the rector's uncompromising speech, without getting himself still more deeply into the mire. He knew what simple, old-fashioned delight it would give the rector to fight in defence of a woman's reputation, — and how unpleasant it would be for his opponent.

"I was wrong, parson," he stammered, looking excessively ashamed. "I ain't going to say I don't *believe* that thing that was told me, for I can't doubt that person's word, no more than I can doubt yours. But for *saying* a thing like that about a girl, without having any call to say it, I'd ought to be right well ashamed of myself, — and I am that, parson. And I'll promise you I won't never say one word more agin the girl, — nor hint it, nor look it, neither. But feeling as I do, I can't see her, of course; an' you mustn't press me to, parson."

"Well, I suppose that's for you to say, Job!" answered the rector, softening at the sight of the captain's repentance, and holding out his hand. "I do know that you believe you are doing right. Let us forget this argument. Even friends as old as you and I can't always see alike. Be sure and get in to see us as soon as you can. I wish you'd drop in and take tea with us to-morrow night, if you can make it convenient. Mrs. Goodridge is eager to see you, and has so much to ask you about."

"All right, parson, I'll come to-morrow night!" replied the captain, his face brightening as he returned the rector's hearty hand-clasp. "Look out, now, where you set your feet, if you ain't used to a rope-ladder!" he added, as the rector went over the side.

"No! I'm not used to them, exactly. We don't use 'em at the parsonage. But I can manage 'em all right!" laughed the rector, — and he went nimbly down one of the side-ropes, hand over hand.

CHAPTER XXI.

SETH AND HIS SCHOOLMATES

LUELLA could not help brooding, for a few days, over Captain Britton's refusal to see her, though the rector had mitigated it as much as he could in the telling. She was unable to make up her mind whether the captain's unfriendliness was due to some treachery of Melissa's, or to something said by Jim himself. Instinct and inclination at length combined to fix the blame on Melissa; and a suspicion dawned upon her that perhaps Melissa had been behind the whole trouble. Thereupon, she felt less dejected about it, and tried to dismiss it from her mind. But she no longer wanted to see Ezra Boltenhouse, lest she should meet a similar snub from him.

She was now, for little Seth's sake, going about the village with somewhat more freedom. She met with frequent coldness, and some blank insolence, but, on the whole, with more kindliness and good-will than she had expected; and several

Seth and His Schoolmates 219

women of the congregation, wishing to stand well with Mrs. Goodridge, came out openly in her support.

From this time onward, however, Luella grew less and less concerned about herself, more and more engrossed in little Seth. The boy was notably tall and strong "of his age," as the phrase went, and full of abounding health. With his dark brown hair, dark skin, and dark slaty-gray eyes, he was "the dead image of Jim Calder's grandfather," according to Mrs. Bembridge. Born as he had been under the shadow of his mother's sorrow, he was rather a sombre, thoughtful child, but joyous enough at times, and good-tempered with the cheer of sound health. Strangers invariably mistook him to be at least two years older than he was.

Till he was seven years old little Seth got all his schooling from his mother, learning to read a little, to make boyish letters and figures on a slate, and to distinguish many kinds of trees and flowers. During this time he had no playmates except little Alfy Russ, of his own age, and Alfy's two rather patronizing sisters, Mandy and Julie, who were nine and eleven respectively. Well cautioned by Mrs. Russ, their mother, who valued Mrs. Bembridge's goodwill, and had a superstitious dread of her anger, these two little girls were careful never to say anything, in any childish quarrel, which might hurt

Luella's feelings if Seth should innocently repeat it at home. But with that sex precocity which is not uncommon among country children, the little girls understood their playmate's equivocal situation very well, and would sometimes hold slightly aloof from him when other children were about. To Seth, who found Alfy always ready to play with him, this changeableness in Julie and Mandy seemed nothing of more importance than girls' whims. Girls were queer, anyway; and when Mandy and Julie did not want to be nice to him he promptly forgot all about them.

But when, at last, his mother and "Granny" (as he had been taught to call Mrs. Bembridge) decided that he was old enough to go to school, there came a difference which he could not understand. At first, of course, he had to put up with the knocking about and snubbing and heartless ridicule which those primitive savages known as children always visit upon a stranger of their own kind. He resisted sturdily the boys and girls of his own size, avoided as best as he could the bigger ones, and sobbed with resentful grief because his attempts to make friends were met with jeers. Alfy, however, who had been going to school for some months, assured him that it was all right, that the new boy always got treated that way, and that it was nothing for him to "feel bad" about. There-

Seth and His Schoolmates 221

fore, being a plucky youngster, Seth fought it out and faced it out as well as he could, and did not let it dwell on his mind after he got home from school. Recess, of course, was the worst time in the school day for him, and, acting on Alfy's advice he managed to get himself "kept in" at recess almost every day. This did not require any serious transgression on his part, for Miss Barnes, the teacher, seemed particularly keen to single him out, on the least excuse, for this punishment. Miss Barnes was an experienced teacher, a shrewd observer of her young charges, and well aware of the ingenious cruelty of which a mob of children can be guilty. She had probably befriended many a "new boy," without his guessing it, by the simple expedient of keeping him in at recess until the children had got used to him and ceased to regard him as their lawful victim.

During this rather distressful period, which so many a child has to go through, Seth's sense of injury was too confused for him to take note of any special form of derision or taunt that was cast upon him. References to his own or his mother's situation glanced off harmlessly from the armour of his innocence. Epithets which were cast at him by precociously knowing and malicious brats had no significance to him, and did not even catch in his memory; and as Alfy did not understand them any better than he did, there was no harsh enlightenment forthcoming from that quarter. Alfy's sisters understood, and because Seth was an accepted playmate of theirs, they resented, and took his part, at times, with a fine little fury of sympathy. This championship was not quite to be depended on, however; for when Mandy took his part with any degree of zeal, Julie was prone to go over to the other side, and *vice versa*. But whichever championed him, toward that one Seth's heart always went out in grateful warmth. Both Julie and Mandy he looked up to with immense respect, in spite of the fact that they allowed him, sometimes, to play with them, — and that he could beat either of them, easily, at wrestling.

As it chanced, among all the children at the school there was none so scornfully and tirelessly vituperative toward poor Seth than the gipsy-eyed little witch, Sadie Babcock, who had been so insulting to Luella a couple of years before. She was a year older than Julie Russ, and prettier than either Julie or Mandy. But in wits she was no match for either. One day at recess she had been particularly nasty to Seth, and Mandy Russ, coming up just in time to catch what was said, saw Seth's grave little mouth quiver with uncomprehending hurt. Mandy proceeded to tell Sadie such home-truths, as to certain near ancestors of hers,

Seth and His Schoolmates

that Sadie, flying into a rage, fell upon her tooth and nail. In a battle of this sort, of course, nine-year-old Mandy was no match for her heavier and equally active opponent; but Julie came to her sister's rescue like a whirlwind, and Sadie was promptly cuffed and clawed into a kind of raging submission. Little Seth stood looking on, his heart bursting with shame at the sight of girls fighting his battles for him. Moreover, he felt a strange pang of regret for the beaten Sadie. Ever afterward he flushed hot at any chance remembrance of it, and, as a sort of compensation, when he grew older he never let slip an opportunity to fight a girl's battles.

It was not long, however, before Seth slipped into his own small niche in the school, ceased to be new boy, and was idly allowed his rights as a member of their turbulent little confraternity. These rights included freedom from mass attack on the part of the rest of the school, freedom to fight his own battles and win or lose as best he might, and tacit permission to join if he would in the persecution of the next newcomer. Having accepted him in this way, the majority of his schoolmates thought no more of his mother, or his lack of a father, and regarded him only in so far as he could make himself felt in their noisy, enthusiastic, capricious sports and ventures. A few, however, were always more or less uncivil to him, or insolently superior in a way that made his heart swell with rage; and, once in awhile, in the event of a quarrel, he was liable to be made the target for epithets which he did not understand, though he vaguely felt them to be insulting. This feeling grew less vague, and more strenuous, as it gradually dawned upon him that none of the other children — save one, a shy, freckle-faced little girl — ever had quite the same taunting epithets applied to them, no matter how violent the quarrel in which they might be involved. Seth had been going to school two years before these things got really under his skin. By reason of his personal prowess in all games, his general kindliness and fairness, and his readiness to take his own part, — or that of any other child who was being bullied, — he was popular among the children of his own age, — and no boy of his own size dared to taunt him. What the bigger ones might say hardly touched him, since he could not do anything about it.

It was from observing the effect of such taunts upon the shy little freckle-faced girl that his eyes were suddenly opened. It had not been really borne in upon him, hitherto, that certain derisive epithets which, upon occasion, had been hurled at himself, were any more peculiarly opprobious than those which his playmates were wont to bandy freely in case of heat. But to the little freckle-faced girl they were evidently different. One showery noon she managed, unwittingly but clumsily enough, to spatter some mud on Sadie Babcock's clean pink calico frock.

"You little fool!" snapped Sadie, angrily, — she was now in the upper class, and counted herself one of the big girls, — "can't you be careful?"

But as she surveyed the extent of the damage her hot temper flared higher. Freckle-face, quite untroubled by being called a fool, had run at once to wet her handkerchief in the pail behind the door.

"Oh, I'm sorry!" she cried, solicitously. "Let me wash it off for you, Sadie!"

Now, as this would have merely made it worse, Sadie turned upon her like a fury, and jumped away.

"Get out, you clumsy little bastard!" she cried. "Don't you dare to come near me!"

Freckle-face started back as if she had been struck. Her small, thin face flushed scarlet, her eyes grew large, with a look of piteous hurt which touched Seth to the heart, and her lips quivered. Then, bursting into a passion of tears, she ran away and hid herself in the spruce bushes behind the schoolhouse. Seth, in secret, admired Sadie Babcock excessively, and was sure there was no one else in the world so beautiful, except his mother. But at this moment he was filled with rage against her, and wished she was a boy, however big, that he might try to avenge poor Freckle-face. Not knowing what else to do, he turned and slipped back into the bushes himself, thinking to find her and comfort her. Not finding her at once, his generous purpose faltered down into a kind of embarrassment, and he returned gloomily to the school.

That same afternoon, as it chanced, the matter was driven home for him. As school came out, and the children, breaking loose, trooped down the steps with shouts and jostling, boisterous challenge and snatching of caps, Seth, on the bottom step, was dexterously tripped, by a girl who admired him and took this primitive method of fixing his attention upon herself. He plunged headlong, clutched wildly to save himself, and sent his next neighbour sprawling face downward in the mud. He had saved himself, — but he trembled at the result, for his victim, Tommy Coxen by name, was a big, violent, hectoring lad of thirteen, with whom none of the other children ventured to take many liberties.

Tommy Coxen was not altogether a bad lot. He was capable, under ordinary circumstances, of taking an accident like this in good part. But as he

Seth and His Schoolmates 227

picked himself up, much decorated with mud, the uproarious laughter that greeted his appearance stung him to sudden rage. He had just been whispering some boyish gallantry to Sadie Babcock, when he fell; and now her shrill laughter rang out above all the rest. It was too much.

"You damn little bastard!" he shouted, turning upon Seth with scarlet, mud-plastered face, "I'll lick hell out o' you fer that."

That mysterious, but hideous word again! Seth had been brooding over it all through the afternoon session. Now, it seemed to smite him between the eyes. Baby though he was, things turned red before him. With a scream of fury he sprang straight for Tommy Coxen's muddy face, striking him in the mouth with one fist, and with both knees in the stomach.

The attack was so utterly unlooked for, and delivered with such force, moreover, from the advantage of the step, that Tommy Coxen was knocked clean over, falling on his back with Seth on top of him. Seth fought like a wildcat, but he was, of course, so outclassed that the struggle was brief. Almost before the other boys could form a ring around the combatants, — the girls peering eagerly but disapprovingly over their shoulders, — Tommy had hurled Seth off, rolled him over, pinned him down, and drawn off to "paste" him. Seth shut his eyes and set his teeth to take the punishment. But Tommy's fist never fell.

"Say, young one!" he said, panting a little. "There ain't nothin' to hender me givin' ye the blamedest lickin' yer ever got in yer life, be there?"

"Lick away!" gasped Seth, with a sob of hysteric rage.

"Well, I ain't a-goin' ter!" was the astonishing reply that made him open his eyes again. "Ye've got the sand all right, kid. Served me jest right, fer callin' yer the name I done. Now we're quits. An' if any other chap, what's too big fer you to lick yerself, calls you that agin, you tell me an' I'll lick him fer ye, *see!*"

Having delivered himself of this long speech, Tommy Coxen got up, his hurts all healed by the consciousness that he had done a fine thing in a very telling way. Jerking Seth to his feet, he held out his hand to him; and Seth, amazed, relieved, and flattered, grasped it shyly, gulping down a sob which would have done grievous discredit to the situation. There was a general clamour of approbation, and Tommy Coxen moved away triumphantly in the centre of a knot of hero-worshippers. Seth was amazed to find himself, too, something of a hero for the moment. Freckle-face gazed at him with luminous eyes. Sadie Babcock gave him a little grin of approval, as it were in spite of herself,

— for she dearly loved courage. Half a dozen of the bigger girls and boys came about him and patted him on the back. But he, child that he was, felt in terrible danger of crying. How to hold back the hated tears was all that he could think of. For a moment or two he grinned rather sheepishly at the compliments he was getting. Then, blurting out, "I mus' be gittin' home now!" he broke from the crowd, and ran away into the bushes as fast as he could go. Once safe in the green, sweet-smelling silence of the firs, well beyond ear-shot, he walked softly, crying off the tension of his spirit. He did not go home till he was quite himself again, because he dreaded to have his mother, or Mrs. Bembridge, ask what he had been crying about.

CHAPTER XXII.

SETH BEGINS TO UNDERSTAND

THAT evening, when Luella, Mrs. Bembridge, and Seth were sitting at their simple supper, of hot saleratus biscuits and blueberries and cream, the boy was unwontedly silent. He was so deep in his musings that his mother and Mrs. Bembridge noticed it, and exchanged smiling looks in regard to it. The old woman was just about to offer him the proverbial penny in exchange for the matter of meditations so profound, when suddenly he spoke what was on his mind.

"Mother," he inquired, scanning her face with anxious eyes, "what does 'bastard' mean?"

Mrs. Bembridge caught her breath and shifted her gaze from Seth's face to his mother's in consternation. Luella went crimson, then pale as death. It was several moments before she could trust her voice to answer.

"Why, dearie," she asked at length, to gain time, "why do you ask such a question?"

Seth Begins to Understand

"Is it so awfully bad, mother?" he continued. Luella did not dare to answer without some knowledge of what was behind the inquiry. Mrs. Bembridge, in her agitation, spilled all the hot tea which she was trying to pour into the saucer, and scalded the cat, which was sitting on the floor beside her, so that she fled out-of-doors with an indignant yowl.

"Tell me why you ask, Seth," insisted Luella. "What's put that word into your head?"

"Well, mother," he answered, slowly, "it seems to make people a lot madder to be called that than if you call 'em 'damn fool,' or 'liar,' or 'son-of-a-bitch.'" Here he hesitated. He had intended to tell all that had happened between himself and Tommy Coxen. He was burning to tell it, because he had so heroically wiped out the insult. But he had not missed that first horror in his mother's face, and out of ardent love for her came a quickness of instinct that led him to keep his counsel, for her sake. "Why, mother," he went on, "just before school went in, this afternoon, Sadie Babcock got mad as hops at Nellie Winters, an' called her a little bastard, — and Nellie felt that bad about it that she ran away into the bushes, crying, — and she was late for school, an' got scolded, — an' didn't seem to mind *that!*"

Luella drew a breath of relief, though by no

means fully reassured. If poor little Nellie Winters got it, she could not dare hope that her own child would escape. Seth had to be answered, however. His dark eyes were on her face, expectant, demanding.

"Dearie boy," she replied, "it is a very bad and cruel name to call any one. I can't explain to you exactly what it means, till you're a little bit older. You mustn't ask me now, boy. But believe me, the badness is in the *calling* people that. *That's* the *badness,* Seth. Don't you ever forget that, dearie. And don't you ever, ever, ever let yourself call *any one* that, no matter what a temper you may be in, or what they have done to you."

"'A' course not, mother! I wouldn't, ever, for anything!" protested the boy, in a tone that carried conviction.

Here Mrs. Bembridge spoke up, unable to hold her tongue any longer.

"An' nobody," she declared, in a voice harsh with emotion, "nobody but a nasty, dirty, low blackguard would call another body that. Anybody as does, they ain't got no right to have other folks speak to 'em, I tell you that, Seth."

The boy bridled at this, and laid down his spoon.

"Well, Granny," said he, positively, "Tommy Coxen ain't a low, dirty blackguard. He's one o'

Seth Begins to Understand

my very best friends, — my bestest friend after Alfy, mother."

"Tommy Coxen!" exclaimed Luella. "Why, Seth, dearie, he's a *big* boy. He must be fourteen or fifteen, — eh, Granny? How do *you* come to be friends with *him?*"

Here was Seth's chance to tell his story, and at the same time divert his mother's mind from the evidently painful subject which he had himself brought up.

"Why," he explained, glancing proudly from his mother's face to Mrs. Bembridge's, and back again, "you know, Granny, he's so much bigger'n me, he could just lambast me into a jell, if he wanted to. But this aft'noon, when school was comin' out, when I jumped right on to him — an' kicked him — an' punched him fair in the mouth with my fist, he didn't do a thing but fling me down an' sit on me so's I couldn't fight him any more. Then he picks me up, an' says to me, he says, ' I ain't a-goin' to hit you, kid, 'cause you done jest right, an' you've got the sand all right!' He said that to me, Granny. Then he shook me by the hand, an' told me — "

But at this point he hesitated, realizing a difficulty ahead if he was not going to explain fully.

"Yes, what did he tell you, dear?" urged Luella, tears in her eyes, thrilling to the achievement of her tiny defender, — while Mrs. Bembridge, under the shelter of the table-cloth, clutched her hand in sympathy.

Seth dropped his eyes for a moment.

"He told me, mother, that if any time I wanted to lick some boy that was too big for me, I was just to let *him* know, an' *he'd* lick him for me, good! I don't think Tommy Coxen's a low, dirty blackguard, Granny!"

"No, that he ain't!" agreed Mrs. Bembridge, emphatically.

Luella sat silent for a few seconds, then she sprang up, seized the boy, — who had resumed his blueberries and cream, — and strained him passionately to her heart. Her bitterness over the insults which he had suffered was mixed with triumph over the manly way he had borne himself, the tribute he had won from the reckless young rowdy, Tommy Coxen.

"Oh, muzz, look out!" protested Seth, wincing, "you hurt my arm!"

Then Luella realized that he had not come unscathed out of the fight which had so briefly been described. Unwillingly the boy submitted to an investigation. When his mother pulled off his jacket, and rolled up the sleeves of his little shirt, one arm was found to be black and blue almost from wrist to elbow. Then a fine large bump was discovered on the back of his head. Seth sturdily

Seth Begins to Understand 235

insisted that these injuries were nothing, — that he did not even know of their existence. He was allowed, indeed, to finish his supper, but immediately afterward he was compelled to submit to being "fussed over," with arnica and cold water and caresses unending, for a whole precious half-hour when he might have been down in Russ's yard playing with Alfy and Mandy and Julie. There was new hay in the Russ's mow, and he was impatient to play in it. To the two women, however, his bumps and bruises were a godsend in disguise. They furnished a safety-valve for the intense emotions which Seth's narrative, with all its implications, had generated. When, at last, bathed, arnicated, and petted to the utmost of his patience, Seth was set free, he ran hallooing down the lane for a romp with Alfy in the wonderful, stimulating, mysterious summer twilight, leaving his mother and Mrs. Bembridge to sit down together by the window and tell his story over again to each other with infinite elaboration and inference.

After this Seth found his position at school somewhat easier. Among children, prestige weighs heavily. Those who persisted in shunning him or snubbing him were less aggressive about it, because it was no longer a popular thing to do. As for taunting him with the unspeakable epithet, no one was likely to do it in mere brutal thoughtlessness, for Seth's outburst of madness had shown the dangers of it. Then the midsummer holidays came. The gray, little, red-doored schoolhouse was locked, its windows were boarded up for protection against stones, and Seth returned to the sole comradeship of Alfy and his sisters, varied by frequent trips through the fir pasture to the parsonage, where both the rector and Mrs. Goodridge made much of him always, and took delight in his quaint, grown-up fashion of speech.

The Russ children were almost as busy in the holidays as in term-time, the girls helping their mother in housework, wool-carding, and flax-spinning on the little wheel. The big wheel used for the spinning of woollen yarn they were not yet tall enough to use. Alfy helped his father with the barn chores, and with light work around the farm. There was little playtime for him till sundown and supper-time, when the cows had been milked and turned out again to pasture. Seth, therefore, was thrown much on his own resources during the day.

His days, however, were never too long. He had certain light daily duties in connection with Mrs. Bembridge's hens, — the beautiful " Blue Creepies," which he so much admired. Then he had time to read, — and ample material, of bewildering fascination, in the books which Mr. Good-

Seth Begins to Understand 237

ridge was always ready to lend him. Then, there was the ever open book of the green world, continually inviting him. Both Luella and Mrs. Bembridge encouraged his interest in all the wild things, plant or tree, beast or bird or insect; and he spent magic hours alone in the fir pasture, silent and moveless as the gray stumps or the green hillocks, watching all the quick-eyed, furtive life that went on around him, or listening to the stealthy wilderness sounds till his ear could unravel every diverse strand in the tenuous but complex tissue. Sometimes, however, he neither watched nor listened, away in his bright retreats, — but fell into troubled brooding over the meaning of the forbidden word, — the subtle difference which a few of his playmates made him feel between himself and them, — and that look in his mother's eyes, which had in some inexplicable way reminded him of the look in the eyes of Freckle-face under Sadie Babcock's insult. These ponderings were not yet frequent enough, or enlightened enough, to cast any gloom over his ordinary cheer. But they caused him some troubled half-hours, and gave him, at rare intervals, a hint of foreboding, which would make his heart sink suddenly, he could not guess why. For the most part, however, he got nothing but wisdom and strength and curious knowledge from his intimacies with the wilderness, — and the gift of the seeing eye, the patient, waiting hand, the controlled and ready nerve. And it came about that not in strength and stature only, but in thought, imagination, and reserve, the child was older than his years.

CHAPTER XXIII.

THE MEANING OF THE WORD

IT was not until the following spring that Seth got any further light on the matter of that mysterious difference between himself and the other boys, — between himself and Alfy, for instance. It was one soft evening at the end of May, when the air was poignant with the far, wistful piping of the frogs. Seth, Alfy, and Mandy were bringing home the Russ's cows from pasture. They were just putting up the bars, when along came three big, rough-looking boys, swaggering and yelling.

"Don't speak to 'em," whispered Mandy, hurriedly, "they're horrid Wood Pointers!"

There was always some enmity between the Westcock boys and those of Wood Point. A boy who seemed to be ringleader of the rowdy strangers promptly gave evidence of this by shying a stone at one of the cows, which had just filed out upon the road. She was one that had but recently "come in," as the phrase goes, and her great udder was swollen with milk. The stone hit her sharply on the leg, cutting her, and putting her on the run. Alfy was outraged, both in his tender-heartedness and in his instincts as a farmer, — for he knew it was injurious to make a new milch-cow run.

"Quit that!" he shouted, angrily. "Don't you go runnin' our cows!" And Seth, who was a little behind, having just put up the last bar, ran forward to stand beside him.

"Aw, go chase yerself!" jeered the boy who had thrown the stone. "Who's a-goin' to stop me?" And he picked up another stone as if to repeat the offence.

Alfy advanced fearlessly. All three of the Wood Pointers were bigger than either himself or Seth; but he was strong in the knowledge that he was in the right, and confident in Seth's fierce courage.

"You let them cows alone, Si Hatch," he shouted, "or I'll tell my father on you. You better bet, 'f *he* hears you've been a-stonin' our cows, or a-runnin' of 'em when they're in milk, he'll tan yer hide fer you, or else have the law on you."

"Aw, go chase yerself!" repeated Si Hatch, who was not gifted with originality. "Who keers fer your father?" But he refrained from throwing the stone. Alfy's threat was an effective one, for no farmer would tolerate having his cows run.

"You'll keer, 'f you don't look smart!" retorted Alfy, quick to follow up his advantage. "My

The Meaning of the Word 241

father's Joe Russ, — an' you don't want to fool with *him*."

This was an unanswerable argument. Joe Russ's violent and implacable temper was well-known. The other two boys, who had been waiting, grinning, to back up their leader in any way that might seem most amusing, were glad they had kept quiet. But Si Hatch could not endure to back down without a struggle to divert attention from his crawl. Swaggering up to Alfy he snapped his fingers in his face, spat on the ground to show his contempt, then turned sarcastically to Seth, who stood waiting, fists and teeth clenched, to hurl himself into the attack at the first sign of Alfy's need.

"An' I s'pose *you've* got a turble kind of a father, too!" he sneered. "Who might *your* father be, sonny?"

Mandy Russ, standing wide-eyed and expectant in the background, caught her breath. She remembered vividly Seth's wildcat assault upon Tommy Coxen. She looked to see him dart straight at Si Hatch's throat. To her amazement, he did not seem to know he was insulted. While obviously resenting Si's manner, he looked puzzled, as if confronted by a new idea. He had never concerned himself about a father, being wholly, and trustingly, contented with his mother. In that seafaring, sea-ravaged community there were plenty of households where the mother had to be father and mother both. There was nothing unusual enough in that situation to make the absence of a father from his own life a conspicuous thing to him. He had never missed a father. So he had never thought of one. A child may go on year after year taking a situation for granted, till suddenly the situation, which had seemed so harmless, turns upon him like a snarling beast.

"Who might *your* father be?"

The idea was such a tremendous one that Seth was astounded out of all anger.

"*My* father?" he faltered. "Why—" he suddenly realized that, somehow, it would never do to say he didn't know. Then an inspiration came to him. "Why, Mr. Warden, of course. Mr. Warden was my father, I'd have you know!"

The Wood Point boy, belonging to another school district, had not recognized Seth. He knew all about him, however. Now he hooted in joyous derision. Here was his triumph, after all.

"Mr. Warden! Mr. *Warden!*" he crowed, with jeering inflections that brought the hot blood to Seth's face he knew not why. "*Mister* Warden! That's yer *mother's* name. *You hain't got no father.*"

Seth just stared at him, with wide dark eyes into which an awful fear was coming. He did not

The Meaning of the Word 243

yet realize how far he should resent this statement, — the truth of which he somehow could not doubt. Not rage, but anguish and amazement, were surging wildly in his heart. The expression of his face stirred Mandy's sympathy to a white heat. She ran up, and blazed out at the young bully.

"Git out of this, you Wood Point loafer!" she cried, "or I'll git my father to whale you half to death."

"Spit cat!" retorted Si, hugely amused, and conscious that Mandy, with her flaming blue eyes and long bright hair, was very pretty, — "I ain't skeered o' yer pretty claws. An' ye know right well he *hain't* got no father. He's jest a little Come-by-chance!"

By this time Seth had understood. He had expected another word than "Come-by-chance." But in a flash he knew that they meant the same thing. He saw that piteous look in the eyes of Freckle-face, — in the eyes of his mother. Then, once more things looked red before him, and he saw only Si Hatch's face, leering. On the instant, he leaped. One fist landed solidly in the bully's eye, the other, a fraction of a second later, on his mouth, knocking out a tooth. Taken by surprise, the big fellow staggered backwards. Recovering himself in an instant, he launched a blow which would have knocked his small opponent clean out had it landed fairly. Seth dodged, however, quick as a cat, so the blow glanced, merely cutting his cheek and making his head spin; and before Si could follow it up, Alfy had closed in, jumping on the bully's neck and trying to choke him.

In a moment the three were rolling on the ground, panting and grappling and crying out like young animals, while the other two Wood Pointers, with a wholesome dread of Farmer Russ before their eyes, stood aloof and assured Mandy that Si Hatch "had brung it on himself all right!" Mandy, however, was badly scared. She felt that Alfy and Seth together were no match for their big, loutish opponent. She screamed at the top of her shrill voice, and gazed around wildly for help.

To her infinite relief, help was coming. She saw a light-footed young farmer running down the hill. She screamed louder than ever. "Oh, oh, Mr. Barnes, come quick! He's killing Alfy!"

The other two boys discreetly took to their heels. Si Hatch, who was finding his hands much fuller than he expected, was now eager to take to his heels also. He struggled to his feet, Seth and Alfy clinging so savagely that he could not strike them with effect. But the moment he was upright, Mandy darted in and tripped him. He went down with a curse. And at this moment William Barnes came up, panting from his run.

The Meaning of the Word 245

"Oh, Mr. Barnes," explained Mandy, sobbing with excitement, but determined to spare Seth's feelings, "they stoned our cows, — an' Seth an' Alfy tried to stop them."

"Well," responded William Barnes, dryly, "I reckon they succeeded." And he dragged the panting combatants apart.

The moment he could regain his feet, Si Hatch ducked his head and ran like a hare. This did not suit Mr. Barnes at all, in whose eyes stoning a new milch-cow and running her when in milk was a heinous crime. He was lithe, and swift of foot. Inside of two score yards he overtook Si, clutched him by the collar, and shook him till his teeth almost rattled. Then he propelled him back to where Seth and Alfy, with bleeding noses, and Mandy with her little white apron assuaging their wounds, awaited him. Forcing the culprit, who was spitting blood from his broken tooth, to confront them, he demanded:

"What d'you mean by stonin' them cows, Si Hatch?"

"I never!" declared Si, sullenly.

"O-o-o-h!" exclaimed the others, in indignant chorus.

"Don't you lie to me, Si!" said Mr. Barnes, shaking him again. "I seen you, leastways, I seen the cows a-runnin'; an' I know Alfy Russ wouldn't 'a' run his own cows."

"I jest shied a stun at 'em," muttered Si, ugly but frightened. "'N' I wasn't the only one. Ther' was two more, 'sides me."

"I seen 'em. An' I'll remember 'em," answered Mr. Barnes, grimly. "But you're the only one I've caught. I'll teach you to stone cows!" and he shook him again. Then, turning him round, he looked at the young lout's puffy eye and bleeding mouth, and burst out laughing.

"I was goin' to give you the all-firedest good lickin' y'ever got in all your darn, loafin' life," he continued. "But I reckon them ere two kids has give' ye all ye want. I reckon ye kin git!"

With a gentle kick of contempt, he let him go; and Si slunk off, too cowed to even mutter.

Then Mr. Barnes turned to Alfy and Seth.

"Ye're a pair o' spunky leetle tarriers, you two, an' no mistake. But look out he don't ketch the one or the tother o' yous alone. He'll be layin' fer yous. Keep yer eyes peeled, now mind I tell yous."

The cows were half-way home, *tonk-tonking* leisurely along the road, and pasturing as they went, before the children overtook them. The children were excited and elated; and, during the telling of the story to Mr. and Mrs. Russ, Seth was too much occupied with the part he had played to let himself dwell on the humiliating knowledge which had come to him. When he started up the lane to his own home, however, it came over him with a whelming rush of shame and pain and doubt. He didn't know how to tell his mother. He could not bear to bring that look of piteous fear and shrinking again into her eyes. Something he would have to tell, because the marks of the battle were upon him, — honourable scars. He would not dare tell his mother exactly how he got them, hungrily as he longed for her admiring sympathy. He would put it all, exclusively, upon the stoning of Alfy's father's cows. He would keep locked in his own heart the bitter fact that he now knew the meaning of the insulting name he had been called. "Come-by-chance," he felt, was just as bad as that other name, which he would not bring himself to even whisper to himself. As he thought of how his mother would wince at it, how her face would flush, then whiten, how her kind, dear mouth would change, how her beautiful eyes would contract with pain, — all which things had been stamped upon his heart ineffaceably, — he had a swift revelation that the insults to himself were far more truly insults to her. Through him, they pierced her tender spirit. It was upon her, more than upon himself, that the mysterious stigma rested. He could not understand it; but a passion of longing to protect her from it sprang up within him from that moment. It was plain to him that in some way it was all connected with his lack of a father. Some day, but not now, — for he was wiser than he had been a year ago, — he would ask about his father. To-night, he would talk only of how Si Hatch had stoned the cows.

There was consternation in the gray cottage when Seth came in and the lamplight fell upon his discoloured little face. But the stoning of Alfy's cows explained everything to the complete satisfaction of both Luella and Mrs. Bembridge. And Luella fell asleep that night with no load of burning shame to crush out her pride in her boy's loyalty and pluck.

CHAPTER XXIV.

HIS FATHER'S NAME

IT was not till several weeks later, when there was no longer a single mark on his face to remind his mother of his fight with Si Hatch, that Seth mustered up courage to ask her about his father. He seized upon a moment when he was alone with her. The two were coming home through the spruce pasture from a visit to the parsonage; and, as it chanced, Mrs. Goodridge had been talking rather enthusiastically about the doings of her grandfather, who had been a Loyalist leader during the American Revolution.

This innocent talk of grandfathers would have been enough to make Seth think of fathers, even if he had not been letting them occupy all his thoughts of late.

Luella had dropped down on a hillock by the path to pick some strawberries. Seth stood before her, regarding her with a look of gloomy solicitude. He was afraid he was going to hurt her. It wrenched his heart to hurt her; but he felt that he must get the burden off his mind.

Suddenly conscious of his silence, of something unusual in his attitude, Luella looked up with an inquiring smile in her deep eyes. The moment he met her look Seth spoke.

"Mother," he asked, almost in the tone of a demand, "where's my father?"

Luella was unprepared. The question was one which she had for some years forgotten to expect. And just now, it came hardest. This was the very day on which, ten years ago, the *G. G. Goodridge* had borne away her life. She gave a little, startled cry, and buried her face in her hands, leaning it far forward on her knees. A heavy coil of her wonderful, flaxen gold hair fell forward over her hands.

Seth's heart smote him at the sight, but for the moment he was implacable. He must be answered.

"Oh, muzz, dear, tell me!" he persisted.

"I don't know, Seth," answered Luella, in a low voice, without lifting her head. "He is very far away, — that's all I know!"

"Is he dead?" demanded the boy.

"No, I believe he's not dead — except to us," replied Luella, hardly above a whisper.

"How do you know he isn't dead, mother?" insisted Seth.

"I know he's alive, he's somewhere on this earth," — and then Luella began to shake with fierce sobs. The scent of lilacs, and salt, and clover blossoms, and Jim's hair, came mysteriously into her nostrils. His bright, adoring eyes seemed to look into hers, as when she saw him last. For Seth's own sake, she could not let herself break down.

"Oh, Seth, don't!" she cried, desperately, springing to her feet, and dashing her hands across her eyes. "I can't stand it, just now. Don't ask me any more now, dearie. Come, let's go home to Granny, now!" and clutching him by the hand she began to run, as if she would escape her memories.

Seth was torn between the longing to spare her and the sense that he ought to know more. He was on the point of asking "What's his name?" but shrank, he knew not why, when the words were fairly on his tongue. Instead, he queried, half-reproachfully: "Don't you think I ought to know about my father, muzz, dear? When will you tell me?"

"Yes, yes, dearie, it's your right to know all I can tell you," answered Luella, her face flushed and averted. "I *will* tell you, Seth. But not to-day — I can't tell you to-day."

"All right, muzz, dear!" conceded Seth. "But just tell me one thing now!"

"What is it?" asked Luella, with a tightening of fear at her heart.

"Is his name — Warden, mother?"

"No!" cried Luella, dropping his hand, and hurrying on still faster. There was something desperate in her voice. But Seth had nothing more to say.

They hastened onward in a heavy, dreadful silence, till the back of the barn appeared, gray through the dark green of the firs; and in a minute more they came to the bars.

"I think I'll go down and see Alfy now, muzz, dear," said Seth, turning into the lane.

"Very well!" agreed Luella, in a muffled voice. "Don't be late for supper."

Seth went down the lane very slowly. He had just grasped a new and tremendous idea, and was struggling to master it. It was terrible to him, but less so than if he had not been prepared for it by what Si Hatch had said. Now that he knew, beyond all possibility of doubt, that Si Hatch had told the truth, he arrived at a definite idea of what a bastard was. A bastard, he concluded, turning the knife in his soul relentlessly, was one who was not permitted to have the same name as his father, — and therefore *he was* a bastard. But, he argued further, he would have borne his father's name if his mother had borne it. He began to wonder what dreadful name people called his mother when they got angry with her. Was it not just as shameful for her to not bear his father's name, as it was for him? This thought filled him with a rage of pity for his mother, so that he could not bring himself to go in and ask for Alfy. He turned from the Russ's gate and walked on up the road, musing passionately. For the first time, the thought presented itself that he was the victim of a terrible wrong, and that his mother was the victim of a terrible wrong. Then, clearly it was this unknown father who had done them both the wrong.

As the enormity of the injury, overshadowing their whole lives, dawned slowly upon him, he felt himself choking. An impulse to avoid all chance of meeting any one made him turn off the road, climb the snake fence, and push his way up through the fir pasture again, where he felt sure of solitude. His hands were clenched, his boyish little face was set hard, his eyes had an unnatural light in them. He went ahead among the young trees unrealizing his direction, consumed with a murderous craving for vengeance on this unknown father. That such a woman as his mother, — so good, so kind, so wise, who was *always* right, — could by any possibility be to blame, never entered his mind. He felt almost as if his heart were going to burst in his bosom from the impotence of his passion to avenge her. His face worked convulsively, and he was quite unaware of the scratching of the hard spruce branches which dashed across it from time to time in his reckless passage among them.

Presently, as he crossed the path, a clear young voice called to him imperatively.

"Seth! Seth! Oh, Seth! Stop! I want you!"

It was Mandy Russ, tripping along the path to the parsonage. Seth could not ignore her. Violently controlling his impulse to dash on into the silences, he stopped and waited without a word, for her to come up. She was a pretty, bright-eyed girl, of about Seth's height, though a good two years his senior.

"Oh, Seth — what *is* the matter?" she gasped, frightened at the strange look in his face.

"Mandy," he demanded, in a voice she did not recognize as his, "who was my father?"

The girl was taken aback. She looked as if she was going to cry.

"Why, Seth — " she stammered, "why, of course, Jim Calder's your father, your mother says. Of course, Seth!"

The significance of that "of course," and "your mother says," was lost on Seth. The name was all that signified to him.

"Who's Jim Calder?" pursued the boy, in a hard

voice. "That cross old woman's son, down by the crick?"

"Yes!" assented Mandy.

"Where is he?" demanded Seth.

"Nobody knows but old Mrs. Calder!" answered Mandy, getting over her fright, and now eager to talk. "An' she's that ugly she won't tell *anything* about him, — not even to Mr. Goodridge. But Mr. Smith at the post-office, *he* tells when she gits letters from him, — letters that have on them all kinds o' queer, lovely stamps, from New Zealand, an' Singapore, an' Manila, an' Shanghai, an' Japan. My, I'd like to have some of those stamps. Wonder what she does with 'em! She gits as much as three an' four letters a year, sometimes."

"Calder," muttered Seth, to himself. "Calder." And he said the name over and over, as if accustoming himself to it. "And do you mean to say, Mandy, that cross old Mrs. Calder, with the great, long upper lip, is *my* grandmother? She doesn't like me one bit!"

"No!" agreed Mandy, naïvely. "But she jest *hates* your *mother*, Seth."

This information was not vital. Seth turned aside from it, as from husks.

"Why — why did he go away?" he demanded, harshly.

This was to Mandy the most embarrassing question he could have asked. She knew the whole story, and all the embroidery of gossip which had been added to it. She knew that certain of the Westcock people, led by Mrs. Ackerley, were wont to say that it was because Luella's child was not Jim Calder's, that Jim Calder had gone away. She had heard the vague rumour about Bud Whalley. These things it was horrible to think of telling Seth. It was inconceivable. Taking a firm grip on herself she lifted her head and looked Seth fair in the eyes.

"I don't know," she answered. "How could I know that, Seth? Liker than not there ain't nobody knows, except Jim Calder, an' your mother!" Mandy paused, then added, with eager interest, "Why don't you ask her, Seth?"

"I will ask her, some day," said the boy, resolutely. "Thank you, Mandy, for what you've told me!" And turning away abruptly, he marched off up the pasture, through the bushes. Mandy gazed after him sympathetically, and with a sudden feeling that he had grown older all at once. She was two whole years older than he, — yet now, she suddenly felt herself the younger. At the same time, a strange little feeling of what she called "lonesomeness" came over her, — as if she had been crowded aside, in Seth's life, by matters too weighty for her to contend with. She hardly understood the feeling; but she could not help having a little cry over it, before she emerged from the privacy of the pasture.

CHAPTER XXV.

THE SEED OF VENGEANCE

FROM this day onward Seth played less childishly, read more intently in the parsonage study, wandered more persistently in the woods or on the marshes, or along the windy dyke-top, alone. He was too healthy in body, too red-blooded and active-muscled, to carry his burden always with him. But when he was alone in the woods, and nothing happening to fix his attention, — or if he was reading, and the matter lost grip upon his interest, then he would begin to brood over his mother's wrongs, and his own. As he brooded, he would grow hot and sick with shame; and then, slowly, the shame would flame into hatred of the remote, unreal figure that was Jim Calder, his father. He pictured this figure as resembling himself, grown up; and sometimes he would plan minutely for his vengeance on this figure resembling himself. The picture thus formèd of his father burned itself so deeply into his mind that no description afterward obtained was able to efface it.

The Seed of Vengeance

Time after time Luella was on the point of volunteering him the answer to his question of that memorable day in the pasture. But always, she weakened at the last. Moreover, she presently became convinced that he knew. And since his sudden maturing she had acquired a curious little dread of him, a dread of what he might think, or say to her. It was, perhaps, more a diffidence than a dread, however, for more and more she realized the depth of his adoring devotion to herself. But once in awhile she surprised in his eyes a look which made her feel that she did not understand him, and she shrank from troubling unnecessary deeps which she might not be able to fathom. Young as he was, she nevertheless felt it better to leave the question of his further enlightenment in his own hands. She would hold herself ready to answer him to the fullest degree; but she would not force upon him any information that he did not demand. In this she was strongly sustained by Mrs. Bembridge, who did not believe in "too much talk," — and also, though with some hesitation, by the rector, who was usually in favour of "a clear understanding" on any difficult point.

Luella was now on very civil terms with her Uncle Abner. Ever since the day of her unexpected visit to his store, both she and Mrs. Bembridge had dealt with him regularly, — and always on a cash basis. This commanded the old shopkeeper's respect, and at length his esteem, also. Little by little, too, the parsonage trade came back, after it had dawned on Mrs. Goodridge that "Old Abner" was no longer unfriendly to Luella. Mr. Baisley's occasional efforts to resume his ancient, half-paternal attitude toward his niece were gently repulsed; but he gradually took to emphasizing his relationship to Seth, whose sturdy self-possession and unfailing respect greatly pleased him. He fell into the way of making little presents to the lad whenever he came into the store. Moreover, he took pains to have something to say to both Luella and Seth whenever he met them coming out of church. Seth was unprejudiced, having never been told how the old man had treated his mother in her trouble. He fell into an attitude of friendliness, therefore, dropped into a habit of sampling the candy and biscuits, and came to regard his great-uncle as one of his few friends in the village.

One day as he and his mother came out of the store, laughing cheerfully, with bundles under their arms, they almost ran into Mrs. Ackerley, who was stalking past with scornful nose in air. Mrs. Ackerley's nose was always high in air as she passed Mr. Baisley's store. Ever since the day when he had sued her for that ancient bill of $7.63, and forced her to pay, she had kept telling her neighbours that he sold rotten fish, and trying to make them imagine there was a bad smell in front of the store. Every one laughed, and it pleased Mrs. Ackerley to stick to the fiction till she came to believe it true.

Now, when she saw Luella and Luella's son come out of the store in manifest good-humour, while she herself had nothing to show for the stand she had taken but an unfortunate lawsuit and considerable loss of prestige, she felt herself deeply outraged. She was never one to suffer in silence, or to content herself with any of the more delicate modes of expression. When confronted by Luella she started back dramatically, her face red and her eyes glaring, and drew her black alpaca skirts close about her.

"Git out o' my way, you slut!" she rasped. "Don't you dare tech a decent woman!" Then, keeping her head turned so that her angry little eyes were fixed upon Luella's as long as possible, she stepped bridling by.

At this unspeakable insult to his mother, Seth felt himself choking. Blindly, not knowing what he intended to do, he lunged forward. But at the same instant Luella's firm hand fell upon his shoulder, holding him with a strength of which he had not dreamed her capable; and he heard her voice saying, calmly:

"Seth, what would you do to a woman? Don't be troubled, dearie. Her foul tongue cannot hurt me."

Submissive instantly, Seth turned, trembling, and lifted a white face to see his mother white also, but smiling at him.

"Oh, mother," he gasped, "if only — I could kill her!"

For his sake, Luella had held herself under rigid control. Now, she laughed gently. It was rather an unnatural little laugh, but it served its purpose in helping Seth to regain his own composure. She could not bear that the neighbours, who might have been watching the encounter from their windows, should see any sign of excitement on the part of either herself or Seth.

"Don't you give her a second thought, boy," she said, in a steady voice. "Everybody knows that old woman's tongue, and nobody cares what she says!"

Seth made no answer. He could not trust himself to speak again. But he possessed himself of her hand, and squeezed it till it hurt her cruelly. In the violence of his impotent craving to protect her from all injury and insult, he found himself suddenly in peril of bursting into tears. He set his teeth hard, and glared unseeingly at the landscape. Soon his emotion changed into a lust for vengeance upon the man who had brought such outrages upon her, — and in a moment the tears within were scorched dry. But he heard his mother talking to him, quietly, sweetly, about little home things and plans for the garden, till, presently, the storm within him grew more manageable. He tried to hear what she was saying. At last, she caught his attention.

"How is it you haven't been trout-fishing yet this spring?" she asked. "Ain't this good weather?"

This was something requiring definite answer, and Seth turned his mind upon it.

"We were planning to fish in Wood Creek Saturday, Alfy an' me —"

"Alfy an' *I!*" corrected his mother, smiling.

"Alfy an' I," assented Seth. "Water's a little high, but it ought to be all right by Saturday. An' that reminds me, mother. I wanted to git some fish-hooks at the store, an' a new line." And he halted, as if he thought of turning back.

"There's no time to go back, now," declared his mother. "Time enough to-morrow afternoon. I'll have to send you down right after school, for some more things for me."

The next afternoon Seth asked to be excused from school five minutes earlier, so that neither Alfy nor any of the others should propose going down to the "Bito" with him. He had another purpose in view, besides the fish-hooks and his mother's commissions. When he ran into the store, to his satisfaction he found Mr. Baisley alone. After a word or two he went direct to his point.

"Uncle Abner," said he, with a gravity that arrested Mr. Baisley's attention, "I came *specially* to ask you to tell me something."

Mr. Baisley wondered what was coming. He laid down the box of fish-hooks and eyed the boy over his spectacles.

"What is it, sonny?" he inquired, in a guarded voice.

"Tell me what like — what kind of a man — is Jim Calder; my father, I mean, Uncle Abner," he added, hastily, to let Mr. Baisley know he knew.

Since Mr. Baisley had become so friendly to Luella and to Luella's boy, his bitterness against Jim, always sharp enough, had increased fourfold. Indeed, he had cause and to spare for hatred of Jim Calder. His thin cheeks grew bricky red through his thin whiskers at Seth's question, and his eyes became like needle points in his indignation.

"Your *father,* indeed! A nice sort of a father he's been to you, that you should go callin' him your '*father*' like that!" he piped, his voice mounting to an even harsher shrillness as he went on.

The Seed of Vengeance

Then he paused, leaned over the counter, and shook a lean, minatory finger at Seth's face. "Don't you go for to gittin' no sentimental trash into your head, Seth," he went on, more quietly, but with greater intensity, "about that dog-goned scoundrel, Jim Calder. If you'd knowed the way he's treated your poor mother, you'd bite your tongue out sooner'n call him 'my father,' like that!"

When Mr. Baisley felt assured of the righteousness of his wrath, his speech was not ineffective.

With a grown-up air which might have been funny had not the resolve in his young face given it dignity, Seth held out his hand to the old storekeeper.

"Thank you, Uncle Abner!" said he. "I've been thinking that's the kind of a man he must be. Now I know. An' *I'll fix him,* one of these days, when I get to be grown up."

Mr. Baisley grasped the strong, square, little hand in his lean grip, ardently.

"I might 'a' knowed it of you, boy!" he exclaimed, in proud approval. "That's the way to talk. An' you're more of a man now than lots o' men I know, for all you're but a kid." Then he lavished upon him more fish-hooks and lines than Seth knew what to do with.

In the curious jumble of sturdy common sense and visionary dreaming which so often constitutes the mind of an intelligent child, those fish-hooks had a kind of sacredness to Seth. He was only eleven years old, though he looked, and talked, so much older. And in his veins was all the superstition which the mysterious, fog-haunted, tide-harassed Bay of Fundy breeds in the folk who dwell about her borders. The fish-hooks were to him a pledge of the secret understanding (secret by intuition, not by any spoken word) between himself and his Uncle Abner, in regard to the purpose lurking in his heart. There was just a suggestion of something sinister in the old storekeeper, which enabled him to touch Seth on this one point, — a point which he could never have allowed the sunny-tempered, transparent Alfy, or any other of his friends, to even approach. When, on the following day, the weather proved soft, sweet-smelling, and showery, with gleams of mitigated sunshine through gray clouds, he felt that those hooks were going to bring him luck. He knew, as the born fisherman does, just by the smell of the air, that the trout were going to bite. And when, though Alfy had luck enough, he had just three times Alfy's luck, as to numbers, besides catching the big fish of the day, — the biggest he had ever caught, — then, with an incongruity only possible to a child's mind, he drew grim conclusions as to the fortune that would follow his far-off purpose of revenge. He was capable, at this time, of fixing his purpose ineradicably in his brain; and he did so. But it was as yet little more than a sprouting seed. The deadliness of the plant which it would grow to be was not yet quite real to him. In spite of all his hours of bitterness, shame, hate, and poignant pity, he was a natural boy, and he could still mix up his passion with a question of fish-hooks.

CHAPTER XXVI.

THE FORESTERS' PICNIC

WHEN Seth had reached the age of fifteen he was the head pupil in the school, though there were boys and girls several years older. He looked, in every way, not younger than seventeen. By reason of his courage, his strength, his quickness of decision, and a reticence which gave him that air of unknown possibilities, so dear to the childish or the childlike heart, his prestige in the school was very great. Within that little world bounded by the school-bell, it protected him completely from all reminders of the stigma upon his birth. No boy dared challenge his prompt fist. As for the girls, big and little, to most of them he was a sort of hero. They admired him openly, as did Mandy Russ (Julie had quit school the year before), or in shy secrecy, like little Freckle-face, toward whom he maintained always an air of half-condescending protection. The few girls who might have liked to cross this current of tribute to Luella's nameless son were checked by a wholesome appreciation of the scorn which came so easily into his steady, dark eyes, of the self-possessed acuteness of his tongue. Had Seth lived no life but that of the school, his bitterness might have sweetened, his hatred of his father faded down, his purpose of vengeance cooled for lack of fuel. But in the village world there was always something coming up, — so slight, so subtle, to be sure, that it could never be taken notice of, — which served to turn the knife continually in his own heart, or in his mother's. His purpose, therefore, kept growing in intensity, ever more and more biting into his soul. Of all his studies, those to which he brought the keenest zest were geography and arithmetic. In studying the first, he felt that he was somehow doing something toward finding out where his father was. In studying the second, he was learning how to reach him. He was preparing himself for the higher study of navigation, having made up his mind to become a sailor, and voyage the Eastern seas in his quest.

During this summer, toward the end of the holidays, the "Foresters" of Sackville and Dorchester combined to hold a great picnic. It was an event, talked about and advertised for weeks, and all Westcock village — which lay between Sackville and Dorchester — was stirred by it. It was held in a field overlooking the upper end of Partlow's

Pond, two or three miles from Dorchester. In carriages, buggies, wagons, and hay-carts people went to it, even from Upper Sackville and the Grantasque Road.

Even Luella went, for a wonder. Seth insisted that she should; and she feared that if she held back too obstinately he would understand her reasons too well. Moreover, Mrs. Goodridge urged her also, and her urgency took the very practical form of an invitation to both Luella and Seth, to go in the rector's two-seated wagon. The rector, who had been away from home a few days, taking duty for a brother clergyman at Shediac, was to meet them at the picnic and drive home with them that night through the Dorchester woods. In all these years Mrs. Goodridge had found no feminine companionship more to her taste than that of the quiet-voiced, calm-eyed, steadfast Luella.

It was a proper August day, dry and hot; but the drive through the deep-shadowed Dorchester woods was pleasant, except where the unusual traffic kicked up too much dust. About a quarter of a mile from the picnic grounds Mrs. Goodridge put up at the farmhouse of a parishioner, where Seth rubbed down and foddered the sweating horse.

They found the grounds already thronged. Along the south side of the field, in the shadow of a spruce grove, were ranged white tents, — chiefly refreshment booths, with a few of the mild entertainments usually furnished at such affairs. Everywhere fluttered the brilliancy of the British and Canadian flags, — chiefly Union Jacks, or the flag of the merchant marine with the Canadian arms in a wreath of green maple leaves on the broad, blood-red field, — with here and there a Stars and Stripes, in token of brotherly good-will. The lower and more level portion of the field, toward the water, was given over to games and athletic sports.

Mrs. Goodridge was not long on the grounds before she was carried off by Dorchester friends, whom she had not seen for some time. Luella and Seth wandered around gaily together, — Luella, fresh and dainty in her pale blue dimity frock and wide, white hat, looking like Seth's sister rather than his mother. Presently they were joined by Jinnie McMinn. Then Luella, observing that Seth had a hungry eye on the sports, gaily drove him off to try his skill.

Though only sixteen, Seth's stature compelled him to compete in the men's events, rather than in those for "boys of sixteen and under." Even if he might have been permitted to enter in the boys' class, he would have disdained the easy triumphs there awaiting him.

Now, however, he found little triumph awaiting him. Pitting his unripe strength against men, he was almost inevitably defeated; but his defeats were honourable, under the circumstances, and he was not discouraged or ashamed. He entered for everything, with the idea of " trying himself out," so to speak, among adversaries stronger and more skilful than himself. And before long, though he had won nothing, except third place in a hard-fought quarter-mile race, he began to attract attention by his untiring endurance and pluck. After having contested every race, from the one hundred yard dash to the mile run, including the hurdle-race, and having then come fourth among twelve stalwart competitors in throwing the hammer, he was made glad by a word of strong commendation from the rector, who had recently arrived and hastened at once to watch the sports.

The rector's eyes, under the brim of a broad black hat, were dancing with enthusiasm. Seth, stripped to his short-sleeved cotton undershirt, with his red and white suspenders twisted around his waist for a belt, his hair matted down in wet strings over his forehead, came up drenched with sweat. The rector grasped his hand with a mighty grip.

" 'Pon my word, old boy," he exclaimed, " you're just doing wonders. You're fairly holding your own with some of the best athletes of the country, and you not fifteen. It's splendid. It makes me feel young again!" and he heaved his deep chest, burning to be in the heat of it himself.

Seth blushed with pleasure and pride. He knew that, however lenient might be the rector's eye in some matters, it was exacting and critical in a question of this sort.

"But I'm way past fifteen. I'm nearly sixteen, sir!" he corrected, deferentially.

"Well, that makes precious little difference, when your opponents are anywhere from twenty to thirty," said the rector. "I tell you what, I'm going to coach you up a little. You must come over before tea, say Tuesday and Thursday evenings, and we'll practise together, you and I. Why, in another year you'll be beating us all out of our boots!"

"Not you, sir!" protested Seth. "I guess you'd have to teach me more'n I can ever learn, before I'd be able to beat you."

"Nonsense, boy! I'm getting too old!" laughed the rector, with a transparent hypocrisy. "Now, what are you going into next?"

"The pole vault, sir!" answered Seth. "I've used the pole quite a bit, long jumping; but I haven't ever tried to see how high I can go. I'll find that out right now."

"Well, don't take too long, or too hard, a run," admonished the rector. "Trust to your spring, —

and then to your arms. And don't forget to drop your pole in time. Now I've got to go, and see some of the people. If I stay here much longer I won't be able to keep myself out of it all." In spite of himself, however, he did stay, long enough to see Seth win second place in the pole vault. Then he went away greatly pleased, shaping his course toward the main tent at the upper end of the field, but stopped every four or five paces of his progress by people who beamed at sight of him, and claimed a hand-shake before he passed.

The next event was putting the stone. At this game, which he had never practised, Seth soon found himself distanced, and dropped out. The champion of Westmorcland County, a brawny Scotchman from Sackville Corners, named MacFall, felt sure of victory. He had soon discouraged all his opponents but one, a splendid young giant who had come over from Truro, in Nova Scotia, for the special purpose of competing in this event, and lowering the crest of MacFall. Between these two the issue hung, on a matter of half inches, till a superb throw of the Nova Scotian's put him a clean foot and a half in the lead, and he rested proudly. Three times more did MacFall throw, straining every muscle, mustering every art, — but the utmost he could do was to cut down that humiliating lead by a scant four inches. Then he acknowledged himself beaten.

There was general chagrin over the triumph of an outsider, from the neighbouring and always rival province of Nova Scotia; and this particular outsider had been rather arrogantly confident from the first, which did not make his victory any the more popular. Suddenly Seth, sensitive to the feeling that was seething inarticulately about him, spoke up in his penetrating young voice.

"That's a mighty fine throw, Mr. Ryan. But there's some one on the grounds here that can beat it, and beat it easy!"

There was a confused murmur, — exclamations of doubt, derision, question, and agreement.

"Bring him right along, then, afore I git my coat on!" cried Ryan, swaggering confidently.

"Wha d'ye mean?" demanded MacFall, incredulously. "I'd like weel to see that one!"

"I mean Parson Goodridge!" announced Seth, with conviction. An instant chorus of approval from men of Sackville, Westcock, and Dorchester who stood about, made it evident that Seth had some foundation for what he claimed.

"That bit mon, what was talking wi' ye the noo, to put the stane wi' *him?*" queried MacFall, shaking his head in disappointment.

But the Nova Scotian was amused.

"I don't *think* there's any *parson* that can lick me at me own game!" said he.

"You dasen't risk it!" cried several voices. Whereupon one of the judges interposed hastily, to prevent hot words.

"The prize is yours, and won with distinction, Mr. Ryan," said he, courteously. "And I'm very sure we none of us grudge you the honour so worthily won. But lest you should think any one has been trying to banter you, I will say that if our rector, Mr. Goodridge, — a much older man than you, by the way, — had been in this contest, your laurels would certainly have been in danger."

"Then I won't take the prize," declared the Nova Scotian, half-angry, "unless I can have a chance at this wonderful parson of yours. Bring him along, says I; and bring him quick."

On the word Seth and two of the Sackville men were off at the run to capture Mr. Goodridge. He was easily found; and their eagerness so prevailed that he came with them before he knew their errand. When they explained it to him, however, hung back, though his eyes sparkled. It would never do, he protested. And what could he do, against a famous athlete like Ryan, who was the champion of his Province, and only twenty-five years old When he was younger, — well, perhaps. But at forty-five — it was absurd! And thus pro-

The Foresters' Picnic 277

testing, he was led up and confronted by the victorious Mr. Ryan, who was duly presented to him.

The rector greeted him with hearty warmth and a little congratulation on his victory. Ryan, surveying the figure before him, of middle height, neither broad nor slender, bearded and grizzled, in long black clerical coat and wide-brimmed black clerical hat, suspected that he was being made game of. His manner was suspicious, his return of the rector's cordial greeting was rather curt. Watchful eyes noted this, — and noted, too, with delight, that the rector's manner changed at once. He was nettled.

"That settles Ryan's hash!" remarked one of the Westcock men; and a faint murmur of contentment went around.

"I shall count it an honour, indeed, to have a try with you," said the rector, gravely, taking off his coat and hat, and delivering them into eager hands. "But, of course, this must be a mere friendly match, for our own amusement. The prize is already yours, — and well won, too, I see!" and he measured with practised eye both the size of the stone and the distance it had been put.

Mr. Ryan was in a bad humour.

"It's for the prize," he retorted, roughly, "or I ain't in it!"

The rector hesitated, eying him sharply. He

didn't quite like this brusque young stranger. Then he smiled sweetly.

"Oh, well, just as you wish, of course," he agreed in a gentle voice. Whereupon Seth chuckled.

By this time word had gone around that the rector was about to try conclusions with the Nova Scotian champion who had just done up Sandy MacFall. The crowd had gathered in hastily; and a silence of tense expectation settled down upon it. The rector took off his waistcoat, carefully and smoothly turned up his shirt-sleeves, and picked up the stone to test it.

"He kens what he's about. He's handled the stane afore," said MacFall, eying him with concentrated interest from under his thick red eyebrows. No one else spoke.

The rector was now forgetful of everything but the heavy stone poised on his palm and the space which he had to make it cover. He no longer saw the watching throng of faces. Standing sidewise to the mark, and about seven feet behind it, he took two elastic, swinging side jumps, as it were, and propelled the stone from the level of his shoulder, springing into the air, but coming down again with both feet behind the mark. A muttered note thrilled over the crowd, as the stone described its long, free curve. It fell exactly in the mark made by the champion.

The Foresters' Picnic

The crowd broke into a cheer. MacFall grunted inarticulate wonder and delight. Ryan's face changed, and he eyed the rector curiously. The rector stood just where he was and waited for some one to bring back the stone to him.

"That was just a try," he explained, modestly, "to get the feeling of the stone!"

"By Gawd, ye've got him beat!" burst out MacFall in a Highland ecstasy. And nobody even smiled.

The rector, poising the stone, now gathered himself for a second effort. His face was grim, his brow furrowed, and his eyes measured the distance shrewdly. In his shirt-sleeves he betrayed, to some extent, the massive strength of his shoulders; and no one could misunderstand the great, elastic muscles of his bare white arms. In his controlled balance, as he sprang to the throw, there was a certain reserve of force which foretold success. The stone seemed to leap from his thrust as if alive.

The throng held its breath as the great missile curved through the air. It fell a clear two feet beyond the Nova Scotian's mark. Dorchester, Sackville, and Westcock yelled themselves hoarse.

The young Nova Scotian came forward, and scanned the distance between his throw and that of his antagonist. Very thoughtfully he picked up the stone, and walked back with it to the scratch.

There he hesitated for a moment. Then he dropped the stone at his feet, and held out his hand bashfully to the rector.

"May I shake hands again, sir?" he asked. "'Tain't no use my tryin', just to amuse the lookers-on. I *might* better my throw by a foot, maybe, — and maybe I mightn't. But I couldn't touch that throw o' yours, if I tried all day."

The rector shook his hand warmly, but seemed disappointed. "Oh, come on!" he protested, like a boy. "Why, I've only just got my coat off!" And he looked around as if hoping for another rival. There was a general laugh, and Ryan drew back.

"I don't think you'll get any one else to tackle you, sir!" said he, admiringly.

"Well, then I suppose I'll have to put on my coat again," sighed the rector, turning down his sleeves and taking the coat from Seth.

"Won't you enter for the jumping, sir?" suggested young Palmer, of Dorchester, who had taken first place in the pole vault.

The rector hesitated. Then he turned away with a decision that was obviously final.

"No, I'll rest on my laurels!" he answered, positively. "Don't you young fellows go thinking you can get me to give you a chance to snatch them from my brow!" And with his frank, gay laugh on his lips he made his escape back to the tents.

For a little there was confusion, all the contestants being so interested in discussing the rector's throw that the contests could not go on. Then, the judges got things running again. Seth kept on striving, doggedly, in quest of experience rather than of fame; and acquired many new "wrinkles" in his jumping. At last he chanced to notice Sadie Babcock, — now twenty, and very much the young lady, — standing near and watching him. Her vivid, dark face and provocative eyes vouchsafed him a look of unmistakable approval, and under the stimulus of it he outdid himself, winning the hop-step-and-jump over the redoubtable young Palmer. She saw his triumph, and smiled upon him again. But when he was free to go and speak to her, she had vanished. Where she had been he found instead an old farmer, in a gray homespun shirt, with a coarse country-straw hat surmounting his fringe of white hair, and a short black clay pipe between his teeth. He beamed approvingly on Seth, and Seth smiled back upon him in a friendly way.

"You done foine!" said the old farmer, removing the short black pipe from his mouth. "They tell me your name's Seth Warden!"

"Yes, that's my name!" assented Seth, pleasantly.

"Luelly Warden's boy?" inquired the old man.

"The same!" said Seth, stiffening with suspicion, as had become his wont at the least mention of his mother's name.

The old man's face became reminiscent.

"Many's the time I've joggled her on my knee," said he. "Her father's father an' me, we was great friends,— when I lived out Frosty Hollow way. I hain't seed her since she was jest a long-legged slip, but I always said as how she were the makin's of a mighty foine woman, said I! An' she's got a mighty foine boy. But ye don't favour *her* none, my lad!" And the old man scrutinized his face critically.

Seth was feeling nervous. His sensitiveness was always on guard for a slight, and this subject was bristling with perils. But the old man was kind, and obviously well-meaning. Seth could not take offence.

"I wish I did look more like mother!" said he, simply.

"Ye might be proud to!" assented the old man. "But yer father's a handsome un, too. Queer, now! Ye don't look a mite like him, neether. Not a mite!"

Seth got red, drew himself up, and looked about for some escape. He could have run away, of course, without rudeness; but the subject held him balefully.

"But there ain't no mistakin' whose son ye be!" went on the old man, musingly. "Let 'em say what they like, the lyin' cats! Lord 'a' mercy, what tongues they got, some o' them backbitin' women! Ye're Jim Calder's son, an' the livin' photygraf of Jim's grandfather, who was jest sech another as you be, in his day."

Seth could not stand another word. That phrase, "Let them say what they like," rang in his brain. It revealed to him another phase of the obloquy under which his mother had been writhing all these years. A hate of his father, that was almost madness, suddenly tore at his heart.

"Excuse me!" he cried, desperately. "I must run! I'm in the next event." But instead of going into the next event, which was merely that farce-comedy called a "potato-race," he ran on down to the shore and plunged his throbbing head into the chill of the water. After sopping his face and eyes for a good ten minutes, he was able to go back and enter for the wrestling, wherein the violence of the effort served as an outlet to his emotion. When he had been thrown twice, — but only after a long, savage, uncompromising struggle, — by a wiry little seaman, from Sackville, named Josh Harper, he felt once more his own master, and resolutely dismissed the black subject from his mind, for the time. But he knew in the back of his brain that one more damning count had been added to the score which he held for settlement. He swore to himself that the day should come when he would see it paid. Then he hurried away to look for his mother. He would not let any dark mood of his overcloud so rare a thing as this her holiday.

CHAPTER XXVII.

INSULT

AMONG the tents Seth looked in vain for his mother. He found, however, Sadie Babcock, radiating brightness among the indeterminate crowd. There was a man with her, of whom Seth was vaguely conscious; but Sadie threw him away, as it were, — so carelessly was it done, — and came forward to greet Seth and congratulate him on his prowess. Sadie had been away in the "States" for a year, and had not expected to find the plucky little boy whom she had half-despised and half-admired so soon grown up into a handsome and powerful young man. Her year away from home had broadened her appreciations, and she perceived in the boy a kind of distinction which made him better worth her interest than any of the ardent but somewhat uncouth swains who were her regular admirers. As for the irregularity of his birth, she was now inclined to laugh at her old censoriousness. She felt that that disadvantage was more than counterbalanced by the intimacy of his relationship with the parsonage folk. Being home only for a few weeks' visit, she decided that to play a little with this grave, handsome, fearless boy would not only amuse her, but be, at the same time, a great and excellent education for him. Now, taking him frankly by the arm, as "old schoolmates, you know, Seth," she led him off down the field again toward the other shore of the pond, where there stood a few scattered benches overlooking the deep water.

Immensely flattered, and thrilling strangely under the spell of Sadie's bewildering eyes, Seth was a willing captive. He did not forget, however, to keep a keen lookout for his mother; and seeing his eyes wander, Sadie was piqued.

"Whom are you looking for?" she demanded, imperiously. "Is there any one you'd rather see than me?" And she flashed her full battery upon him.

The tribute the boy's eyes paid her in return was sufficient, even for her. But his words were more qualified.

"Yes, one, Sadie!" he answered, with a little teasing laugh. "But only one," he hastened to add. "I'm looking for mother. I want to be sure she's having a real good time!"

"That's dear of you, Seth," responded Sadie, with feminine wisdom. "You've got such a beautiful mother, I don't wonder you want to take care of her. I never saw such hair. Women in the States would give fortunes for hair like that. An' her eyes, — did you ever see such blue? An' her girlish figure. She doesn't look much older than you, Seth, I declare!"

"When I was a little mite of a boy," said the delighted Seth, "an' you a sassy little girl with your nose in the air an' always looking out for a chance to snub me, — even then I knew enough to think that, next to mother, you were the prettiest thing in the world. But I didn't *like* you much then, Sadie!"

"I was an impertinent little fool then, Seth," said Sadie, dropping her eyes with a fascinating show of penitence. Then, lifting them again immediately, she gave a pretty cry of delight.

"Oh, *there* she is! There is your mother, away down by the shore, sitting on the green bench. She's all right. That's the rector with her, and Mrs. Goodridge. So, you see, you don't *have to* leave *me,* just yet, — if you don't want to, Seth!"

Seth did not want to; and the two seated themselves on a bench among some slim bushes, where they could see everything that went on around the shore, without being themselves conspicuous.

Hitherto the picnic had been an unqualified success, with no smallest touch of rowdyism to disturb its ordered gaiety. But about this time in the afternoon a rougher element began to drift in, from the quarries and the mines across the Memramcook River. On the grounds there was no drink sold stronger than lemon soda and spruce beer; but the quarrymen, equipped with a generous thirst, found opportunity to gratify it generously at the saloons of Dorchester Corner on their way down to the picnic. They were mostly decent fellows, when sober; but when about half "loaded" some of them were not to be depended on.

There was one big miner, in particular, who began to make himself unpopular as soon as he entered the picnic-grounds. He was not so much quarrelsome, as too aggressively familiar; and when his familiarities were not well received, he grew resentful. He was particularly anxious for feminine society, but by no means discriminating, or persuasive, in his efforts to gain it. And he reeked blatantly of bad gin.

About half an hour before Seth discovered his mother sitting with Mr. and Mrs. Goodridge, Luella, who was just then wandering about alone, had had an encounter with the overexuberant miner. Her striking good looks, her unusual flax-gold hair, and her graceful figure had caught his fancy at once. Sidling up to her in the shifting crowd, he had suddenly slipped a great arm about her waist, and stuttered close at her ear, with his fuming breath: "Come an' set on the grass with me over yonder, my daisy."

Speechless and scarlet with indignation, Luella gave him one look of withering scorn, then struck him in the face with her open hand, wrenched herself free, and walked off with her head up. The blow was a smart one. It left Dolan blinking and grinning sheepishly. One of his comrades, who had been near by, fell to jeering him over the sharpness of his rebuff, till presently his embarrassment gave place to rage.

"I'll git even with the pretty slut for that!" he swore. Then, clutching his jeering comrade by the arm, he led him away into the bushes, for another stiff drink out of the flask he carried in his pocket. From this fellow, who had worked a few weeks in the quarry below Wood Point, Dolan now acquired a rank perversion of Luella's story, which added fuel to his boorish wrath. He felt not only injured, but outraged. That he, Nick Dolan, should be rebuffed by any woman, was not an easy thing for him to believe; but to be flouted by a hussy like that, it was more than his drunken dignity was going to endure. He fortified himself with a drink or two more, then started off to find Luella again, vowing he would *teach her* to slap a decent man's face!

Trembling from the indignity she had suffered, — which she naturally attributed to the irregularity of her situation, — Luella had found Mrs. Goodridge, and carried her off to a secluded seat on the other side of the pond, to tell her about it. Mrs. Goodridge, however, had not taken the matter quite so seriously.

"It's outrageous, of course, child!" she said, soothingly. "Such people as that ought to be put right off the grounds. But what he did, Luella, was not personal to you. You must not think that. It meant nothing more than that he was drunk, and at the same time not *too* drunk to know the prettiest woman at the picnic when he saw her. You must not think anything more of it, child."

And with this consideration Luella wisely allowed herself to be consoled.

A few minutes later the rector came looking for Mrs. Goodridge, and seated himself beside her on the bench. When he heard what had happened to Luella he sprang up, hot with indignation, and was for having Dolan put off the grounds at once. Mrs. Goodridge, however, caught him by the coat and emphatically refused to let him go. She hated "a fuss;" and she did not want attention called to the fact that it was Luella who had suffered the insult.

"What nonsense, George!" she exclaimed. "I wish you'd just stay here with us, and let well

Insult 291

enough alone. It's all over now, and the man has probably forgotten what he did. Why, I haven't seen *anything* of you, all this blessed day. Luella's none the worse. And really, it's her own fault, as I've been telling her, for looking so sweet as she does to-day. I wonder *all* the men haven't been trying to hug her."

The rector laughed, yielded, and sat down again. He had much to tell about the sports; but it was Seth's achievements that he talked about, not his own.

A little later, as Seth and Sadie Babcock, hand in hand, peered out from their seclusion, they noticed two rough-looking men come up the path by the pond, and stop at the seat where Mr. and Mrs. Goodridge and Luella were sitting.

The bank of the pond at this point was about eight feet high and very steep, with deep water close in shore. The path ran parallel to the water, within six or seven feet of the edge.

The rector observed the two men approaching, one of them, apparently, rather drunk; but not knowing Dolan by sight he did not give them a second thought. Mrs. Goodridge and Luella, facing partly the other way, did not notice them at all. The path was only wide enough for one, so Dolan came swaggering on ahead, his companion, who was merely out to see what might happen, following cautiously, three or four paces in the rear. He, for his part, was not drunk enough to be looking for trouble.

Stopping abruptly in front of the green bench, Dolan seized Luella by the arm and dragged her to her feet. As she looked up, amazed, and saw who it was, she gave a startled cry, which was echoed by Mrs. Goodridge. The rector was on his feet at the same instant.

"Hands off!" he ordered. The order was loud and sharp, like a gunshot; and its authority was so convincing that Dolan obeyed instinctively, on the instant, and released Luella's arm. Looking around, however, and perceiving that the order had come from a man very much smaller than himself, and in the peaceful garb of the Church, he snarled, "Garrrn! You go to hell!" and turned his attention again to Luella.

"So ye think ye kin slap my face, like a decent woman, eh?" he stormed, clutching her arm again, half-amorous, half-angry. "Ye little tow-headed slut! I'll — "

But the sentence ended inarticulately. The rector's fist shot forth like a catapult, caught the ruffian square in the right eye, and sent him staggering half-way to the edge of the bank. Then the rector's left hand caught him in the throat of his collar, swinging him around; the right gripped him by the waist-band; and in a second he was hurled headlong out into the pond.

His companion ran up, aghast.

"He can't swim, sir. Nick can't swim a stroke, an' no more kin I!" he cried.

It was plain he spoke the truth, from the aimless fashion in which the big miner was beating the water.

"Can't swim!" exclaimed the rector, in a tone of angry impatience. "What a confounded nuisance!" But even as he spoke he was flinging off his long coat and kicking off his low summer shoes. The next moment, forgetting his broad hat, he had plunged in, and was circling warily around the wildly clutching Dolan. Excited, but not alarmed (such was their confidence in the rector's ability to do what he started out to do), Mrs. Goodridge and Luella had rushed to the edge of the bank.

"Look out he doesn't grab you, George," cautioned Mrs. Goodridge.

The next moment the rector saw his chance. With his left hand he seized Dolan by the back of the collar, with a grip so inflexible that the fellow could not turn. Pulling him backwards, the rector towed him slowly ashore, and jerked him roughly out upon the grass.

"There!" said the rector, brusquely. "Perhaps

that will do you good. Now clear out, and be thankful I don't have you locked up."

Thoroughly sobered, Dolan rose to his feet, shook himself, and looked at his conqueror with unbounded respect.

"Jiminy, parson!" he exclaimed, his oath modulated to his idea of what would suit the cloth. "But ye're a hot one! I ax yer pardon, I do, — an' I ax the young lady's pardon!"

Then turning fiercely on his companion, he roared, "Jeph, ye fool, what're ye gawkin' at? Git a pole, quick, an' fish out that there hat fer his Reverence, er I'll lick the hide offen ye."

He glared at Jeph till the latter hurried off to do his bidding. Then he picked up his own hat, — which had flown off when the rector struck him, — made a sweeping bow with it to the ladies, and strode off as steadily as if he had not been drunk for a week.

Meanwhile Seth and Sadie had arrived, exultant but solicitous; and the crowds were hurrying up from all over the field.

"What was it all about, mother?" asked Seth, in a low voice. "I saw him grab your arm. Did he hurt you?"

Luella's horror at the thought of Seth learning just what had been said to her, and understanding all that it implied, steadied her shaken nerves like a plunge into ice-water. With a masterly self-control she smiled upon him as if it was all a casual matter. But to save her the embarrassment of an explanation, Mrs. Goodridge intervened.

"He was drunk, and insulted your mother grossly," she said, with a tranquil face. "So, of course, Mr. Goodridge had to thrash him, or do something; and it was kinder just to throw him into the pond. Mr. Goodridge thought, of course, he could swim."

"The man was *very* drunk, or he would never have said it!" explained the rector, rather blunderingly, as he squeezed the water out of his clothes. "The ducking sobered him; and when he's sober he seems to be a decent enough fellow. He was penitent, and apologized to your mother very nicely — didn't he, Luella? I must look that man up. — Oh, thank you! I'm sorry to have given you so much trouble. Thank you very much!" And he smilingly accepted the dripping hat which the man called "Jeph" had fished out of the pond for him. "By the way," he continued, holding out his hand to the miner, "I wish you'd bring that big friend of yours over to Dorchester church next Sunday morning. I'd like to see you both after service. He seems a manly chap. Tell him I like a man that's not ashamed to say he's sorry, when he's done wrong."

The little party was now surrounded by an eager and gaping crowd; and Jeph was embarrassed.

"Yes, sir," he answered, bowing two or three times. "I reckon as how it'll be Nick as'll bring me, sir, 'stead o' me bringin' him. He's never met a man afore as could handle him like you done; an' he'll be thinkin' as how you're a mighty fine parson."

"Well," said the rector, "tell him I'll be very glad to see him, — and you, too."

Whereupon, feeling himself dismissed, Jeph retired with an air of great relief.

"Now, George," said Mrs. Goodridge, with decision, to divert attention from the cause of the disturbance, "you must go right up to Judge Harrington's and get some dry clothes on. You'll catch your death of cold."

"Nonsense, dear! I'll not do anything of the sort," replied the rector. "What do you think I'd look like in the Judge's clothes? I'll be dry as a bone in no time. Why, I wasn't in the water long, anyway. Now I must run off. There are some people here I want to speak to."

"Of course, George, you *will* have your own way," retorted Mrs. Goodridge, with some warmth, as the rector made off through the crowd. "Don't blame me if you're sick to-morrow!" But as he was already out of ear-shot these last words seemed rather to be directed at Luella.

"Isn't he *awful* hard to take care of?" exclaimed Luella, smiling sympathetically, while she clung, rather tremulously, to Seth's arm. Then Sadie Babcock, with a tact which Luella gratefully recognized, came to the rescue with a vivacious, highly picturesque account of the rector's achievement in putting the stone, and the tension was gradually relieved.

CHAPTER XXVIII.

SETH GOES TO SEA

SETH needed no telling, in order to understand the nature of the insult to his mother, which Mr. Goodridge had so swiftly chastised. He asked no questions about it; but all the more, for this silence, it burned within him. At the moment when the thing happened his boyish heart had been melting rapidly under the magic warmth of Sadie's wiles. Now, however, the girl's innocent spell was broken. He knew that she would never be able to make him forget the one grim purpose to which he had devoted himself. He liked her. His eyes might be intoxicated by her wild beauty. His blood might thrill to her caressing touch. He might seek her companionship, — but it would be primarily that she might make his days pass more quickly. There could be but one prime object in his life, — to avenge his mother's wrongs. All else was secondary and incidental. This attitude made him doubly interesting to Sadie, who was piqued into exercising all her lively charms upon him. But when she went back to " the States " again, in September, she had to acknowledge to herself that the boy was the victor, — that he had held a secret citadel in his heart against her, so securely that she had never been able even to guess what was in it. She had planned to amuse herself by making a boy fall in love with her. But she went away with the chagrin of realizing that it was she, for all her twenty years and worldly wisdom, whose heart had been most troubled. She had been at pains to conciliate Luella, who had proved easily — perhaps amusedly — gracious; and with a little touch of self-scorn she yielded, just before leaving, to the sentimental impulse to send Luella a basket of flowers, with a farewell note. Secure in an intuition that Seth was not in any grave danger of heart-break, Luella acknowledged the tribute with a serene complacency; and Sadie went away full of thoughts — which she knew to be foolish — of the net she would weave around Seth when the next summer should bring her again to the banks of Tantramar.

The next summer, however, did not bring her to the green plains of Tantramar, but kept her languishing, instead, in the high, white wards of a New England hospital. And when again her homesick eyes beheld the yellow foam and tumult of the "Bito," Seth was just about sailing on his first voyage. She could do nothing more than see him for greeting and farewell, and flash upon him the picture of a vivid, piquing face and dark eyes grown wistful, which she hoped he might bear with him in his memory.

It was on his sixteenth birthday, that Seth confided to his mother his intention of going to sea. Luella was bitterly disappointed. She had been cherishing an ardent hope that he would go to the academy at Sackville, attend college, either there, at Mount Allison University, or at the University of New Brunswick at Fredericton, and take up one of the learned professions. She had been saving carefully from her little income all these sixteen years, with a view to giving her boy an education. And because of Seth's reticence, she had been flattering herself that he had escaped the call of the sea. She tried, passionately, and at last with tears, to dissuade him, never guessing that the lure which was in his blood by inheritance was the least of the forces which were compelling him. When, however, she found him inflexible, she dried her eyes and accepted the situation once and for all, with that scorn of all petty nagging which was part of her strength and charm. The point settled, Seth knew she would never keep fretting at him about it; and, boy though he was, he had seen enough of women folk, old and young, to appreciate his mother's rare distinction in that regard.

"Don't think I don't understand you, dearie," she said, at last, with a long sigh. "I know well enough it's inevitable as fate. It's in *my* blood, too, — so that even I long to roam a bit before I get too old to enjoy it. And God knows it's in your blood, still worse, for your father's fathers were roamers for generations back." Here she watched Seth's face closely, for this was the first time she had voluntarily referred to his father; but Seth gave no sign that she had said anything unusual.

"Yes, Muzz dear," he answered, "it's in my blood, an' it's got to come out. It breaks my heart to think of leaving you, — and to break up all the plans you had made for me. But those plans — it just chokes me to think of them. After I've had my fill of the sea, though, an' after I've seen the world a bit, it'll let go of me, likely. Look at Captain Barnes here, an' Jerry Smith, an' Jim-Ed Coxen, — they got their fill of it, an' see how they've settled down, so there's no better farmers in Westcock. You wouldn't think they'd ever been further than the Joggins, — yet they say Jim-Ed Coxen ran a hotel in Singapore for two years an' can talk Malay like a native."

Here Mrs. Bembridge — who throughout the whole conversation had been knitting on a new majenta sontag, and apparently paying no heed —

laid down her big wooden needles, hitched her chair nearer the stove, and broke in.

"Fancy yer ever thinkin', Luelly, that ye could keep that young hawk o' yourn from flyin', when his wings got strong! I knowed Tantramar'ld never hold him, — an' all New Brunswick'ld be a cage too narrer for his wings. We'll have to let him go, Sweetie, — tho' Lord, Lord, it'll be lonesome without him!" And she brusquely dashed off two big tears which were just starting down her nose.

Seth jumped up, ran around to her chair, and gave her a strenuous hug.

"But I'm not going yet, Granny!" said he deprecatingly. "And you bet, I'm not going for long, when I do go. I couldn't stop away long from you an' mother. An' besides, when I'm home I'm going to make long, long visits, studying, you know, for I want to get to be captain right away quick, while I'm still real young. Oh, I'm going to do a lot of things, Granny, as soon as I'm captain. But first thing I do, Muzz, when I've got my own ship, will be to take you all 'round the world. You *shall* go roaming — away beyond the tides of Tantramar!"

"And will you take Sadie Babcock, too?" asked Luella, with a teasing smile which disguised the seriousness of her inquiry.

"Oh, I'm not thinking any about Sadie!"

laughed Seth, without embarrassment. The question, however, did set him thinking of her. He pictured her dark radiance beside his mother's cool, fresh, Northern colouring, tranquil eyes of deep azure, and classic mould of face and head, which reminded him of pictures in the old copy of Lemprière's Classical Dictionary in the rector's library. The keen but admiring scrutiny which he was bestowing upon her features brought a little flush to Luella's face, and she demanded, laughingly:

"Well, if you're *not* thinking about Sadie, what is it you are thinking about your poor old mother, I'd like to know?"

For answer, Seth turned to Mrs. Bembridge.

"Granny," said he, "do you think any ship would be safe, with two such beauties aboard her as mother an' Sadie? We'd have to carry big guns, to keep off the pirates. No, Muzz, I guess you'd be just about all I could take proper care of!"

Thus it was settled that Seth was going to sea, — but not for another year. He left school, sent to St. John for the latest text-books in navigation, and buckled down to hard study. When he got into difficulties with problems yet too complex for his knowledge, he went confidently to the rector for enlightenment; and presently the rector was giving him a lesson once a week, helping him just as he had helped his father before him. The closeness of the parallel gave Luella a tightening of the heart, and was a matter of discreet comment at the parsonage. But neither Luella nor Mrs. Bembridge, neither the rector nor Mrs. Goodridge, nor Mary Dugan, allowed any hint of it to drop in Seth's hearing. They all felt that he might resent it. This reserve was difficult for no one but the rector, whose natural candour would have led him to speak of it at about every other lesson; for if he had found Jim Calder a ready pupil, he found Seth a still readier one, and felt continually prompted to tell him so. Late the following summer, when Seth was nearing eighteen, he sailed on his first voyage. It was a comparatively short one, on a 200-ton brig called the *Dolphin*. The *Dolphin* was bound for the West Indies and Guiana, and in December she got back to St. John with a cargo of molasses, rum, and mahogany. Seth was home in Westcock in time for Christmas, his face deeply bronzed, his tall frame considerably filled out. All through the stormy Tantramar winter, when the roads were deep with drifts, and the scattered houses isles of warmth and life in the dead, bright wilderness of snow, he stayed at home, studying, brooding, tramping the muffled woods on his snow-shoes. He was restless; and with a pang Luella told herself that the lure of the sea had laid fast hold upon him. In this she misunderstood him, however. On the sea, in night watches, and when the winds raved in the ropes, he had seemed to come nearer to discovering his father, and his long-cherished dream of vengeance had grown real. It had become a living lust. He felt that he had now actually set his hand to the deadly task to which, under all his boyish plays and interests, he had been dedicated since that day in the fir pasture. From now on, he told himself, there was to be no halting, no going back. Not until he had secured a berth on a Dorchester ship, of Hickman's, which was loading deals in St. John for the long voyage round the Horn to Calcutta, could he be at ease in his heart. Then, for the fortnight that remained to him before leaving to join his ship at St. John, he suddenly brightened, and made a spell of summer sunshine for his mother and Mrs. Bembridge in the old gray house in the fields. He felt that now, at last, he was fairly on the way to his vengeance. This idea, curiously enough, instead of making him more sombre, gave him a sense as of relief from a crushing burden. He grew more boyish, more gaily care-free and natural than he had been for years. With something that seemed like a near promise of fulfilment, his deadly purpose ceased to urge him for awhile, and his heart was able to grasp a little rest. Those two weeks were a happy time for Luella, except for the pang it gave her to think that the prospect of getting away again was able to make him so glad. As for Mrs. Bembridge, she felt a touch of grievance at his frank gaiety. "Ef he's so *mighty* glad to git quit of us," she grumbled, strictly to herself, "he might have the decency not to shout it to all Westcock!"

The ship which carried Seth from St. John was a fine barque, named the *Silver Queen,* one of a fleet of *Queens,* — *Fundy Queen, Sackville Queen, Dorchester Queen, Hopewell Queen,* — built in Dorchester, registered in Dorchester, and owned by the Hickmans. Her captain was William Estabrooks, one of the Sackville Estabrookses, and a member of Mr. Goodridge's congregation. Seth had been strongly commended to him by the rector, so he kept an interested eye on the lad. Beyond this, however,— which might be of service to him in case of any unexpected need, — Seth had no favours, no privileges, not shared by all the other hands "before the mast." Nor did he want either favour or privilege. There was no particular hardship in faring as a mere "able-bodied seaman" on one of these well-built, well-found, well-sailed Bay of Fundy ships.

The voyage, from Seth's point of view, — since he already had visited the purple seas of the tropics, watched the palms wave against the turquoise sky, and thrilled to the rosy glory of the oleander blooms against white, sun-lit walls, — was comparatively uneventful. Off Hatteras they encountered a blow which taught Seth what a storm at sea was really like, and drove the *Silver Queen* about five days off her course. But Captain Estabrooks knew how to handle his ship, and the ship was staunch, and there was at no time any imminent peril. They touched at Barbados for fresh water. About ten degrees south of the equator they ran into a series of dead calms, wherein they would sizzle for a week at a time, with slatting sails and groaning spars, rolling like a log on an oily swell. Then, with the decks blistering their feet, the crew would curse in complicated, ingenious, hair-raising oaths, and express themselves ready to sell their immortal souls for a sniff of Fundy fog. In the struggle to round the Horn they were driven far south, buffeted by swooping gales, and staggering amid the mountainous leaden seas, roaring up from the Antarctic, for nearly six weeks. Then, at last, the great Cape relented and let them pass. With half a gale behind them, and a clear sky overhead, they ran up the Pacific coast and shaped their course across the vast for India. Thenceforward winds favoured them, and without delay or misadventure they raced free up the Bay of Bengal and made for the mouth of the Hoogly.

At Calcutta the *Silver Queen* got a cargo of tea,

spices, sandalwood, and Indian rugs and stuffs, for Liverpool. But here Seth parted company with her. He had shipped for the voyage only. Captain Estabrooks tried to induce him to sign again, saying that from Liverpool he would probably get freight for St. John. But this was no part of Seth's plan, and he was obdurate. He explained to the captain that he was resolved to see the East thoroughly before turning his face again toward Tantramar. He got his discharge, with a strong letter from the captain to help him in case of emergency, and disappeared into the seething, heated hive of humanity known as Calcutta.

Taking refuge in a Sailors' Home, where he could lodge and board for a modest sum, without being cheated or robbed, he devoted himself for a month to making inquiries for one Jim Calder. He tried all the sailors' boarding-houses, the quays, the ships themselves. As there had been no such person as Jim Calder, however, for about seventeen years, his inquiry was not fruitful of result. Had he asked for news of one Jim Callahan, on the other hand, his search would not have gone long unrewarded. There were many in Calcutta who knew the moody, reckless, popular Jim Callahan.

CHAPTER XXIX.

THE MATE OF THE MARY OF TECK

SATISFIED that it was useless to make further search in Calcutta, Seth decided to try Singapore next, and then work his way around to Shanghai, Hongkong, and Yokohama. He had no difficulty in finding a ship. Young, strong, alert, educated far beyond the standard of an " A. B.," he belonged to a class of sailors for whom the demand is always far in excess of the supply. Moreover, when it was known that he was a Canadian, the fact counted heavily for him, the sailors of Nova Scotia and New Brunswick having a reputation among shipmasters all over the world for steadiness and capability. Seth was in no hurry to sign papers. And his deliberation was most unexpectedly rewarded. A huge East-Indiaman, from Bristol, with a shrewd-eyed Scotchman for captain, and an inharmonious crew of Lascars and Finns, was in need of a quartermaster. Captain Duff was a reader of men, and cared more for what he read in their faces than in their papers. Meeting the clean-cut, intelligent-looking young sailor on the quays, he fell to talking with him. Seth's speech and manner were a testimonial of the highest class. A few searching questions revealed his schooling to Captain Duff's satisfaction. The tone of his discharge from the *Silver Queen* was guarantee, if the keen Scotchman had needed any, as to his character. In an amazingly short time Seth found himself signing papers as quartermaster, no less, on the crack ship *Mary of Teck*. Elated beyond measure, he could not wait till he got back to the Sailors' Home, but had to stop in at a little shop on the way, and write a line to his mother, telling her of his great good fortune.

Though the *Mary of Teck* was not to sail for two or three weeks, the new quartermaster's duties began at once, so Seth hastened to get his chest aboard that very day. He had never before been on board a sailing ship of the size of the *Mary of Teck*,—and for the moment he was so well satisfied that he almost forgot his dark purpose. His work, his success, his sense of achievement, filled his heart, and the joy of life downed the bitterness in his healthy young brain.

Except the captain, the first and second mates, the quartermaster, the ship's carpenter, and the bo'sun, every man on the *Mary of Teck* was a foreigner. This, of course, threw the English-speaking members of the ship's company more or less together. The bo'sun and the carpenter were both

The Mate of the Mary of Teck

from Biddeford, in Devon, — grizzled, weather-beaten old seamen, talking a dialect which to Seth seemed hardly English at all. They were heavy-built, silent men, endlessly smoking their short, black wooden pipes, very deferential in their manner toward their superiors,— of whom it delighted Seth to find himself one, — but curtly masterful with the crew. Seth felt that they were men to be depended on in any kind of a tight place, but not to be cultivated with profit in time of ease. They were both called Bill, — the bo'sun Bill Jenkins, and the carpenter Bill Lipsett. They camped together on the borderland, as it were, between the foreign crew and the quarter-deck.

The second mate, Mr. Tinker, was a ginger-haired, dapper, diligent little cockney, quick as a steel trap, who knew a little of everything and talked about it confidently all the time, strewing the deck with his H's. For all his noisy brag, however, his eye was steady and honest; and Seth concluded that his qualities in all probability surpassed his charms. Seth recalled how once, at school, Mandy Russ had attempted to teach him the language of flowers. All he remembered now was that the significance of mignonette, as Mandy had expounded it, was "your qualities surpass your charms." Whimsically enough, he now thought of Mr. Tinker as Mignonette; and ever afterward calling him by that name in his mind, he came to see a grotesque outward resemblance between the eminently unbashful man and the eminently modest flower.

But the man who particularly excited Seth's interest was the first mate, who seemed to have all the strong efficiency of the captain, with a charm that the shrewd, dogmatic Scotchman absolutely lacked. This man was either an American or a Canadian, — Seth could not make up his mind which. The crew seemed to like him no less than they feared him. The prompt and exact obedience which they rendered to the captain had something impersonal about it, as if they recognized in him a swift, efficient force, with whose workings they must keep up at any cost. They neither knew nor cared whether he smiled at them or not. But with the mate it was different. It was impossible to obey him more promptly than they obeyed Captain Duff; but they could obey him more enthusiastically, and they did. He managed to meet every man's eye, with a certain brusque understanding, demand, and good-will. Each member of the crew was to him an individual, not a machine; and he knew each one by his strange, foreign name. Seth felt that this man's authority was inherent, personal to himself, and not dependent upon his office.

He was a man not above middle stature, this first

mate of the *Mary of Teck*, — a man, say, five feet eight in height, slim-hipped, wide-shouldered, muscular-looking, yet lithe, and weighing perhaps a hundred and fifty pounds. His face was tanned to a deep, clear, ruddy brown, almost as dark as his short-curled, elastic-looking, ruddy-brown hair. This thick hair, and the thick, golden-brown moustache, were ever so lightly touched with gray; and Seth judged their owner to be about forty years old. His eyes were a clear greenish brown, turning to a cold gray when he was impatient or stern, filling with sympathetic light when he smiled, sinking into a darkness as of dream when he brooded, which he seemed prone to do when unoccupied. In repose, his mouth showed harsh, sorrowful lines drawn deeply about it, but it was almost boyish when he talked or laughed. Left to his own thoughts, his face would all at once take on ten years of age. Upon this man Seth could look down from his four inches' superiority of height; but in spirit he instinctively looked up to him.

The three weeks before the ship sailed were too busy for the formation of any intimacies. Seth felt himself in an atmosphere of friendliness, and was more genuinely at peace with himself than he had been at any time during the last nine years. When, in the quiet of his bunk, he found time to dwell upon his vengeance, his slumbering hate would flame up again with sickening intensity. He would turn, and toss, and break out in a nervous sweat, and clench his hands in the hot dark, till the weariness of his hard day's work would save him in spite of himself, and quiet him in the baths of sleep. But in the morning, rather to his surprise, he would wake contented, instead of hag-ridden by the curse upon his life. This state of mind he examined solicitously, viewing it with some distrust, until he satisfied himself that it was the nearing of his hour of vengeance that gave him his unlooked-for peace. His lean, dark face was grave, as always; but there was now a cheer in his smile which would have made it hard for any one to believe that his one reason for being here on the *Mary of Teck,* his one present purpose in life, indeed, was that of wiping out in blood the stain of his mother's dishonour.

When at last the *Mary of Teck* put out to sea once more, squaring away with a fair wind behind her and overrunning the long, white-crested seas, she passed a trim-built barquentine beating up for the Hoogly mouth. The mate was standing at the rail, watching her intently. Seth came up and stood beside him.

"Can you make her out yet, Mr. Callahan?" he asked, in a voice that thrilled with eagerness.

The mate's face was stern and haggard.

The Mate of the Mary of Teck

"Not — yet, — quite!" he answered, with seemingly some difficulty in his speech.

Seth looked at him curiously, but was too absorbed in the ship to think much about anything else.

"I'd know as far off as I could see her, she'd come from a Fundy shipyard!" he cried, enthusiastically. "Or else from the Miramichi, or Richibucto."

At this moment the stranger went about on the port tack, showing her stern, and the mate lifted his glasses.

"I guess you're right!" said he, in a very low voice, handing the glasses over to Seth.

"Why, if it ain't the old *G. G. Goodridge*. She hails from Sackville, New Brunswick," cried Seth, while a sudden pang of homesickness contracted his heart. A mist came into his eyes, and he did not see the piercing look which the mate turned upon him.

"Your name's Warden, ain't it?" he demanded, quickly. "May I ask, how do you spell it?"

Seth came to himself at once, under this need of protecting himself against possible inquiry about his parentage. Instinct and preparation both served him.

"W-*a*-r-d-e-n!" he answered, easily. "There's quite a family of us, up Tidnish way, where I come from. It's quite a drive, down from Tidnish, but I used to get in to Sackville pretty often. I tell you, Mr. Callahan, it made me kind of homesick, to see that there ship, so unexpectedly."

"Yes, I should think, — I should think it might, — homesick's no name for it!" replied the mate, repossessing himself of the glasses and fixing his gaze intently on the retreating vessel. His interest was so absorbing that Seth, even through his own absorption, could not but notice it. Seth was not at all given to asking questions, because, in addition to his native reticence, he had such a dread of having questions put to him. Now, however, he yielded to a sudden craving for sympathy.

"Have *you* ever been in those parts, Mr. Callahan?" he asked.

The mate did not turn his head, or desist from watching the flight of the *G. G. Goodridge*. For a moment he made no reply. Then he said, slowly:

"Not in a — not in a lifetime, Mr. Warden. But I belong there. I was born at Minudie, not far from Amherst. An' my heart goes back to them windy, wide green marshes, and them copper-red flats, glistening in the sun as the tide goes out, and them great yellow tumbling tides. Seeing that there Sackville ship takes me back, so I can smell the smell of the hay an' the smell of the salt-flats, the way they used to mix together!"

"Oh, but it's a long ways off," cried Seth, his eyes brimming. And he held out a hand which the mate grasped warmly. "An' that there barquentine yonder," pursued the mate, "maybe you could tell me who she's named for! It ain't a common name, the name of Goodridge."

A flood of homesick enthusiasm rushed to Seth's lips, — but he checked it back, and resumed his grave composure.

"She's named for Parson Goodridge," he replied, "him that's rector of Sackville, an' Westcock, down by the Tantramar mouth. They say he's thought a lot of, down Sackville way."

"Oh, ay!" said the mate, with apparent indifference; and fell therewith into so deep a reverie that Seth moved away without disturbing it. He was torn by strong emotion. His heart went out to this man of his own country, almost of his own village. Had it only been possible for him to be frank, what a comfort it would have been to unloose his lonely heart to one who could so sympathize! What a delight unspeakable, to talk of Westcock, and the Tantramar, and the rector, freely and without misgiving! Any other man could have done so. But he, he was different. He had been set apart from his fellows, and cursed, by the man who had wronged his mother. As he brooded thus, and realized that even here, on the opposite side of the world and among strangers, he could not escape the blight upon his life, the hate which had been of late but smouldering burst into a new and fiercer flame.

CHAPTER XXX.

THE FIGHT IN THE DANCE - HALL

AFTER this conversation the first mate and Seth seemed to gravitate naturally toward each other whenever they were both at leisure. They did not talk any more of their native marshes and the yellow tides of Fundy, — Seth being shy of the subject, and Callahan seeming to have laid it away in the secret closets of his memory with the passing of the *G. G. Goodridge*. But the sympathy between them was such as apparently needed no expression beyond propinquity. They talked together on every other subject in life but those which touched their own lives most closely. And Seth, in particular, found it strengthening to seek the mate's companionship whenever a night of brooding on his vengeance had left him shaken in nerve. His hate had now so fierce a grip upon his spirit that he sometimes feared lest the black mood should obtrude itself upon his duties and impair his usefulness. When it threatened to tyrannize over him in his daily routine, he found that there was nothing like a talk with the mate to bring him back to a saner mood.

The voyage to Singapore was sweltering but uneventful, with winds light, but favouring. The *Mary of Teck* was to discharge only a portion of her cargo here, take in a small new consignment, and then continue around into the China Sea, to Hongkong. The plan of her voyage could not have been more adapted to Seth's quest if he had arranged it himself. There would be all the time he needed at Singapore.

The strange, seething vortex of races, called Singapore, caught Seth's imagination. It held in itself all the smells, colours, noises, mysterious suggestions of the East, heightened by sharp contrasts from the West. Yellow, and white, and brown, and black, European, Chinaman, Malay, Parsee, and negro, all strove here in trade and in intrigue, bluntly domineering, coldly shrewd, suavely insidious, according to their race and type, but all held back from each other's throats by the impartial and inflexible hand of England. For his curiosity, he wandered in the native Mohammedan bazaars, incense-perfumed Chinese shops, and quaint, lanterned, flowery tea-houses, with an occasional incursion into the prosperous European quarter to convince himself he was not walking in a dream. But most of his time was spent in the hotels and

The Fight in the Dance-hall

drinking-places frequented by the English-speaking seamen, — places kept usually by red, perspiring, methodical Germans, or else by lean, keen-eyed, adventurous Americans ready to turn their energy, on the slightest provocation, from running a bar to organizing a real estate boom in the suburbs, or getting up an expedition against some rich pirate stronghold among the southern islands. Besides these, however, he found a sprinkling of places managed by Italians, Greeks, Portuguese, or half-breeds, with here and there an English-looking "pub," presided over by some immutable Britisher who scorned to change his ideas of how a public-house should be run at any mere dictates of climate, custom, or expediency. His way was best, — had been proved so in Hammersmith. It was right that these foreigners should learn to like it.

In all these places Seth drank little, — just enough to buy the freedom of the company, — observed and listened much, and asked a discreet question now and then as occasion offered. But never a trace was uncovered of any one by the name of Jim Calder. With the officers of the *Mary of Teck,* of course, he gave no sign that he was looking for any one, that he was thinking of anything but his duties and his amusements. He had ever before his sensitive spirit the danger of exciting Mr. Callahan's curiosity, and so opening the way to a discovery of his maimed parentage, his distaff naming. He valued the mate's friendship so deeply that he had a morbid fear of anything that might happen to mar it. Moreover, he felt that if the mate had ever chanced to know Jim Calder (and the low hills of Minudie were in plain sight from Westcock), he would be likely to speak of him of his own accord. It never occurred to Seth to doubt that his father, however much of a scoundrel, must be a man of a personality not to be disregarded.

Boy though he was in years and in experience of life, Seth had unlimited reliance in his own resources, and in the course of his solitary explorations he continually went into places where an older or more prudent man would hardly have ventured alone. Partly this was his native courage and self-confidence, and partly it was a certain faith in his star. He believed that it was his destiny to take vengeance on his father. Till that fated task was done, nothing could happen to him. It had never been his custom to wear any weapons except his own effective fists. But here, in this roaring vortex of the Orient, he allowed himself to carry a handy Colts 32 in his hip pocket. His quiet, grave manner, his cool, unwavering eye, and his six-foot, sinewy stature were all, taken together, an excellent preventive of trouble.

The Fight in the Dance-hall

One night, when Seth was returning to the ship, oppressed by the long fruitlessness of his search, and with more than wonted hatred in his heart, his attention was caught by a sudden babel of shouts, and oaths, and women's screams from down a little side street. He ran that way at once. The noise came from the lighted doorway of a sort of beer-garden and dance-hall. Seth recognized the place as one where he had already made his profitless inquiries. As he ran up to the door the hubbub increased. It was evident that something serious was happening in there amid the lights and the curses. Seth darted in, swiftly but quietly, and tried to make out what was going on. The sudden light dazzled him, however. Before he knew it he was upon the fringes of a wildly excited crowd of foreign-looking men and gaudy women. He stopped and shaded his eyes, and took his bearings, having no fancy for leaping blind.

In his anxiety, — for what he heard told him that some one was fighting against heavy odds, — his blindness seemed to last minutes. In reality, it was not half a dozen seconds before his eyes cleared. Right ahead of him, about ten paces distant, his back to the wall, stood Callahan, making lightning-swift slashes and lunges with the steel-shod blackthorn which he always carried when ashore. At his feet, with pallid, unseeing face turned upward, lay the body of big Steffan, one of the sailors of the *Mary of Teck*. The mate stood over Steffan's body, defending it. His face was stained with blood. A few feet in front of him, in a widening pool of blood, lay a twitching black figure, stabbed through the throat by that steel-shod, darting weapon in the mate's hand. All this Seth's eyes took in at a flash; and also that Callahan was hard-pressed, with swarthy men that looked like natives assailing him from right and left at once, — his front being protected by that quivering figure on the floor. Every detail, and the meaning of it, stamped itself on Seth's brain in the smallest fraction of a second. The next instant he had torn the crowd apart violently, ploughed his way through, dropped the nearest assailant with a straight left-hander, like a bullet, back of the ear, and shot the next through the body. Before he had time to think, he found himself beside the mate, menacing the mob with his smoking Colts.

At the sound of the shot fell a silence, followed by a restrained murmur as the throng widened away. The dark-faced assailants — Seth remembered afterward that some had rings in their ears — seemed to fade back and efface themselves.

"You got here just in time. They were six to one agin me, and the blood was getting into my

The Fight in the Dance-hall 325

eyes!" said Callahan, pleasantly, wiping his eyes with his handkerchief. Seth was excited, and did not trust himself to reply at once. That cheerful coolness of the mate's was what he longed to emulate.

Every one seemed to be trying to slip away from the place as fast as possible. The mate looked down at Steffan's body, deftly and gently felt at his heart, and half-rolled him over.

"Dead as a door-nail, poor devil!" he said. "I might's well have saved myself all this bother. But we've avenged him, eh? He'll sleep easy on that score!"

There was a tramp of heavy feet outside, in the street, and some of the crowd came scurrying back, seeking another exit.

"What's up now?" inquired Seth, his hand going to his hip pocket.

"Oh, the police! Let's git! Come this way!" and with the air of one who knew his way thoroughly he caught Seth's arm and led him back through a small door, and into a long, narrow, unlighted court.

"But, why?" demanded Seth, in amazement. "What 'ave we got to be afraid of the police for? Shouldn't we stop an' tell them all we can?"

"'Twouldn't be fair to the ship!" answered the mate, with decision, "We've got no time to waste in court. Let the police find out for themselves. They didn't help us any! Come on!"

As they ran, softly, Seth kept turning the matter over in his mind, and realized what it might mean to him to get arrested and have to await the slow, relentless course of a trial. Whether as a principal or a witness, the prospect was not attractive. He felt very ready to follow a leader like this, who could be at the same time both reckless and prudent, and whose wisdom seemed to balance with his strength and his nerve.

At the further end of the court Seth saw a door standing half-open, and apparently giving upon another street. But the mate had no concern for that half-open door. Before reaching it he turned to the left under a low brick arch, and into a stable. At the inner end of the stable a ladder led up to the loft. They ran up the ladder, pulled it up after them, carried it across the loft, and lowered it into another court. When they had descended they took down the ladder and laid it along the wall. Then the mate led through an open space filled with all kinds of rubbish and débris, and came to a gate in a high wall. This was bolted. He drew the bolt, motioned Seth out, and closed the gate behind them. Seth saw that they were in an alley which he remembered as branching off from

The Fight in the Dance-hall

the street leading down to their own pier. All was quiet around them.

"I don't think those lads will follow our trail," said Callahan, with a laugh.

"You seem to know this place pretty well," remarked Seth, with admiration. The flight had made him think he was playing a part from one of the romances which he had pored over in the rector's library.

"Oh, I'd ought to know it, God knows!" answered the mate, rather wearily, the cool, restrained excitement dying out of him.

"I'd give anything, Mr. Callahan," said Seth, as the two started in a leisurely way down the pier, the mate indifferently holding his handkerchief to a nasty slash on his head, — "I'd give most *anything,* to be able to handle a stick like you handled that blackthorn o' yours to-night. It was cutlass and rapier in one. I never saw anything so slick."

"The *point's* the thing. Give 'em the point, lad, every time, when you've got a crowd agin you, — an' aim at their faces. That scares them. But I may say, *you* weren't, so to speak, what you'd call anyways slow. You were as handy with your gun as you were with your fist, — and that's saying a heap, I can tell you. That was one thing scared those black hell-cats so. I tell you one thing, lad, there's few men I know, — an' I've met a lot of likely scrappers, — that would have sailed into a hostile crowd all alone, like you did this night. An' there's still fewer that could have made good, like you did. I owe you my life, that's sure. 'Tain't much good to *me*, — but it's something to the fellow that does it, to save a friend's life. Shake, lad!" And he held out his right hand, which Seth now, in the starlight, saw to be bleeding profusely from a long knife-cut. As he grasped it, and the blood went warm over his hand, he felt a strange thrill of pride, — of a pride that brought tears to his eyes, — in the cool, unfaltering bravery and masterful sufficiency of this man, his vagrant fellow countryman from the green uplands of Minudie.

"It's a proud day for me, Mr. Callahan," he said, steadying his voice with an effort, "to have stood by the side of a man like you, in a scrape like that. I'll be proud of that, just as long as I live."

And as he spoke, his high emotion suddenly went out under a rush of black, vengeful rage. This man might be his friend, his close, intimate comrade, but for the fact that he could never be frank with him. Here, too, the hand of the man who had stained his life from its beginning intervened again, branding him, denying him the kindly, human solace of a friend. The bastard must keep his heart hidden behind his mask.

CHAPTER XXXI.

THE BO'SUN'S BELAYING-PIN

THE mate's cuts were none of them dangerous, but the one on his head was enough to have laid up for weeks a man with less clean and vital blood, a constitution less resilient and indomitable. Under Captain Duff's rough-and-ready, but essentially rational doctoring, he was not laid up at all, and the wounds healed " by first intention," as the surgeons would have said. The investigations of the Singapore police traced the slain Steffan, of course, to the roll of the *Mary of Teck*. But there was absolutely nothing to suggest to them that the first mate or the quartermaster had been mixed up in the fatal quarrel. The trouble, it came out in the trial, had started over a girl, as usual, — a slim, gold-bangled brown creature, whom the big blue-eyed Finn, Steffan, had taken away from the leader of a band of piratical Malay sailors. The leader was dead, of Seth's bullet. Another of the band was dead, of Callahan's thrust in the throat. Of the rest of the band the police caught four, — and of these two were hanged. The crew of the *Mary of Teck* were well content, holding that Steffan himself could hardly have asked for an ampler revenge. But not a soul, save the captain and the second mate, had a suspicion that Mr. Callahan and the quartermaster knew anything of the matter. The captain, who himself liked a fight well enough when it did not interfere with business, appreciated the good turn they had done him in dodging the police. And little Tinker was consumed with admiring envy because he had not had the luck to be in the scrap with them.

A few days later the *Mary of Teck* was under way again, heading out into the treacherous China Sea.

Both Captain Duff and the first mate knew these waters well, — the shifting and perfidious currents, the thick-sewn reefs, and the wiles of the piratical inhabitants of the inhospitable shore, who were cunning in the use of lying lights to lure ships to their doom. As for the pirate junks which would sometimes swoop out from secret and inaccessible harbours, the *Mary of Teck* cared little for them. She had speed for flight when she wanted to flee. She was manned and armed for fight, in case she should want to give battle. At bow and astern she carried a serviceable little Maxim.

On this voyage, however, as it proved, there was need of neither flight nor fight for the *Mary of*

Teck. Her only mischance was a spell of calm, off the coast to northward of Sai-gun, in French Cochin China. Here, on account of a dangerous current setting toward a group of reefs and rocky islets, Captain Duff found it necessary to drop anchor and await a breeze. This was the kind of opportunity which Tonquinese pirates loved to take advantage of, — but, probably forewarned by their spies in Singapore that the big East-Indiaman had no reason to dread a battle, they never showed a sign of their existence. The far-off shores and headlands remained as peaceful in appearance as they were unalluring.

But the enforced idleness, on that blistering sea, became almost intolerable. Some of the Malays among the crew, grown weary of gambling, went back to their opium on the sly, in spite of all watchfulness. This was a vice in regard to which Captain Duff's discipline was rigid. He knew that unless it was kept down with an iron hand it was sure to interfere with the efficiency of some of the men just when they were most needed, — and you never could be sure which ones. Two men who were caught under the influence of the poppy siren, when it was time for them to do their trick at holystoning the deck, were put in irons down in the stifling hold, to sober and repent; and their plight made others more careful, if not altogether abstemious. One fellow, however, whose indulgence was not opium but the deadlier Indian hemp, and who, through cunning and constitution combined, had been tampering with it for two or three days without outward betrayal of its effects, went suddenly mad in the heat. Without warning, he sprang upon his nearest comrade and stabbed him behind the bare, brown shoulder, right through to the heart. Then, with a screech, he set out to run amuck down the deck, slashing this way and that with the bloody knife.

That screeching yell, with the uproar that followed it, need no explaining to the captain and the mates, who knew their East. They rushed forward. Seth, on the other hand, was amazed and startled. He was engrossed in writing a letter to his mother, under a bit of awning near the starboard rail, hidden from view by a pile of teak timbers of which the ship carried a partial deckload. As he jumped to his feet one of the Lascars fled by, his black eyes starting from his head, his face blanched to a dirty pallor. Almost on his heels bounded the madman with the bloody knife.

That was something Seth understood. He darted forth to hurl himself upon the maniac's back. At the same instant, however, the English bo'sun, Bill Jenkins, who was readier with his hands than with his heels, hurled a heavy belaying-pin. At this game Bill Jenkins was unerring. The belaying-pin would have caught the madman full in the back of the neck, — had not Seth at that moment intervened. Fortunately for him, he was not in the exact line of the hurtling missile. It struck him a glancing but stunning blow, on the side of the head just over the ear, where the skull was substantial. The force of the blow joined with that of his own momentum, and, plunging onward as he lost consciousness, he pitched head foremost over the rail. In the same moment, Mr. Tinker's revolver rang out. The madman went down sprawling and kicking, shot through the loins.

As Seth pitched overboard, the boatswain, who could not swim, gave a yell of consternation, and rushed to lower away a boat. The first mate, however, who had seen the accident, dropped his revolver, sprang to the rail, and without hesitation dived in. Seth, being unconscious, had sunk. But the mate was like a seal in the water; and the water was clear. Slowly, waveringly, the dark form sank through the deepening green as the momentum of the fall spent itself. But the mate's clean dive carried him deep and swift. He caught the body, turned, and struck out for the surface, emerging about twenty paces from the ship's side. The moment he appeared he shouted for help, and began thrashing the water violently with his free arm to scare off any sharks that might be about. A few seconds more and the boat splashed down, and shot toward them; and he and his unconscious burden were hurriedly hauled in.

"Be he aloive, sir?" appealed the boatswain, with anxious countenance.

The mate was feeling for Seth's heart. A look of infinite relief passed over his face, and he smiled whimsically.

"I guess he'll come round all right, Bill. It takes more'n a belayin'-pin an' a few sharks to kill one of these Canadians."

But it was not till he had been laid on deck under an awning, and stripped, and ammonia put to his nose, and ice put on his head, that Seth came to. As he opened his eyes he met the mate's eyes, bending over him; and the look of unfathomable tenderness, of half-wistful love, which he encountered there, sank into his heart. Instinctively, and with a smile, he grasped the mate's hand, and sat up.

"He'll be sound as a bell in no time!" said the captain, in a tone of satisfaction.

"What's happened?" demanded Seth, amazed to find himself stripped. Then he clapped his hand to his aching head.

"Oh, I remember! Something hit me an awful clip! Did you git that lunatic with the knife?"

The Bo'sun's Belaying-pin 335

"I jolly well plugged *him!*" cried Mr. Tinker, cheerfully.

"It was Bill here did *you* up!" said the mate, indicating the bo'sun's troubled countenance. "But I don't think it was you he was trying to hit with that handy belayin'-pin of his. He's going to practise with it a bit, an' try an' not hit the wrong man on the head the next time!"

"Knocked you clean overboard," explained the captain. "And Mr. Callahan had to go over after you and keep the sharks shooed off till we could get the boat lowered."

Seth's eyes met Callahan's again, with a look of ardour that was more than gratitude; and the mate said:

"That was nothing! It was as easy as falling off a log. But I'm powerful glad it was me that had the chance to do it for you, lad, instead of the captain here, or Mr. Tinker, who could have done the same thing just as well as me. It's sort o' tit for tat between us now!"

Seth struggled resolutely to his feet, but kept the towel of crushed ice held closely to his head.

"That ice feels mighty good," he declared. "But I reckon I'll get some clothes on now. A bag of ice ain't enough for a man to wear, even in a climate like this. What's become of that lunatic that made all the trouble?"

"Oh," said the captain, "when his friends whom he tried to murder saw that the sharks had been cheated out of your carcass, they threw him over to them, just for good luck. But he wasn't taking notice any more, so it didn't matter. There was no fancy funeral coming to him, anyhow!"

CHAPTER XXXII.

THE RECTOR AND TIM LARSEN

THAT night, under the vivid tropic stars, Seth lay in his hammock on deck, his throbbing head still bound with an ice-pack, while the captain and the mate lounged close by in their long, cool, reclining-chairs of cane, smoking, and sipping shingaree. It was the second mate's watch; but in the starlit calm, with the glass showing "Steady, Fair," Mr. Tinker was allowing himself some latitude. The talk between Captain Duff and Mr. Callahan was interesting, and from time to time he would turn up and join in.

The captain, when a boy, had been coldly and mercilessly cheated out of a little inheritance, by an executor-trustee whose name carried before it the title of "Reverend." Being a man of somewhat narrow and unvarying mental process, he had it settled firmly in his mind that priests and parsons in general were "no good." With his dry, caustic Scotch wit, he told pungent stories against them, all aiming to show that when they were sincere they were milksops, and when they were strong they were self-seeking hypocrites. Seth listened with growing impatience. He had known but two clergymen. One of these two was his adored rector, whom he felt to be no less " good," in the deepest spiritual sense, than he was manly and strong in a worldly sense. The other, Mr. Sawyer, the Baptist minister, all Westcock and Wood Point knew for an honest, sincere, kindly man, for whose presence the community was the better. His head throbbed too painfully to let him join issue with the dogmatical captain, who had all a Scotchman's skill in dialectic. He would have flamed out presently, however, in defence of the cloth, had not Callahan at length stepped into the breach.

The mate, in argument, was persuasive where the captain was assertive. He began by a strategic undermining of his opponent's sweeping universal. He recited cases, which the captain would try ingeniously to discredit. When the second mate joined in, it was to support the captain, with coarse but witty anecdote or comment. Warmed up by the argument, the mate at length became insistent, demanding credence on the ground of his own, direct, personal observation. He set himself to paint, in detail, with lavish illustration and convincing fervour, a parish priest whose life in every way gave the lie to the captain's strictures upon his calling. The picture he presented was that of one who was a man among men, tireless in his work and in his sympathies, tolerant and charitable in his judgments, yet fearless in rebuke, forgetful of self, unfailing in tenderness; very human, too, in his sensitive, quick temper, his hearty mirth, his frank pride in his muscular strength, which was phenomenal, and his boyish readiness to take the law into his own hands when any question of a woman's honour or the protection of the weak was at stake. As the picture grew, Seth began to wonder where in all the world the mate could have met a clergyman so amazingly like the rector. While he was mulling this idea over in his troubled brain, the captain and Mr. Tinker were reluctantly confessing that this particular parson, at all events, must be not only a parson but a gentleman. Then, to clinch the matter in the minds of these scoffers, he launched into a picturesque story of this parson's dauntless courage, and of his ascendency over the roughest and most dangerous characters that came within reach of his influence.

"This parson I'm telling you about," went on the mate, with a kind of admiring passion in his voice, "which I want you to know was more of a man than any of us, and could do up any one of us on this ship, easy, and was at the same time tender as a mother, and simple, some ways, as a child, — he lived, with his wife and the servant-girl, in a lonely kind of a house a good ways off into the country. One winter night he got home from a long journey. He'd been away a week, and got back a couple of days sooner than he expected.

"Now, as it happened, in a neighbouring parish there was miners, and a mighty rough, big-limbed, brawling lot of chaps the miners were, always lookin' for trouble, an' makin' it when they couldn't find it. And the biggest, strongest, quarrelsomest bully of the whole crowd was big Tim Larsen, who was part Swede, an' part Irish, an' the rest plain s-n of a-b-tch. Just about the time the parson was gettin' home Tim gets on a tearin' spree an' comes over to parson's parish, — which we'll call Kouchibouguac, — an' begins kickin' up trouble at the little tavern down in the village. He licks everybody that'll fight him, an' some that try not to, an' then, to make more fun, he takes 'em on by twos an' threes; an' as some of the Wes— Kouchibouguac boys was pretty husky lads, he gets pretty well cut up before he gets enough licked to satisfy him. As he has plenty of cash in his pockets, he then squares himself with the barkeep an' the rest o' the boys by buying the drinks several times round, an' spite of black eyes and broken teeth everybody's having a fine time.

"'I kin lick any two men to oncet, any two men

The Rector and Tim Larsen 341

in this 'ere county!' announced Tim, in the course of the enlightening conversation.

"'Humph,' says one chap, with both his eyes blacked up, 'there's one man right here in Kouchibouguac you *can't* lick!'

"'Show 'im to me!' shouts Tim.

"'I mean the parson,' says the other. 'We got a little parson here as kin do you up, Tim Larsen, with one hand, an' not half-try!'

"'Show 'im to me!' yells Tim again. 'I've hearn tell o' yer parson. I'll make his mouth sich a quare shape he won't be preachin' to yez for a month. Where's he live?' An' with that he starts for the door without his cap.

"'I don't know as he's home,' explains the barkeep. 'He's been away these three or four days back.'

"'I don't keer about *that!*' shouts Tim, very wrathy. 'Jest tell me where he lives. 'F he ain't to home, I'll wait for 'im.'

"So the boys directed Big Tim, drunk as he was an' murdering mad, to the parsonage. They didn't mean any harm by it at all, they were that drunk. But they made sure the parson was home all right; and they wanted Tim to run into the biggest licking he'd ever got in his life. That's the kind of confidence they had in the parson, — that though they all loved him, loved every hair of his head, they thought it was all right to run this drunken giant up against him in the middle of a winter's night. It never occurred to them that it might give the parson any inconvenience to have to get up and lick Big Tim. They likely thought he'd be writing on his sermon, — this being Saturday night, — and Tim would just do to warm up his ideas a bit.

"Well, the parson wasn't writing on his sermon. He'd gone to bed, and just got to sleep, pretty tired, — when he was awakened by a tremendous battering on the back door, down-stairs. He sat up.

"'What *can* that be?' he inquired.

"'Why, it's somebody trying to break in the back door with an axe,' said his wife. 'I wonder why they didn't ring!'

"The parson jumped out of bed, pretty mad at being disturbed. He lit the lamp, and was marching off in his nightshirt, and bare feet, to see about it, when there was a crash, and they heard the back door come down slam.

"'*George*,' cried his wife, indignantly, 'put on your slippers and dressing-gown. You'll catch your death of cold that way!'

"The parson did put on his slippers; but he hadn't any time to bother about dressing-gowns. In his short white nightshirt, and carrying the lamp, he hurried down-stairs.

"At this old parsonage, you must understand,

The Rector and Tim Larsen

there was an outer kitchen, used in summer, and an inner kitchen, used as a kitchen only in winter. It was the outer kitchen door that had been smashed in. Now, just as the parson opened the door leadin' from the hall to the inner kitchen, the door opposite was burst in with a crash, an' there before him stood Big Tim Larsen, his face all bloody, an' in his hands the axe which the parson used to chop wood with when the chore-boy came late.

"The parson was pretty mad. 'Put down that axe!' he ordered, his voice like bullets, an' the look in his eyes, under his high, white forehead, hittin' Big Tim's brain like a couple o' Mauser balls. The parson couldn't have *looked* very dignified, one would think, with his nightshirt flappin' about his bare legs; but he's the kind of a man that carries his dignity inside, so's it don't depend on his clothes. Any ways, it was enough for Big Tim. He stood the axe in the corner as quick as he could, an' felt for his cap to take it off respectfully.

"'What do you mean by breaking into my house that way?' demanded the parson, sternly, — but now there was something in his voice as if he was talkin' to a very bad child. Big Tim shifted his feet bashfully. Those eyes of the parson's were makin' him feel as if he was about two foot high.

"'Beg pardon, sir! But I didn't know you was to home!' he stammered.

"This being just the rottenest, damnedest excuse he could possibly have given, the parson saw it was certainly honest.

"'The next time you come to my house,' said he, severely, 'whether I'm home or not, you ring the bell, remember. You're very drunk, so I'll overlook it this time. Now you go and fix up that back door you've knocked down. It's letting enough cold in to freeze the whole house out.'

"Big Tim stood the door in place, ran the bolt, and piled some wood against it to keep it steady. On the inner door the lock had given way, so the hinges weren't broke. Very much ashamed of himself, he fumbled at the broken lock, then turned round, fished out two handfuls of money from his pants' pockets, and shyly shoved them at the parson as a kind of peace-offering.

"'No, thank you, my man!' says the parson, a little more gently. 'Put it back into your pockets, and go to the sink there and wash the blood off your face. You are a sight!'

"Tim felt of his face.

"'Bin fightin',"' he explained, apologetically.

"'So I should fancy,' says the parson, with a little bit of a quizzical smile.

"'Thank you fur yer kindness, parson,' says Big Tim, now mighty anxious to get away. 'But I don't like fur to go messin' up the sink. I'm goin'

The Rector and Tim Larsen   345

now, an' I'll git cleaned up down to the Corners!'

"'No, you're not going now!' said the parson, with a sweetness that was kind of sharp underneath. 'I don't let any man go from my door on a night like this. Moreover, I can't trust you away from me till you're sober. I can't tell what mischief you might get into before daylight, what harm you might do to yourself or others. Bring those buffalo robes, from the outer kitchen, and I'll spread them in here by the hall stove for you, and you can get a good sleep. What's your name?'

"'Tim Larsen, sir!' answered Tim, very nervous. 'But I couldn't think of puttin' ye to so much trouble, sir. I'll git a bed down to Billy Hicks's, sir.'

"'Not much, Tim! You don't see Hicks's again to-night!' responded the parson, that hard edge comin' on to his voice again. 'I've heard of you, and all the trouble you make for other people when you get on one of your sprees. You'll sleep right here the rest of the night. And after breakfast, when you are quite yourself again, and washed up so you'll look respectable, perhaps you'll feel like doing me a favour and signing the pledge, say for six months, on trial. But that, of course, you must decide for yourself. Only for the rest of the night you've got to be my guest. I didn't ask you to come, but having come, you've got to stay. Bring along those buffalos, now, and we'll make you comfortable.'

"There was nothing for Tim to do but do as he was told. He didn't like it a bit; but, somehow, he couldn't have said exactly why, he liked it better, by a long chalk, than getting into a disagreement with the parson about it. The parson kind of fixed him up in the buffalos, comfortable, as if he'd been a baby. Then, turning the keys in the front door and the door leading into the inner kitchen, he gave Tim a cheerful 'good night,' and carried the keys up-stairs with him.

"And there Tim laid, meek as a lamb, knowing the doors were locked, and the windows all double sashed, so he couldn't get out *that* way without bringing the parson down again. And he went to sleep, — and up at the head of the stairs the parson an' his wife slept as contented as you please, — and in the morning Tim was the soberest man he'd ever been. Breakfast, and lots of strong coffee, — which the parson, somehow, knew he needed, — steadied him up; and the parson's wife was as sweet as pie to him. An' then he wanted to sign the pledge for good an' all. But the parson wouldn't hear of it.

"'No, Tim,' said he, as if they were old friends, 'you don't want to push yourself too hard at first.

The Rector and Tim Larsen

A promise is a sacred thing, and you want to try an easy one first. If you give me your word of honour not to touch a drop of liquor for six months, I know you'll keep it. When the six months is up, we'll talk about another pledge, if you like.'

"Then Tim, well slicked and brushed up, and with a fur cap of the parson's on his head, went off, and told all about it, braggin' on the parson, and offering to lick anybody that thought the parson couldn't lick any man in the Province. For the six months he never tasted a drop. When the time was up he went on a spree just for cussedness; but when it was over he was kind of disgusted with himself. He went and told the parson, and said he was ready to take the pledge for any length of time. The parson looked at him hard a bit, then he held out his hand to him.

"'Tim,' says he, 'I think you're the sort of a man that's strong enough just to keep straight without any pledge at all. Some men are so weak, or drink has got such a hold on them, they *have to* have a solemn pledge, to lean on, as it were. But I want to see you, Tim, stand up four-square, all by yourself, and set an example to the rest of the boys, and just keep clear of the drink because it makes a beast of you, not because you've made a promise to me!'

"'Parson,' says Tim, 'I'll do it.' And from that day on, as I've heard, nobody could say they'd ever seen Big Tim the worse of liquor. Once in awhile, maybe, he'd take a drink, but never to hurt. From being the worst, he panned out one of the very best men in the mines, — and it was to the parson he owed it, there's no getting around that!"

When the mate came to an end, there was a moment's pause.

"You must acknowledge, Mr. Callahan," said the captain, cautiously, "that your friend is not only an exceptional parson, but a most exceptional man. It's plain we've come across two very different varieties of the species, you and I."

CHAPTER XXXIII.

SETH'S FATHER

As Seth lay in his hammock, now listening to the mate's voice, — which was music to his ears, — now hearing nothing for the pounding pains in his head, it suddenly reached his consciousness that the mate's story was a familiar one to him. Undoubtedly, the mate's parson was none other than his own rector. The story of Tim Larsen was an old and oft-told one in Westcock, — plainly it had reached around by the Isthmus to Minudie, in the days when Mr. Callahan was a boy there. But as the story went on, his attention was caught by the intimate little personal details of the rector's character, of the household, of the house. It was impossible that any one should know all these things by hearsay. This was no Minudie man, but a Westcock man, claiming the rector with the same loving enthusiasm with which he himself might have claimed him. This man had evidently lived in close touch with the rector. Then Seth's brain, already whirling and staggering before the impact of a truth which he did not yet acknowledge, began to recall the mate's strange emotions at the sight of the *G. G. Goodridge,* that day when they were just out from the Hoogly. He recalled the mate's haggard face, his first eager questions, — and then his utter silence on the subject of Tantramar and all connected therewith. "Why," thought Seth, "it's been him that's fought shy of it, all this time, just as much as me!" Then, on a sudden, with what seemed like a thunderclap in his brain, everything came clear to him. A faint groan burst from his lips, — which he turned to a cough. He caught hard at the edges of the hammock; and for a few moments the starlit sky, the masts, the deck, and the lounging figures before him, seemed to go round in a pulsing mist. This man, — whose voice still went on, — this man's name was not Jim Callahan at all. IT WAS JIM CALDER.

The truth came to him, when it did come, as an absolute certainty. It explained the fruitlessness of his search. In Calcutta, or in Singapore, he would have heard of Jim Callahan everywhere, as one of the best known seamen in the East, with every one wondering what the mystery was that hindered him having a ship of his own. In seeking for Jim Calder, he was seeking a lost and forgotten name.

When the story was done, Seth gathered his wits and his strength, got up out of his hammock, and started for the cabin.

"Anything I can do for you?" inquired both the captain and the mate, together.

"No, Sir, thank you, nothing! I'll be back in a minute!" he answered, — and as he spoke he could not help wondering that his voice — at that moment when his heart was cracking, and his soul raging in torment — should sound so natural, so easy, so cool.

Reaching his bunk, he threw himself down for a moment, unmindful of the stifling heat, striving to order his thoughts.

This man Callahan, then, — this was his father! This was the man who had dishonoured his mother. This was the man who had put a stigma on two lives. This was the man whom he had been planning and scheming, all these years, to kill like a dog on sight. And now, to add to the intolerable injuries which he had done him in the past, he had tricked him into admiration, — into love, he had almost said to himself, but that thought he repudiated in a blaze of hate. Well, *that* was past! It was hate now, and swift revenge. To Seth's chaotic, distraught brain it counted as less than nothing that the man, his father, had that day risked his life — faced a very hideous form of death — for him. All such considerations were eaten up in the cruel flame now scorching through brain and vein and nerve. Presently his madness concentrated itself to a purpose. He got out his revolver, examined it, slipped it into his hip pocket, and slowly returned to his hammock on the deck.

The mate had left for his own hammock. The captain ordered his slung near Seth's, imagining he felt a current of air there. Before he fell into it, he renewed the ice-pack on Seth's head, felt his pulse, grumbled, and gave him a bitter dose to ward off what he regarded as a threatened fever. The dose contained a strong opiate; and in spite of himself, with his hand resting on the weapon in his pocket, Seth fell into a heavy sleep which lasted till broad daylight. He awoke bewildered, with bloodshot eyes and a sense of some terrible, but inescapable business left too long undone.

He was not much more than well awake when he saw the mate approaching,—but not alone. The second mate, who had just been having himself sluiced down with the deck-hose, came with him, draped in a bath-sheet. Seth reluctantly removed his hand from his pocket, and answered their civil inquiries civilly enough, as he thought. But there was something in his eyes, and in his voice, which made the mate instantly solicitous. His eyes softened with anxious concern. He scrutinized Seth's face, felt his pulse, smiled at him tenderly, and went at once for the captain and the captain's medicine-chest.

Seth's Father

"Knows more than most doctors, he does!" said Mr. Tinker, with confidence, jerking his thumb admiringly toward Callahan's retreating form.

Seth looked at the assured little cockney with a sense of confused rage and something like a snarl on his lips.

"Feelin' pretty bad, aren't you?" said Tinker, sympathetically. "That belayin'-pin on your nut's given you a touch of fever, eh? You're lookin' a bit wild this mornin'. But Callahan'll fix you up all right, — him an' the captain. What the one don't know, t'other does." And Mr. Tinker, in his white toga, drifted off to get into his proper clothes.

With the pain still thumping in his head, with the bewilderment of the opiate, with the anguish of rage in his heart confused with another anguish which he had not yet differentiated or comprehended, Seth was indeed, as Mr. Tinker said he looked, "a bit wild." The suggestion caught him. Hitherto he had had but one thought, that of wiping out in blood the dishonour of his mother and of himself. He had not troubled to think of the penalty he would himself have to pay. He took it as a matter of course that he would hang for it; and in the grip of his black obsession he had not let himself think of the awful, lifelong misery he would himself be inflicting upon the mother whom he was trying to avenge. Now, however, it occurred to him that he ought to save himself, for his mother's sake. They thought him out of his head. He would let them think so. If he killed any one now, his delirium, not he, would bear the blame. He shrank, blind and warped though his brain was, — he shrank from the cowardliness of taking shelter behind his sickness. But, thinking of his mother's lonely sorrow, if she should lose him, he threw that scruple to the winds. He was going to punish her betrayer, at whatever cost. But, also, he was going to save himself for her, if he could.

At this point in his toilsome pondering, when every thought seemed like a thumping hammer in his brain, a new idea caught at him. What real *proof* had he that this man was Jim Calder? He was sure, of course, — but his assurance had nothing to depend on but intuition. Could he kill such a man as the mate, on the strength of an intuition? Did he not know himself to be half out of his head, with pain and hate and misery? Might not his very certainty be a figment of his delirium? When first this thought took hold upon him, he resented it, feverishly, because it seemed to deny him the release he craved, the release of immediate, irremediable action, and then — rest. But as soon as he had convinced himself that he was no longer capable of such action, without proofs more tangible than he possessed, then he clutched passionately at the hope that this man Callahan might, after all, not be his father. If only that might be, he thought, how he would love him, the tender comrade, the strong, indomitable friend!

In the semi-tranced condition to which he had wrought himself, Seth felt positive that he would find the proofs he sought, which would settle the matter one way or the other beyond possibility of doubt, in the mate's bunk or in his chest. This idea came to him with a certainty which, if he had been quite himself, would have seemed to him absurd. Now, however, he simply waited, in trembling eagerness, till the captain had brought him some medicine, which he swallowed without opening his eyes or taking the trouble to say thank you.

No sooner had the captain gone than Seth slipped from his hammock. For a moment he had to steady himself, and things turned black before his eyes. This dizziness passed at once, however; and he stole down to the cabin. He found it deserted, of course, every one being on deck for the sake of whatever air was to be had. It was the mate's watch, and Seth felt himself safe, for a few minutes at least, from all surveillance.

Seth went straight to Callahan's chest and flung it open. With the curious intuition which sometimes seems to serve those who are in an unnatural condition of nerves and brain, he plunged his hand down deep into the right front corner of the box, through garments of various kinds, till his fingers closed confidently on a small book. He pulled it forth. It was a worn and battered little Bible, bound in dark red leather. Seth felt, for an instant, afraid to open it. Shaking so that he could hardly control his fingers, he turned to the yellow fly-leaf. There he saw, in a handwriting that was dear and familiar, a somewhat faded inscription.

> *To James Ellison Calder*
> *on the Day of his Confirmation*
> *with the loving friendship of*
> *G. G. Goodridge.*

Westcock,
July 27th, 1871.

Seth dropped the worn little book back into the chest, closed the lid with a kind of anguished awe, and fled back upon deck. For an hour he lay motionless in his hammock, with his face covered so that no one might see it.

He had now no longer any shadow of hesitation. His purpose was so focussed and so fixed that he experienced a certain sense of relief. What he had to do seemed so inevitable that he no longer had to think at all, but only to wait. He had drawn up about him the folds of a brilliant silk shawl which he had bought for his mother in Calcutta. Under the shelter of this he kept his right hand in his trousers' pocket, gripping the butt of his revolver.

Presently he heard some one coming. He knew the steps. They set his heart turning over and over like a falling paper. It was the mate, coming to give him another dose of medicine. When he spoke, Seth looked up at him with a red-eyed, sullen stare, — in answer to which the mate but smiled the more gently.

"You must take this, lad," said he, "though I reckon you'll find it don't taste very good. It'll cool down the fever that's setting your blood afire."

His whole being centred upon his deadly purpose, Seth had no power or even thought to resist the administering of the medicine. He swallowed the dose obediently, but in dogged silence, giving the mate a look of strange, lurking menace, which the latter took for an impersonal flash of delirium. As the mate, with a little smile of understanding comradeship, turned away and started up the deck, Seth slowly drew the revolver from his pocket. The mate's straight back presented a fair target. Seth thought of his mother, of the misery and dishonour this man had wrought upon her life, of the ineffaceable stigma ruthlessly branded upon himself. His fevered face went white as death, his mouth set itself savagely, and he half-raised himself in the hammock. But even at that instant, in spite of himself, something seemed to take him in the throat. He saw again that look of tender, almost brooding love which he had surprised in the mate's eyes as they bent over him, on his return to consciousness. That look, in some inexplicable way, disarmed him, turning him weak and helpless. He stuck the revolver back into his pocket, trembling, and hid his face again with a corner of the bright shawl. To his amazement — for he did not realize how sick he was — he found his eyes overflowing.

For some time he lay, with his face covered, cursing and wondering at the incomprehensible weakness which had plucked him back from vengeance. He could not get rid of the memory of that look in the mate's eyes. Then another memory came up beside it, — of the high, gay, dauntless courage in the mate's face as he stood there under the dance-hall lanterns, fighting single-handed the ruffians who had murdered poor Steffan. He thought, too, of the confident joy which had sprung into the mate's eyes, at the sight of him darting to the rescue. He found himself, even, thrilling with pride, at the knowledge that this brave yet tender man, this incomparable and smiling fighter, was his father. When he realized this emotion in himself, rage, at himself as well as at the mate, almost overwhelmed him. Already half-hysterical, half-delirious, with his hurt, the drugs he had taken, and the mad warfare convulsing his heart, he with difficulty restrained himself from springing up and rushing to find the mate, and shooting him down before the eyes of all. But he thought of his mother, not only dishonoured, but then childless also. And with the thought of her, he steadied himself once more. She was his great love. It was not enough, he told himself, over and over again, that he should avenge her honour. He must try and save her happiness, by saving himself for her. And yet, even through the semi-insanity of the lust for revenge, which was now regaining its grip upon him, he realized that after killing this man, — his father, as he now kept calling him, — he would crave nothing so much as instant death for himself. With this realization an intense longing grasped him and shook him, an intolerable longing for the touch of the man's hand, the sound of his voice. He buried his head deeper under the shawl, and found himself weeping like a child, in his weakness.

Then he checked himself, stiffening up his whole body, in the violent recovery of his resolve. Setting his teeth till the ache in them seemed to numb the ache in his head, he gripped the butt of his revolver again, and waited.

In this tense stillness, with the confusion in his head mingling curiously with the confusion of sounds which now arose all over the ship as a light breeze began to ruffle the glassy water, he fell into a feverish sleep. Suddenly, he was awakened. His last thought, as he fell asleep, had been his vengeance. It was his first, his instant thought, now, as he awoke.

The mate's solicitous face was bending over him, in his hand a glass of medicine. Dashing the glass across the deck, Seth struck upward with his left fist, catching Callahan fair in the mouth, though at such close quarters that the blow had small force. At the same moment he jerked the revolver from his pocket. Before he could turn the muzzle up, however, both his wrists were seized, in such a grip of steel that his fingers opened straight out, and the revolver dropped from the hammock to the deck.

"There, lad! Steady! Steady! It's all right, lad. There! There!" murmured the mate, softly, with soothing and command. Under the spell of his words, and of that compelling grip, the boy's desperate tension gave way. Nerve and muscle fell to utter slackness. His wild and drawn face relaxed, as wax melts in a flame; and he looked up piteously. The mate let go of his wrists.

"Poor lad," he said, smiling down at him. "I woke you too quick. You were in a fever dream, I reckon. Were you back in the dance-hall at Singapore?"

Seth's Father

When Seth looked up at his father's bruised and bleeding lips, something seemed to break in his heart, or in his brain, he knew not which. He suddenly felt as if he were a little boy, long lost, whose father had just found him.

"Oh," he exclaimed, with a sobbing gasp, " I've hurt you!" and catching the mate's hand in both of his he crushed it to his mouth, and clung to it passionately, and hid his face with it.

For a moment or two the mate said nothing, and did not move. Then he passed his hand caressingly over Seth's hands.

"There, dear lad, don't worry about it!" said he. "The way you were lying, and me so close, you didn't get any strength into the blow, — lucky for me, for I've seen what that left of yours can do when it's got a fair show! You didn't know what you were doing. You were clear out of your head for a minute. I saw that in your eyes. What can a little thing like that matter, between comrades like us two, that's stood for each other with our lives? Let me go now, lad, an' get you some more of the medicine you spilt. I guess you'll be better soon, anyway, now the heat's broke, and we've got a good fresh breeze on our beam!"

But Seth still clung tight to his hand, while he furtively dried his eyes on his shirt-sleeve. Then, looking up with a ghost of a smile, he let the man see a glimpse of the ardour of devotion that was surging up within him.

"I *am* better, already," said he. "You've saved more than my life, I think! I feel *well*. I feel as if, all of a sudden, I'd never been so well before. I don't need any more medicine."

But the mate shook his head positively, and laughed.

"Not five minutes ago," he protested, "you were that luny you were trying to smash in my face, and you wanted to shoot me, in the bargain. Now, you're feeling so well you think you'll get out of takin' any more medicine. No, sir-ree! I'm going for another dose for you. And don't you fall asleep again while I'm gone, or I'll be scared to give it to you!"

"All right!" laughed Seth, his heart leaping with such sudden gladness that he *had* to laugh, though half-fearful that his joy might be mistaken for light-headedness. "I'll take anything *you* have to give me!" he added, cryptically.

CHAPTER XXXIV.

WHAT THE HEART KNOWS

THOUGH Seth knew that he was now in no more need of medicine, that his body's sickness was no longer anything, since the deadly sickness of the spirit had passed from him, he felt that it was only reasonable that he should not seem to recover too instantaneously. He took his dose, sat up and commented on the breeze that was driving the *Mary of Teck* through the roughened and white-capped water, then lay down again and closed his eyes. He was grateful for the opportunity to think, to adjust himself to the overwhelming change which he knew had taken place within his heart.

With a vast illumination lightening every dark corner of his soul, it had come to him that he loved this man, Jim Callahan, or Jim Calder, who was his father, with a like great love to that which he bore his mother. It had come to him that his life-purpose of revenge was for ever and ever made impossible. He could no more kill his father than he could kill his mother. If his father had been guilty of an unspeakable wrong, then it was evident in his face that he had borne long and bitter sorrow on account of it. If his father deserved more punishment than he had yet received, then let life, or fate, or God, inflict it. He felt that he could no longer even judge between his father and his mother. But of one thing he grew presently assured; and the more he thought of it, the more assured he grew. Such a man as this could never have wilfully betrayed such a woman as Luella Warden. If he had done it in a moment of obsession, in the clutch of some overwhelming temptation, such a man as this would not have hesitated to come back, and humble himself, and devote his life to reparation. Seth saw that there had been some frightful mistake. And in his new vision, in the inspiration of his love and hope, he came very near the truth. He told himself that both his father and his mother had been the victims of some third person's treachery. They had both been betrayed. As it all cleared itself so in his mind, he saw himself so clearing it in their minds, also. Then such a great hope, such a glad confidence for the future arose in him that he could no longer contain himself in his hammock. He could no longer play the invalid, with his heart-shouting triumph and his eyes bright with happiness. He sprang up, threw away the ice-pack from his head, and started for the cabin, intending to wash up, and shave, and dress, and enter upon a new life clean. But he had not gone half a dozen paces when Callahan, who had been keeping watch, hurried up with anxiety in his face, evidently fearing a return of the madness.

"What're you up to, lad?" he demanded. "You mustn't be running round. An' you mustn't take the ice off your head yet!"

Seth turned upon him the face of a well and happy man.

"I can't help it, but I'm *well!*" he answered, gaily. "There ain't a thing the matter with me now, but a little bump on the back of my head. The reason I'm well so quick is because you're such a great doctor, Mr. Callahan."

His father looked at him searchingly. There was no delirium in his face. His eyes were steady. He felt his pulse, and found it almost normal.

"You *do* seem pretty fit!" he acknowledged. "I guess you'll have to have your own way. But you needn't 'Mister' me, lad. If any two men have a right to be comrades, it's you an' me. Call me Jim."

Seth flushed, in an embarrassment that seemed to amuse the mate.

"Well, Jim, if you don't mind," said he, "I'm going to fix up a bit, and be right as a trivet. I guess this wind has blowed the vapours out of my brain."

He turned and went below, leaving Jim smitten with a pang of memory and longing. That phrase, "right as a trivet," was one which he had never heard any but the rector use.

During the rest of the voyage to Hongkong, both the captain and Mr. Tinker commented on Seth's high spirits, as compared with his former sombre mood.

"Belaying-pins will work wonders, once in a while!" remarked Mr. Tinker. And the captain suggested that Seth was very much indebted to Bill Jenkins's lucky shot.

Before reaching Hongkong, Seth wrote a long, jubilant letter to his mother and Mrs. Bembridge conjointly. No small portion of it was occupied with an account of his new comrade, Jim Callahan, the mate of the *Mary of Teck*. The mate's courage and brilliancy in the single-hand fight in defence of Steffan's body, his heroism in jumping overboard among the sharks to save so unimportant a life as that of the quartermaster, his skill, and tenderness, and care as a nurse, all these matters lost nothing in Seth's enthusiastic telling. And when, nearly two months later, the two lonely women read and re-read that letter together, Mrs. Bembridge's little black cap and magenta sontag beside Luella's abundant fair hair and broad white brow, there were tears of wondering gratitude for the stranger who had saved for them their boy.

When the ship reached Hongkong, Seth put his letter into the box in the cabin, with the rest of the mail, which the captain was going to take ashore, and stamp, and post. Now, as it chanced, into the same mail the mate had dropped a letter addressed to his tailor in Singapore. An hour later he happened to remember that he had addressed it wrongly. Hurrying into the cabin, he began to sort the mail over, looking for his own letter.

At this moment Seth came along, saw what the mate was doing, and halted at the door in great trepidation. He was not yet prepared to reveal himself to his father.

"That you, Seth?" asked the mate, without looking up, as he ran the letters over beneath his fingers.

Suddenly he stopped, starting as though he had been struck in the face. All the letters but one dropped from his hands on to the cabin table. That one he lifted up, staring at the address. Seth saw his father grow as white as chalk, his mouth twitch with pain. The address was:

    Mrs. Luella Warden,
        Westcock,
             Westmoreland Co.,
                New Brunswick, Canada.

For what seemed to Seth an age Callahan stared at that address. Then he looked up. In his eyes was a bitterness of pain which Seth had never seen on any face before.

"You know —?" he began, in a strained voice, which failed him before he could complete the question.

But it did not need completion.

"Yes," said Seth, softly, looking deep into his eyes. "She is my mother!" And he hungered to throw his arms around the man's shoulders.

But to this he had small encouragement. His father stared at him wildly for several seconds, in dead silence. Then he dropped the letter on the pile, and hurriedly, half-blindly, left the cabin.

For hours the mate avoided Seth, with obvious intention. The captain went ashore and returned. The *Mary of Teck* was towed to her berth. Every one was busy. But Seth hardly knew what his hands were doing, so terrible were his excitement and anxiety. What his father's attitude meant, he dared not try to guess. He could only wait, tortured by his suspense.

At last, in the evening, when he was standing alone by the rail, far away from all the rest, his father came up suddenly and stood beside him.

"You must have thought it queer, lad," said he,

"the way I acted this morning. It *was* queer. But I couldn't help it. Forgive me, lad!"

"I'd forgive you anything, I guess!" replied Seth. "But it did hurt," he added, boyishly.

"You're my comrade!" said his father. "I haven't known you long, it's true, but some way I've come to care more for you than for any other man on earth. I couldn't stand it, now, to let anything come between us, for I've seen it in your face that you — kind of like me, too, you know, lad. Such things show themselves, without much bein' said. But now it seems to me — I ought to tell you something."

Here he paused. And Seth, after waiting breathlessly for a moment, thrust out his hand.

"Tell me — what?" he asked, in a trembling voice.

"Your mother!" said the man, grasping Seth's hand strongly. "Your mother! I knew her once. I knew her well!"

"You knew her," repeated Seth, in a voice of assent.

"I loved her," said the man. "I loved her with all my heart. An' she took my heart in her hands, an' broke it to little bits, an' all my life with it."

Seth started to withdraw his hand, but gently.

"Oh, it ain't *that*," went on the mate, in haste, tightening his grip. "It wasn't *that* made me keep clear of you, when I found out you were her son. I forgave her; an' I love her now, an' I've never in all these years loved any other woman but her. It wasn't *that* made me so queer to you, till I'd got a chance to see into my own heart."

"Then — won't you tell me what it was?" asked Seth, his heart beating so quickly that he could hardly speak.

"It was — knowing something that can't make any difference to me now, lad. You're just Luella Warden's son, the son of the woman I love, — and you're my chum, ain't you, lad?"

Before Seth's mind came up now certain words which the old farmer had spoken on the day of the picnic. He understood.

"Yes, always, I believe," he answered, soberly, returning the grip of Callahan's hand. "But I want you to tell what that something was, that can't make any difference now."

"Why," responded the mate, with difficulty, "if you insist, — it was knowing that you were the son of that man, — the man that had wronged your mother and ruined my life. But let us forget all that, dear lad. He's dead and gone, long years ago. You never knew him. You're just *her* son! An' maybe that's why I loved you first; though I know it's for your own sake I love you now!"

What the Heart Knows

Seth disengaged his hand, and caught both the man's shoulders.

"The man that wronged my mother, an' ruined your life, — an' hers, an' mine, — he's *not dead.* He's right here, before me now! Before God, I am your son, *father.*"

At these words Callahan drew back, and stood staring. Then he began to shake, so that he could hardly stand.

"It ain't possible! No, no, it *ain't* possible!" he muttered. "Would to God that it could be true! Lad, lad, I'd give my right hand if it could be true! I'd give my life, so gladly! But I saw her letter to him, — with my own eyes I saw it!"

"Oh, father," pleaded Seth, "what are letters? They can be forged. What's anything, in comparison with what the heart knows? Don't you *know* I'm your son, your own son? Don't I *know* you're my own, my very own father? Somebody has lied to you, father. Somebody has cheated us all, hideously, vilely. Somebody has *forged* letters, if it's letters you are thinking of. Think, think how easy some one could forge a letter, some one that wanted to get you away from her. But I'm your son, and your heart knows it, father. We've known each other from the start, haven't we, father?" And Seth strove to draw his father to him.

But his father held back, though tenderly, and

looked at him with hungry, wondering, doubting eyes.

"Is it possible she could have forged that letter?" he muttered, searching Seth's face as if to find the answer there. "Oh, lad, if it could be possible!"

"Who, father?" demanded Seth, breathlessly. But his father did not notice the question.

"It *is* possible," he went on, the conviction breaking in upon his heart. "She was very clever. She was clever enough to do it. And she loved me enough to do anything. I see it all now. But, oh, lad, lad, what bitter wrong, what cruel wrong, I've been doing your mother all these years! An' thinkin' it was *me* was the wronged one! It was like a murder! And you, lad, — you, my own boy, how can you bear to look at me, after what I've done to you an' her?" And he turned away, that Seth might not see the working of his face.

But Seth put his arms around him. "Don't let's think of the past, father! Let's just think of the future, — an' of how our hearts knew each other in spite of everything — and of what it's going to mean to mother!"

His father turned, held him close, and looked at him.

"Yes, indeed, lad, you *are* my son," said he. "My heart was trying to tell it to me all the time, ever since I met you; but I didn't know the language! Boy, we will go home to your mother; and together, you and I, we will make her understand, — and, perhaps, forgive me!"

CHAPTER XXXV.

THE BREATH OF THE TIDE AND LILAC BLOOMS

It was two months later when Jim and Seth found themselves once more approaching the country of the Tantramar. It had been Jim's wish to start for home as soon as the ship reached Hongkong, leaving by the very first steamer for Vancouver. But Seth had appealed for delay. It had been his argument that letters should be allowed time to reach Westcock two or three weeks ahead of them, to prepare their way. The wisdom of this was obvious. And Jim, having waited twenty years at his own instance, had reluctantly compelled himself to wait two weeks at Seth's.

In these twenty years there had been changes at Tantramar. Instead of coming by schooner up the Bay of Fundy from St. John, they came all the way through by rail, getting off at the little way station of Bulmer's Mills, at the head of Frosty Hollow, about half-past four o'clock in the morning. Bulmer's Mills was about a mile behind Westcock church, in the Dorchester woods.

They started to walk homeward through the first

phantasmal gray of the June dawn. As they stood alone together in the narrow, forest road, the trees, bushes, and roadside weeds loaded down with dew, the still air cool and pungent with wild essences loosed by the wet, Seth and his father turned to each other, by one impulse, looked happily into each other's eyes, and clasped hands.

"About a half-hour's walk, eh, lad, an' we'll be home!" said Jim.

"Yes, father," Seth answered, with a soft laugh, "it's just about as far now, from Bulmer's Mills in to the parsonage, as it was twenty years ago, I guess! An' our place is about three hundred yards from the parsonage, through the fir-pasture."

As they passed Westcock church, pale fingers of saffron light were just beginning to touch the cloud-wisps in the eastern sky, above the fir-woods of Westcock hill; but the little gray church by the roadside was still sunken in the dewy shadow of its grove.

They passed quietly between the silent cottages which clustered near the church, hearing no sound but the crowing of the cocks who were now beginning to stir on their roosts, and the twitter of a few awaking birds. Onward up the rough, rain-gullied road over Westcock Hill they climbed, pausing to pick a few wintergreen leaves as they had each done so many times when children. Then they passed the old cemetery, with its graceful, sheltering, white birch-trees; and presently, coming out on the open crest of the ridge, they looked down, with the sunrise in their faces, upon slumbering Westcock village and the mystical wide-flung levels of Tantramar.

Here they paused a few moments. They could see the chimneys of the parsonage rising among its dark and ancient groves, — and further to the right, beyond the fir-pasture, the little gray house in the fields which Seth called home. As Jim looked down at the lonely gray house, and thought of Luella, — now surely up, and dressed, and waiting, in response to their telegram from Montreal, — his heart shook with doubt, and hope, and penitence, and overwhelming love. But Seth had no doubts whatever. He felt very sure of his mother, and very sure of the thoroughness with which his letters had prepared the way for this home-coming. Then, suddenly, beyond the pale levels of the marshes, beyond the vapourous channels of the river and the creeks, beyond the gray and golden bosom of the windless bay, over the low ridge of Beauséjour the sun came up, flooding the spaces with a tide of aerial fire. The sudden glory thrilled and dazzled them. Without a word they hurried on down the hill to within a couple of hundred yards of the parsonage gate. Here they turned in, along

The Breath of the Tide

the rector's "Upper Field," now light green with young barley. From the Upper Field they turned down through the fir-pasture, and came so, over the snake fence and past the barn, to the little gray house in the fields, — and to Luella, standing alone in the open doorway, with arms outstretched to meet them.

From Luella, Jim went to his mother. The hard old woman, melted to gentleness by the joy of his return, made her peace with Luella and with Seth. That evening — although, as it was Tuesday, there was no regular service — the little Westcock church was opened up. As the rector remarked, there had already been somewhat more delay in the matter than occasion seemed to warrant; so he was willing even to disturb the routine of the grumbling old sexton. On the edge of twilight, therefore, the bell began to pulse out its mellow summons, while the night-hawks were swooping and twanging across the hollow of the green and violet sky. As the little party moved up the hill from the big white gate of the parsonage, Mrs. Bembridge pulled Luella aside, ostensibly to retie a defective bow, but in reality to steal a chance — as she whispered confidentially to Mrs. Goodridge — to wipe what she was pleased to call her "drivelling old eyes" without "that old Mrs. Calder" seeing her. A soft air breathed up the hillside from Tantramar, bearing with it the rush of the tide as it returned to the empty channels. And with the sound came the mingled smell of the salt, the purple lilac blooms, and the heavy, honey-laden clover.

THE END.

Formac Fiction Treasures

ALSO IN THE SERIES

By Evelyn Eaton

Quietly My Captain Waits
This historical romance, set during the years of French-English struggle in New France, draws two lovers out of the shadows of history — Louise de Freneuse, married and widowed twice, and Pierre de Bonaventure, Fleet Captain in the French navy. Their almost impossible relationship helps them endure the day-to-day struggle in the fated settlement of Port Royal. ISBN 0-88780-544-2

The Sea is So Wide
In the summer of 1755, Barbe Comeau offers her family home in the lush farmland of the Annapolis Valley as overnight shelter to an English officer and his surly companion. The Comeaus are unaware of the treacherous plans to confiscate the Acadian farms and send them all into exile. A few weeks later, they are crammed into the hold of a ship and sent south. In Virginia she patiently rebuilds her life, never expecting that the friend she believed had betrayed her and her family would search until he found her. ISBN 0-88780-573-6

By W. Albert Hickman

The Sacrifice of the Shannon
In the heart of Frederick Ashburn, sea captain and sportsman, there glows a secret fire of love for young Gertrude MacMichael. But her interests lie with Ashburn's fellow adventurer, the dashing and slightly mysterious Dave Wilson. From their hometown of Caribou (real-life Pictou) all three set out on a perilous journey to the ice fields in the Gulf of St. Lawrence to save a ship and its precious cargo — Gertrude's father. In almost constant danger, Wilson is willing to risk everything to bring the ship and crew to safety. ISBN 0-88780-542-6

By Alice Jones (Alix John)

The Night Hawk
Set in Halifax during the American Civil War, a wealthy Southerner — beautiful, poised, intelligent and divorced — poses as a refugee while

using her social success to work undercover. The conviviality of the town's social elite, especially the British garrison officers is more than just a diversion when there is a war to be won.

A Privateer's Fortune
When Gilbert Clinch discovers a very valuable painting and statue in his deceased grandfather's attic, he begins to uncover some of his ancestor's secrets, including a will that allows Clinch to become a wealthy man, while at the same time disinheriting his cousins. His grandfather's business as a privateer and slave trader helped him amass wealth, power and prestige. Clinch has secrets of his own, including a clandestine love affair. From Nova Scotia to the art salons in Paris and finally the gentility of English country mansions, Clinch and his lover, Isabel Broderick, become entangled in a haunting legacy. ISBN 0-88780-572-8

By Margaret Marshall Saunders

Beautiful Joe
Cruelly mutilated by his master, Beautiful Joe, a mongrel dog, is at death's door when he finds himself in the loving care of Laura Morris. A tale of tender devotion between dog and owner, this novel is the framework for the author's astute and timeless observations on farming methods, including animal care, and rural living. This Canadian classic, written by a woman once acclaimed as "Canada's Most Revered Writer," has been popular with readers, including young adults, for almost a century. ISBN 0-88780-540-X

Rose of Acadia
One hundred and fifty years have past since the Acadians were sent into exile; now, Vesper Nimmo, a Bostonian, sets out for Nova Scotia's French shore with the intention of carrying out his great-grandfather's wish to make amends to the descendants of Agapit LeNoir. Nimmo immerses himself in the struggles of the Acadians to preserve their culture and language while the lure of money and modern conveniences draws young people to the Boston states. He meets beautiful, angelic Rose à Charlitte, the innkeeper where he makes his temporary home. When he becomes ill she cares for him, but when he falls in love with her, she cannot marry him — not until she is freed from her past. ISBN 0-88780-571-X